"I WANT YOU, REBECCA"

"I want you more than any woman I've ever known. You have bewitched me." He kissed her. At first it was the barest brush of his lips against hers, but his lips returned to explore the corners of her mouth before seeking it fully and hungrily. She was lost, completely and utterly lost. She knew only one thing—he had not lied about his need, and she could no longer hide the truth about her own.

Joan Avery

HarperPaperbacks
A Division of HarperCollins*Publishers*

This is a work of fiction. The characters, incidents, and dialogues are products of the author's imagination and are not to be construed as real. Any resemblance to actual events or persons, living or dead, is entirely coincidental.

HarperPaperbacks *A Division of* HarperCollins*Publishers*
10 East 53rd Street, New York, N.Y. 10022

Cover illustration by Marin

First printing: May 1993

Printed in the United States of America

❖ 10 9 8 7 6 5 4 3 2 1

For my mother—
my first editor and my morale booster.

With thanks to Bill, Beth, Chris, and Steve
for their patience, love, and support.

1

"Thou shalt not deliver unto his master the servant
that has escaped from his master unto thee."
Deut.23:16

Detroit, 1860

Like the Angel of Death, the menacing figure crouched in the dampness, senses alert, on guard. A monklike cowl hid all but the barest outline of its features. A heavy cloak served to muffle the sounds that still emanated from the small laudanum-drugged babe in its arms.

Behind the grim figure, four pairs of frightened eyes stared into the darkness. The hooded head moved slightly, straining to hear. Footsteps, at one point almost atop them, now retreated. Angry voices, once too close, now grew distant. In the small, dank space, muffled sobs joined the quiet fussing of the baby.

The seconds became minutes and the minutes

seemingly hours, before soft footsteps approached. Cellar doors flew open, and the brilliance of the full moon hit the huddled figures. The outline of a man moved to block the invading light.

"They've gone. Be quick about it! You've lost precious time. The moon will be your worst enemy."

The five shadows climbed slowly from the hole, their limbs stiff from the effects of the cold, sodden earth. They moved quickly, without a word, through the eerie stillness of the deserted back streets. Every sound, however small, grew in intensity, magnified a hundredfold by their sensitive ears. As they moved, the air grew increasingly damp. The unmistakable odor of the water joined the overpowering smell of fungi, mildew, and rotting wood. The screech of a gull marked their arrival.

At a nod from the cowled head, the two large and two smaller figures struggled into the boat. The sleek craft shifted erratically with the insistent lap of the waves. With each dull crash of the frigid water, it strained, desperate to free itself from the lines that kept it moored in the shadows of the decrepit warehouse.

The sleeping babe was passed on. The hooded form leapt into the sloop and released the lines. The sail went up, and the sheeting caught the wind. The small craft flew out from the shadows into the moonlight.

"Get below! If you value your lives, keep quiet." Cursing the fate that sent them out at risk this early in the night, the shadowy apparition stood erect, all senses alert to the darkness.

Then, in the distance, came a faint cry that grew in intensity, deep and rumbling, striking terror in the huddled figures below deck. It was an order to stop—an order to stop or else. A yellow flash in the darkness, then the report of a gun.

Once more the deep voice, this time clear and commanding across the water. "Stop! I order you to stop!"

The cowled head turned to take measure of the enemy. He stood on shore, dark hair ruffled by the wind, like some avenging old world god. Towering over the men in his command, his dark eyes blazed in anger and frustration. The brilliance of the full moon showed the solid line of his rugged jaw, set in determination. His broad shoulders in the blue serge uniform flashed the silver bars of a captain.

The creature beneath the cowl surveyed him grimly. They could be complacent no longer. Though the city of Detroit turned a blind eye to their movement, here was a new threat—evidence that Washington was no longer going to let the citizens of the city ignore the movement of slaves across the river to freedom.

A new game had begun, its rules yet to be set. And a new enemy had made himself known.

"Thank God! I had begun to worry." The woman's distress was evident as she greeted the hooded figure in the doorway.

"There was no need to worry, Rachel," a deep, throaty voice responded. "We were only slightly delayed." The black cowl was thrown back, and waves of hair the color of ripened wheat cascaded out.

Rebecca Cunningham worked quickly to unfasten

the clasp that held the damp cloak at her throat. Once free of its confines, she strode across the room.

"Quickly, Rachel, help me dress. Has Father been asking about me?"

"I told him that you had a headache and were resting. He said he hoped you could make it down before the evening was over." The wonderfully warm and well-modulated voice of the slender black woman, some fifteen years her senior, brought a smile to Rebecca's face.

"We shall have to hurry." She began to strip off the simple shirt and pants the heavy cloak had covered. That accomplished, she moved toward a basin that rested on a beautifully inlaid table in one corner of the bedroom. After washing her face, she turned to the freed slave who was both friend and confidante. "There was no problem, Rachel. Do not look so worried. The river was free of ice, though damnably cold. The family is safe in good hands. They were still waiting for us, despite the late hour. Even the baby seemed to sense the danger. The poor thing saved its wailing until it was safely ashore in Canada."

Rachel slowly moved her hand to cover her mouth. Her eyes, glassy with unshed tears, mirrored her relief. "Thank God!"

"I left the *Deliverance* with Jacob. He'll see that she gets back to the dock before morning." Rebecca's thoughts went to the sailboat that had served her so well these past two years, and to Rachel's husband, who had more than once saved her from discovery.

She grabbed a brush and began to attack her golden mane. Satisfied that she had removed all the tangles, she pulled it up, hurriedly anchoring the large curls high on the back of her head.

"Did Father believe your story about the last-minute fitting?" Rebecca asked.

"I believe so. He was distracted. Major Harcourt has just arrived with a new officer . . . a Captain Taylor."

Rebecca abruptly stopped her toilette and looked up. "Captain Taylor?"

"Yes, he's newly arrived from Washington. Your father has been questioning him on the possibility of war."

Rebecca shook her golden head. Not wishing to alarm Rachel, she forced a laugh. "You mean grilling him mercilessly! I shall have to go and save the man from Father's ardent interrogation."

Rachel held out an exquisite sea-green gown for Rebecca to slip into. After helping her into it, she began to expertly fasten the row of small buttons down the back of the bodice.

"Oh, it's marvelous, Rachel!" Rebecca stared at her reflection in the mirror. She smoothed the expensive taffeta with her hands. "I knew the moment I saw the fabric unloaded from Father's ship that it would make up beautifully, and it has. You are absolutely the most talented couturiere in Detroit, my friend."

Rebecca pirouetted, and the gown moved in a graceful swirl around her tall figure. The hand-sewn seed pearls at its neckline and sleeves shimmered iridescently. As she turned, her shoulders caught the lamplight. Her flesh was as smooth and unblemished as the pearls, with the same pale lustre.

"I should go," Rachel said. "Jacob will want some dinner if he is to be up tonight moving the *Deliverance.* I am concerned, Rebecca, that someone at the party will notice the boat is not at her moorings."

"I doubt anyone will be out this late, Rachel. Certainly not beyond the patio. There's still winter in the air."

As Rachel turned to go, she caught her friend studying her decolletage in the mirror. "Be good!" she said, a gentle reprimand.

The younger woman smiled, thinking of the new captain. Then she twirled around and headed downstairs, toward the dull murmur of voices.

Captain Bradford Taylor stared out the French doors that led to the terraced stone patio and the elaborate gardens of the Cunningham home. In the clear March night, he could see the stables in the distance. Beyond them, glistening in the full moonlight, lay the Detroit River. Still farther, beyond the shimmering ribbon of the river, he could just make out the dark stretches of the Canadian shoreline.

He turned back from his thoughtful perusal to survey the ornate mansion. It was a far cry from the simple, two-room wooden structure he had called home. It was difficult to believe he had grown up less than two miles from where he stood now.

It had been a long time since he'd been home. The city had changed. He had changed. When he left for West Point, he had been a bitter and naive boy. The years had tempered him, hardened him. He had shed no tears when his father died, and when his mother died his tears fed his anger and determination. After her death, there had been no reason to return to the place of his birth, until now.

He studied the illustrious crowd with a practiced eye. Before him were people who had been only names to him when he was growing up. Old Joseph Campau, craggy faced and bent with age, still remained a driving force in the city. He was holding court in one corner of the ballroom. Christopher Buhl, who he had heard would be running for mayor in the fall, spoke agitatedly with several of his political supporters in the center of the room. Near the stairs, Major Harcourt and their host, George Cunningham, stopped in the midst of a conversation to look up the wide staircase. He followed their gaze.

"Rebecca! I'm glad you felt well enough to join us." George Cunningham's enthusiastic greeting caused everyone in the room to direct their attention to the stairwell.

Brad Taylor waited with a certain detached curiosity for the appearance of the woman who dominated Detroit society. If he had learned one thing in his short week in the city, it was that nothing of any social significance happened in Detroit without the support and approval of the renowned Miss Rebecca Cunningham. Brad had already formed a picture of her as haughty and superficial. Of her physical attributes, he had not thought much at all, so it was not surprising that the woman who slowly materialized in a gown the color of a clear ocean jolted the captain out of his reveries.

Never in his life had he seen such a stunning beauty as the woman who was serenely surveying the crowded ballroom. She looked like some Nordic goddess. He followed her as she completed her descent and greeted her father with a warm kiss. She stood as tall as any man in the room except himself, and a good head taller than any woman. Her figure was magnificent—this was the only word he could think of. Her creamy breasts and shoulders begged admiration. Studying her clothed form, he tried to imagine the long, elegantly formed limbs that the pale green skirt concealed. He felt his body react to this intimate thought and inwardly laughed at himself. He would have to find himself a woman once he was settled.

Bradford Taylor was well aware of the effect he had on women. There would certainly be more than one willing to satisfy his body's cravings in return for the pleasure of his attentions. His last mistress had been one of Washington's fairest, and he had been hard-pressed to convince her not to confess everything to her husband and follow him to Detroit.

He watched as Major Harcourt laughed and pointed him out to the bewitching creature. She in turn directed her attention toward him. Her look was neither timid nor arrogant, and he felt suddenly uncomfortable as she continued her scrutiny.

He was fascinated by the approach of the tawny-haired beauty. She displayed a feline grace that made him think of a lioness stalking her prey. His face registered his appreciation of her beauty, and he was rewarded with a curious but nonetheless dazzling smile. His last thought before she spoke was a serious reconsideration of his new policy against dallying with society belles.

"Captain Taylor, I believe?" Rebecca extended her hand.

"A pleasure, Miss Cunningham." Brad lifted her hand to his lips in a studied gesture.

The richness of Rebecca's laughter elicited even more admiration. "I'm sorry, Captain. I've totally ignored propriety in my eagerness to welcome you to Detroit."

"I would have felt anguish indeed if propriety had prevented me from accepting such a warm welcome, Miss Cunningham."

Brad doubted this young woman ever bothered to contemplate propriety. She was the picture of grace and elegance at the moment, and yet he sensed an undercurrent of something untamed.

Rebecca laughed again. "You are as gracious as you are handsome, my dear Captain. That is a rare combination. I shall have to watch you closely if I am to prevent all females of my acquaintance from falling prey to your charms."

"Under your watchful eye, my dear Miss Cunningham, I would no doubt be more than happy."

Rebecca took stock of the stranger. His dark hair and penetrating onyx eyes were all too familiar. With his hard jawline relaxed and a smile softening his full lips, he was even more handsome than he had appeared earlier that night. He was also much taller than he had looked on shore, she noted as his shoulders dwarfed her. For such a statuesque woman, it was a unique experience to feel petite. Still, she did not forget he was the enemy. There was much she could learn if she were careful.

"How long have you been in Detroit, Captain? I can't believe Major Harcourt could have kept you concealed from the female population for very long."

"I arrived a week ago today. Far from being hidden, I have been reacquainting myself with my hometown."

She studied the man more closely. He could not be more than thirty, she estimated, not so terribly older than her twenty-one. With something over forty-five thousand people, Detroit was no longer a small town, yet she found it difficult to imagine having missed such an attractive man. She could feel him studying her now, as if assessing her strengths and weaknesses.

"You are originally from Detroit, Captain? My memory must be failing me."

"I'm afraid I did not travel in such illustrious circles when I was growing up."

She watched as he raked the room with his eyes. There was a certain coldness in them, a certain unwarranted animosity. It was the same look she had seen in them earlier.

Quickly dismissing her anxiety, she continued. "Well, Captain, I am pleased that you do now. You will have to permit me to show you how the city has changed in your absence, but I must go greet our other guests. It's getting quite late."

"It has been a pleasure, Miss Cunningham." Once more, he delivered a kiss to her hand. He watched her glide off toward the corner where Joseph Campau still stood, and then he headed toward the Waterford punch bowl surrounded by a sumptuous array of delicacies.

"I see you've met our charming hostess," Major Harcourt said as he joined Taylor at the refreshment table.

"Yes, a most remarkable woman. I shall enjoy getting to know her better."

"I would tread lightly, Captain, if I were you. Once the nature of your work here becomes known, you will not be a popular figure. There are many here who stand strongly opposed to returning escaped slaves to their owners. Many more actively support the movement to see that they reach the freedom of Canada."

Captain Taylor's cold stare unnerved the smaller man. "There is no need for anyone to know the nature of my duties here, Major. I thought that was made perfectly clear in the instructions you received from Washington."

"Yes, of course . . . of course, Captain." The major struggled to recover his composure. The letter from Washington had made it clear, indeed. Captain Taylor reported not to Major Harcourt but directly back to Washington, and Harcourt was not to obstruct the captain's investigation. The captain, it appeared, was a law unto himself.

"I am here to uphold Federal law, Major. Do you find something wrong with that?"

"No, of course not."

"But let me pursue this further. Are you telling me, Major, that the illustrious citizens of Detroit knowingly break a Federal law?"

Harcourt looked flustered. "It's not as simple as you make it seem, Captain Taylor. Feelings run high that divine law takes precedence in this case." He wondered if this man recognized any such law. Suddenly he pitied the poor fleeing slaves, who would no longer be pursued only by slave hunters but by this grim and enigmatic man as well.

"What do you know, Major, of the Angel of Passage?"

Major Harcourt was startled by the question. How could this man know, in less than a week, what it had taken him months to discover? "I know little, Captain. His existence is little more than rumor and superstition."

"He seems a very effective rumor, does he not?"

The major cleared his throat before replying. "We have been pursuing all leads in regard to this 'person,' Captain. If he exists, we will find him and arrest him."

There was a long pause before Captain Taylor spoke again. "That is exactly what I am here to see done, Major." Setting his punch cup down, the captain headed toward the door.

Major Harcourt contemplated the back of the departing figure. Captain Bradford Taylor would certainly be a match for the stygian apparition known as the Angel of Passage. The next few months would prove interesting, he thought with a strange foreboding.

2

"Well, I'll be damned, Captain! Them niggers sure got nerve. Meetin' plain as can be, as if there ain't a thing wrong with what they're doin'."

The captain looked down with a certain disgust at the dirty, pock-faced man who barely came up to his shoulders. For a brief moment he felt repulsed by the necessity of using paid informants, but experience had taught him it was sometimes the most expedient way to gain certain information.

Frustration haunted him. How could the better part of a city conspire to keep alive illegal activity? The conscience of the city had become well-known to him in the week following the reception at the Cunninghams'. Word of his mission seemed to have spread over the city, leaving a pall on any relationships he attempted to establish. Not a citizen remained who didn't know he pursued not only escaped slaves but their local folk hero as well. Everywhere he went, he was greeted courteously but warily. Ironically, it was as if he were the enemy. Didn't these fools know that if the fugitive slave laws weren't enforced, war would be almost inevitable? They would end up forfeiting their lives, and who would risk life for some unwritten law, some "divine law"? If war came, everyone would lose.

Damn them, damn them all to hell! Especially that devil whom these fools call the Angel of Passage.

The two men stood deep in the shadows of a building along East Congress Street. The captain studied the small, two-story house across from them whose lights burned urgently, despite the late hour. The house belonged to William Webb. Its beautiful fretwork and cozy bay window belied its tragic significance. As he waited, Brad thought of the men who had met here in this house a little over a year ago, most notably the avid abolitionist John Brown.

The fanatical abolitionist had arrived in Detroit with his usual contingent of escaped slaves and met with Frederick Douglass and a group of sympathizers in this house. That March night had rung with discord as Brown tried to get the others to support his plan to raise a small army and march into Virginia to free the slaves. It was here that Brown, unsuccessful and totally discouraged, had begun to formulate a different plan, a raid on the national arsenal at Harpers Ferry, West Virginia.

Brad still remembered vividly the reports that had poured into Washington late last year when a certain Colonel Robert E. Lee forced Brown and his followers to surrender. Despite Northern efforts to have him declared insane, Brown had been hanged. The whole affair had left a bitter taste in many mouths, and Brad wondered what toll it still might take.

Suddenly, the small house became alive with activity as several people moved quickly and quietly from it. Brad recognized most of them. George DeBaptiste, a former valet to President Harrison and the acknowledged leader of the Underground Railroad in Detroit, moved off toward Larned Street. He was closely followed by William Lambert, who had been educated in the East at a Quaker school and who, with DeBaptiste, headed efforts by the Negro citizens of Detroit to see that no slave reaching Detroit would be returned to his master.

It was the third man who brought the captain quickly to the alert. The caped and cowled figure was impossible to identify.

"I'll be damned, Captain, if it ain't him!" The small man's voice reverberated with sudden fear. His outburst earned him a sharp reprimand from the man who shared the shadows with him.

Once the figure had distanced itself from the house, Captain Taylor turned to the man he knew only as Pock.

"Stay and watch the house. I want to know the name of everyone who leaves. That shouldn't be too dangerous." The condescending tone was not lost, even on Pock.

The captain waited until the heavily cloaked figure had turned the first corner before he followed with practiced ease. He moved among the shadows, almost one with them. Still, it took a great deal of effort to keep up with the black shape, whose knowledge of the city's nooks and crannies kept him almost invisible. If this were the Angel of Passage, he was earning Brad's respect. The strange apparition became more difficult to trail with each block covered. Brad barely managed to see the figure float through a back door of the Finney Hotel, the very hotel in which Brad himself had taken residence while awaiting the completion of Fort Wayne on the city's south side.

Seymour Finney looked up from his ledger books as the cloaked figure hurried in.

"I'm being followed!" Rebecca threw back the cowl. Her amber eyes were alive with excitement.

The innkeeper acknowledged her communication with a curt nod before returning to his books.

Rebecca moved through the darkened corridors at the back of the building. Once she reached the kitchen, she entered the small room the hotel used as its larder and eased the door closed behind her. Straining, she moved several sacks of flour. Her breath now came in short pants. She felt a certain exhilarating tension in her body, as if all her senses were heightened. Praying silently, she lifted a small, concealed trapdoor. In answer to her prayers, it opened without a sound. She lowered herself into the darkened shaft and gently let the heavy door back down. She heard the flour sacks she had propped against the open door fall with a reassuring thud. They would conceal the cracks that might betray the opening.

She counted the steps as she descended in the darkness. When she had reached twenty she stopped, satisfied when the smooth texture of the wooden steps gave way to uneven ground. She turned and extended her hand to the right. Exploration of the cool, damp earth soon brought her fingers in contact with the familiar glass and metal of a lamp. She found the flint and lit the lamp. She moved through the narrow space, and at the end of the long passage she hung the lantern at the foot of yet another ladder. She blew out her only source of light and moved with certainty up the ladder, once more counting the steps. She stopped at twenty-two and felt above her for a metal clasp. She released it and slowly pushed up on the trapdoor. Straw dropped down on her, and she shook her head to get rid of it. She allowed the door to settle quietly in the straw before she pulled herself up into the Finney barn. She was well over a block away from the hotel and her pursuer. Slowly, a smile crossed her lips.

The back door of the Finney Hotel flew open with such force that it was left banging against the wall. Seymour Finney looked up once more, appearing startled by the sudden interruption of his work.

"Captain Taylor! Is something wrong?"

The captain paused for a moment, assessing the quietness of the building.

"Mr. Finney. Who was it that just entered by this door?"

"You say someone just entered here, Captain?" A puzzled look furrowed Seymour Finney's normally friendly brow. "I'm sure I couldn't miss anyone using the door, and I've been here since closing time working on my ledgers. Are you sure it was by this door, Captain? It's a new moon tonight, and the darkness, as well as other factors, can have us imagining all kinds of things."

Finney's seemingly good-natured insinuation riled Brad. The man was lying, of that there was little doubt, but to make a scene would gain nothing, since he had no proof.

"As you say, Mr. Finney, it would be hard to miss someone entering less than ten feet from you."

"Good night, Captain." Finney smiled cordially at the captain before turning his attention once more to the ledger.

The conversation was obviously over, but Brad was not accustomed to being dismissed. The gall of the man! If these people thought they could protect the Angel of Passage from discovery, they were sadly mistaken.

Long after he had undressed in his suite of rooms at the Finney Hotel, Brad lay awake, thinking.

"Rebecca!"

Rebecca started at the familiar voice. She had let herself in the servants' entrance of her home and was trailing her cape across the well-scrubbed floor of the large kitchen.

"Rachel, you startled me! What are you doing here at this hour?" A puzzled look crossed Rebecca's face before panic replaced it. "Has something gone wrong? Have they been discovered?"

"No, no. Everything is fine." Rachel slipped into their secret code of communication. "All the packages are intact and ready for final shipment. But when Jacob returned home a short time ago, he said you had been at the Finney barn. You told him you were being followed. Who was it?"

"I don't know. It was dark, and I was hard-pressed to stay ahead of him."

"It was that new captain, wasn't it, that Captain Taylor."

"I really don't know, Rachel. I didn't stop to ask

his name. It doesn't really matter, does it?" The irritation in her voice was evident.

"Rebecca, have you no knowledge of the kind of danger you put yourself in every time you go out? If you are caught, they will make an example of you. You will be imprisoned!"

"I know that, Rachel. I'm not an innocent. In two years I've had my share of frights. Tonight was nothing more, nothing less. What would you have me do?" She was angry now. "Abandon those people when I have the means of doing so much to help them? Shall I leave those hiding in Finney's barn to the mercies of the slave catchers who sit a stone's throw away, laughing and drinking at the hotel? You can't want that, Rachel, not after all you've done yourself!"

There was a long pause after this passionate outburst. Finally, Rachel responded. "No, I would not have you stop. The good Lord knows that there would have been dozens returned to lives of cruelty but for you and the *Deliverance.* But you make me nervous. I fear . . ." she stopped, as if searching for the right words. "I fear you enjoy it! When you come so close to touching death, you come alive. There is something about the danger. It pulls you like a moth lured by the beauty of a flame. Only too late does the moth find out the fire's touch is fatal. You are too passionate for your own good."

Rebecca laughed to dismiss the woman's fears. "Too passionate? I don't believe one can be too passionate."

Rachel studied her obstinate friend. "Then perhaps you have much to learn yet about life. Passion can be one's downfall as well as one's driving force.

Passion can easily teach humility, a virtue I fear you sorely could use more of."

Rebecca bristled at this accusation. "I risk my life for others, and you say I am proud. You are being cruel and unfair. How can you say such things?"

"I say them because I love you. I love you as well as my own flesh and blood. You say you risk your life for others, and yet that is only part of the truth, Rebecca. You also risk your life for you! It is like some mysterious love potion. It excites you as a man would."

"Yes, it excites me! Is that what you want to hear? Maybe I should find a man! Do you think that would be a less dangerous way to satisfy my passions?"

There was a long pause as the two old friends suddenly regretted the direction in which their disagreement had taken them.

Finally, Rachel spoke. "For you, my dear friend, a man might prove even more dangerous." She turned quietly and left, leaving Rebecca in total confusion.

Rebecca's earlier elation was gone. Damn Rachel, she thought. Why did she have to know her so well? A man was something she had not thought of in over two years, not since she had joined the "railroad." She had forgotten the long, tearful evenings she had spent looking for something, or someone, to satisfy the longing within her. With her introduction to the "railroad," all those tears had been forgotten. Rachel's accusation touched so close to the mark that it hurt even to think about it.

Rachel was right. The excitement that the work engendered in her was a sop thrown to soothe other still unsatisfied urges. Perhaps she should take her own advice. Until recently, there had been no man in

Detroit who had piqued her interest. Now, perhaps, there was one.

She chose to ignore the fact that she could not possibly have selected anyone more dangerous than the man she had in mind.

3

Brad awoke with a start at the soft knock on the door. He was not expecting anyone. He quickly pulled on his pants and jerked the door open to find Seymour Finney's stableboy. No more than ten years old, the boy stood terrified at the door with a delicate white missive clenched in his dirty hand.

There were several moments of silence before Brad realized he would have to speak first.

"You have something for me?" He tried not to smile.

"Yessir, Captain!" the boy blurted out. "Miss Cunningham's maid, Maddie, just brought this for you. Mr. Finney said to bring it right up." Brad studied the lad closely. His clothes were filthy and at least two sizes too small. His face was streaked with grime, and what remained of a large bruise shaded one side of the boy's face. Brad was suddenly brought back to painful memories of his own boyhood.

He extended his hand to the boy, but the note remained firmly in the grasp of the small dirty fingers. The lad seemed to have forgotten about it entirely.

Suddenly regaining his wits, the child looked down. His face colored to a shade of red just slightly less vibrant than the color of his hair. He proffered the small note, now slightly smudged. Too embarrassed for further words, he turned to go.

"Wait a moment, lad."

The boy stood frozen in his tracks.

"For your trouble." Brad tossed him a shiny quarter and was rewarded by a look of disbelief. "Spend it only on yourself. Do you understand?"

"Yes, sir." A broad smile cracked the dirt on the boy's face. He fled down the stairs.

Watching him, Brad unconsciously rubbed his arms as if to rid himself of past bruises. He wondered if the boy's life was anything like his own had been.

He shifted his gaze to the note in his hand. The heady scent of jasmine drifted up to him. He broke the seal and opened it. The handwriting was graceful and reflected a genteel upbringing, and yet the strokes were stronger than any female's of his acquaintance. The message itself was short.

"Dear Captain Taylor,

I promised to show you the city. Meet me this morning at ten in front of City Hall.

Rebecca Cunningham"

There was no acknowledgment in the short missive that he might decline. It was, rather, an order. Brad smiled.

"Jeez, Miss Cunningham! Isn't it about the most exciting thing you ever did see?"

Rebecca laughed at the boy's exuberance. "Yes, Joey. I believe it is."

"Do you think they'll stoke it up?"

"I believe the mayor did mention plans for a demonstration of sorts. Look! I think Mr. Roberts is about to do just that."

"Can I go look closer?"

"If you're careful. I told Mr. Finney I would take full responsibility for you this afternoon."

"Yes, Ma'am, I mean, miss. I'll be careful . . . and thank you again, Miss Cunningham. No one's ever done nothin' so nice for me before."

"It's my pleasure, Joey. Consider it a thank you for delivering that message to the captain this morning."

As Rebecca watched the boy run across Woodward Avenue, it hurt her to think that her little kindness was probably the best thing that had happened to the boy in all his nine or ten years. For some unknown reason, her thoughts of the boy segued into thoughts of Captain Taylor. It was an unlikely juxtaposition, a dirty waif of a child and a self-assured, sophisticated officer.

"I see I've been jilted for a younger man."

The slow, resonant voice stirred the loose hairs on the back of Rebecca's neck. The voice and its possessor were both tauntingly close. She dared not turn. She fought for mastery of the sensations that unexpectedly ran out of control. Her response, when it finally came, was well-modulated. It showed none of the intensity of the feelings that rioted within her.

"Ah! You've arrived, Captain. You are in for a real treat." She tried to keep her voice light and teasing as she turned to face him.

"I'm sure I am."

A faint blush colored Rebecca's cheeks. She hoped vainly that it would escape the observant captain's notice, but she feared it would not.

"We are celebrating, Captain, and you, sir, are to be my guest."

"Reason enough to celebrate, then." Much to Rebecca's relief, he smiled. So the teasing had been mutual. Or had it?

"As a stranger to our fair city, you will have the opportunity to see progress at work." She nodded across Woodward Avenue. The captain did not follow her gaze, but instead continued to study her.

"But I am no stranger, don't you remember? I grew up on the streets of Detroit." His words carried a chilling undertone.

"You are a stranger to this Detroit, Captain. We have changed dramatically in the last few years." Once more she tried to redirect his gaze. "Do you see? It is our first steam fire engine! By the end of the month we will actually have a paid fire company, one of the few cities this far west to boast such a novelty." She was babbling, and she knew it, but she could not break the intensity of his stare. Suddenly, she wondered why the reference to his childhood had changed his mood so dramatically.

"Someday, Captain, you must tell me about your childhood."

"It bore no resemblance to yours, I am sure, dear lady." There was the same coldness in his voice as on the evening of the party—the same dismissal, the same bitterness. His black eyes were in careful control of his emotions. She knew the look. It was one that she herself used to hide her soul.

Her smile vanished. "Do you treat everyone with such disdain, Captain?"

"Only when I deem them worthy." He executed a slight bow.

"I am not sure whether I should feel insulted or flattered, sir. Would you care to explain?"

His answer was to change the subject.

"And what is your role in today's festivities, Miss Cunningham?"

"Why would you assume that I have one, Captain?"

"As the belle of Detroit, I find it unthinkable that you would be forgotten on such an auspicious occasion." His tone was teasing once again.

"Now, Captain, I really feel as if you are unfavorably comparing us to some of the grander of your postings. Can Washington be that much more sophisticated? Have you not heard the Prince of Wales will visit us this fall? You will then have an opportunity to see the city shine."

"I doubt I will be here this fall, Miss Cunningham. Although that thought, in your lovely presence, saddens me."

Rebecca knew the words were perfunctory, yet the thought saddened her as well. For in this man's presence, she found herself breathing a little faster. Around him, her skin tingled, and the fine hairs on her arms stood up. Captain Bradford Taylor excited her as no man ever had, and the fact that he was the enemy only heightened the excitement.

She needed to get close to him to seek information, yet it was more than that, much more.

"In answer to your question, Captain, I am to christen the engine. Try to think of it as a ship." She laughed suddenly at the poor comparison. "Well, at least be kind to us in our modest endeavors."

"Being kind to you is my earnest desire." Once more his tone was too familiar, and once more Rebecca felt an irksome blush color her complexion.

"I think you are a little too practiced, Captain. I can see why the women flock to you."

"What makes you think women *flock* to me, as you so daintily put it?"

Surely she couldn't admit her own attraction to him. That would be too dangerous.

"I have my sources." She hoped the falseness of her bravado would escape him.

"And do your sources also tell you why I am here?"

"They say you have come to stop the slaves fleeing to Canada."

"And what do you say?"

"I say you are a fool, Captain, if you think you can stop what God intends."

"You have a personal dialogue with God, then, Miss Cunningham?"

Rebecca said nothing.

"Perhaps you also have a personal acquaintance with the Angel of Passage?"

She forced herself to stay calm. He didn't know anything; he was simply fishing for information.

"If you'll excuse me, Captain, I must join the festivities. You'll have a good view from here. We shall commence our tour as soon as I've completed my task."

He had not expected her to answer his pointed question. He knew that society mavens did not involve themselves in a city's underworld, however noble the cause. Brad watched as she moved across the busy street and through the throng. It was as if the waters were parting for Moses. Carriages stopped, and people stepped aside for her, all exchanging pleasant greetings with her. A marching band had reached a point in front of the dais, and Brad had to move slightly so as not to lose sight of her. He felt compelled to follow her with his eyes.

She lifted her skirts to climb the three short steps to the makeshift podium. He found himself aroused even by this simple act and wondered how experienced she was. She acted more self-assured than most young women her age, and she seemed unflustered by his pursuit.

There was something else as well, an attitude that conveyed a certain nonconformity. It was something he had always been attuned to in women. It usually meant they did not bind themselves to the usual social and moral restrictions. He had learned, through years of experience, that these women made exciting lovers. They were eager to please and took pleasure eagerly. Was Rebecca Cunningham such a woman?

After the champagne bottle had been broken and the band had played yet again, he watched Rebecca take her leave of the mayor and move back through the crowd. Again she was delayed by warm interchanges with fellow citizens, male and female, young and old. But something about her did not fit the picture of society dame that Brad had first envisioned. He definitely would have to get to know Rebecca Cunningham better.

4

"Well, Captain, if you have not had enough excitement for the day, we can be on our way. Before you concern yourself with propriety, I must warn you we will have a chaperone."

"I'm coming, Ma'am . . . I mean, Miss." Brad saw the small red-haired boy who had delivered his morning message struggling to follow Rebecca through the crowd.

Brad looked questioningly at Rebecca.

"Captain Taylor, I believe you already know Joe Whiton. He is an employee of Mr. Finney, and he has kindly consented to accompany us this afternoon."

Brad studied Rebecca for a moment before extending a formal hand to the small boy.

"A pleasure."

Joey hesitantly shook the captain's hand. "Me, too, Captain, sir."

Brad took Rebecca's arm as Joey ran off to the Cunningham carriage which awaited them.

"Do you make it a habit to pick up strays?" he asked her.

Rebecca stopped short. "No, Captain, I make it a habit to care about people." Freeing herself from his arm, she hurried after Joey.

Inside the carriage, Brad felt the chill of Rebecca's anger. He had intended the question merely in jest and was surprised at her response. With Joey safely ensconced in a corner of the opposite seat, it would be difficult to recover from his gaffe.

"I'm sorry if the question was poorly phrased."

"It was not the phrasing, as you put it, Captain, that was so irritating. It was the question itself. I can see your profession suits you!"

"My profession as a United States Army officer is a far cry from the squalor of my childhood, Madam, and it is something in which I hold great pride. I would not belittle it, if I were you."

There was a long silence during which neither one spoke. Joey eyed the couple warily, understanding the belligerence of their interchange, if not the actual meaning.

"I'm sorry, Captain. I did not mean to belittle your accomplishments, but I would prefer that you not prejudge me as a woman who spends her days primping and flirting. My concerns are as deeply felt as yours."

"And what are those concerns, Miss Cunningham?" Brad asked. His interest in the answer, he realized, was more than merely professional. This woman stirred his mind as well as his body, and that was unusual.

"I think we should know each other a little better, Captain, before I bare my soul to you." She smiled for the first time since their angry words.

"No doubt any part you bared would be lovely."

Rebecca was shocked. The color rose in her cheeks. His meaning was not lost on her. One would have had to be a complete idiot not to have understood its lewd implications.

She was supposed to be a sophisticated woman, and she would not let this man destroy that image. He would not know how his words made her acutely aware of every part of her body. It was as if an invisible hand were drawing itself teasingly across her flesh.

"Oh, look, Miss Cunningham!"

The carriage had reached a point where the view to the river was no longer blocked by warehouses or stately homes. The day was unusually warm for so early in the spring, but the trees were still bare except for the occasional bud. The bright spring sun ran across the surface of the river, highlighting each wave. Amidst the sparkling ripples ran a small schooner. It was this that had attracted the young boy.

"It's Captain Fenton. He's headin' around Hog Island and into the lake."

"Yes, Joey, it is the *Good Fortune,* and she's got a good wind at her back today. Captain Fenton ought to make good time."

Brad watched the sleek schooner slip behind the island that dominated the river at this point.

"I fear, Miss Cunningham, that I'm being kidnapped." Captain Taylor's deep voice disturbed the rapt attention both Joey and Rebecca had directed toward the boat.

"And why is that, Captain?"

"You promised to show me the city, and if I'm not mistaken the city is long left behind us."

"Not so, Captain. Surely you recognize Hog Island."

"As a child it was not a part of my world. The island was always in the distance, as far away as a dream."

There was something about his tone. She studied him. Whatever she had heard was not visible on his face.

"Well, we will just have to make it a part of your world."

"Joey, tell Samuel we will stop across from the island for lunch."

The boy jumped into action, thrusting the upper part of his body out the carriage window. Before Rebecca's gasp could materialize into a warning, he had hauled himself atop the carriage and installed himself next to the driver.

Brad laughed. "I think your fears are unwarranted. Joey seems to be able to take care of himself."

Rebecca returned the smile. "Weren't you always able to take care of yourself as a child, Captain? Somehow I find it impossible to imagine you victimized. Perhaps that is why you show little sympathy toward victims." Rebecca did not know why she was baiting him. Perhaps it was the richness of his laugh, or the intensity of his eyes. It was a self-protective measure, of that she was sure. She studied his impassive face and knew, although his features were unchanged, that she had hurt him.

"You have much to learn, Miss Cunningham, about victims and their victimizers. It is an area I would not venture too far into without an intimate knowledge."

Joey's upside-down face appeared suddenly in the

window. "We're here, Miss Cunningham. I'll be helping Samuel, if that's all right."

"Of course, Joey, and thank you."

Brad descended from the carriage first, then turned to help Rebecca descend. The ground was uneven near the side of the road, and he gallantly placed his hands around her waist to lift her away from the roughness. In truth, he had wanted to touch her. He was shocked when he felt the warmth of her body penetrate the thin layers of her clothing. Beneath his fingers he could feel none of the stays and corsets he expected to find on any woman of breeding. There was only the warmth and fluidity of flesh. He felt himself reacting to the feel of her. Once he set her down on the ground he studied her. He saw recognition in her face, but this time there was no blush.

"I'm sorry if I've embarrassed you, Captain. I abandon corsets and stays most of the time. I see no need for so many of the restrictions women put on themselves. You see, my mother died when I was still very young, and Father was too involved in his business to inflict a stern hand. In effect, I was indulged—spoiled, really—and I took full advantage of it, running roughshod over my governesses. I ignored propriety and enjoyed anything that was the least bit rebellious."

"And do you still?" There was a challenge in his question.

She studied him, aware of what her answer might imply, but unable to answer any other way. "Yes, Captain, I do."

Joey ran up to them, interrupting the awkward moment. "Samuel says to tell you we've found a place for lunch. It's right near the water. You can see all the way to the lake! Captain Fenton's schooner's still in sight. It's beautiful to see, Miss."

"Yes, Joey, I'll bet it is. Let's hurry, maybe we can see the *Good Fortune* one more time before she's out of sight." With that, Rebecca took the boy's hand and ran toward the water. For the first time in his adult life, Brad wished he were still a child.

When Rebecca and Joey returned, it was to find that much of the picnic lunch had been laid out. Brad, having rid himself of his pistol and hat, lay with his head cradled in his hands, studying the sky.

"Have you found anything interesting, Captain?"

"I believe an elephant passed by not long ago, followed by a galloping horse and a minstrel with a banjo." He rose up on one elbow and patted the blanket beside him. "Would you care to join me?"

The invitation was a little unusual, but Rebecca assured herself any impropriety was unintentional on his part. Sitting down beside him, she smoothed her skirts to assure she was well covered and then lay back on the blanket. The sky was a wonderful sight. Large overstuffed clouds lay against a background of brilliant blue. Even as she watched, they metamorphosed into fantastic shapes.

Rebecca and Brad lay in silence. The spring sun was warm and the air pungent with the odor of new life. Rebecca was so acutely aware of Brad's body stretched out beside her that she found it difficult to make any conversation whatsoever.

"I believe I see a wagon, Captain, just there. Do you see? It is piled high with snow." She thought she heard some sort of affirmation, but she was too self-conscious to turn her head. "And there it looks like old Joseph Campau, and . . ." She stopped.

He was up on one elbow. The shadow of his face fell across hers. Still, he did not touch her. Yet the intimacy of the moment begged for a touch. She felt that if he did not touch her, she would have to touch him, to caress the line of his jaw, to stroke his unruly black hair, to touch his lips. . . .

"Miss Cunningham, we've the last of it now. Can we eat?" Rebecca rolled to the opposite side and sat up. Young Joey was eagerly awaiting her response, eyeing the assortment of fine food provided for their enjoyment.

"Of course, Joey, go ahead." She turned to the captain. "I fear waiting is unbearable when such delicacies are laid out before a small boy."

His response was whispered close to her ear. "I don't think it is small boys alone who are anxious when they await delicacies."

Once more she felt a blush stain her cheeks. Again, she chose to ignore it. Instead, she stared out at the river. "It's an awful name for such a beautiful place, don't you think? The island, I mean. Hog Island. Did you know it got its name from the Indians who kept their livestock safe from marauders by grazing them there?"

There was no response. Brad lay with his head still propped on one hand. Rebecca had to turn away from his stare. She found herself babbling on, even as her flesh tingled deliciously with the tension between them. "The city fathers talk of changing its name. Belle Isle has been suggested. It is a beautiful island. You will have to come with me when the weather is warmer. I know every corner of it. As a girl I would defy my father and sail my boat over for the day. I'd explore until dusk and sail back to my father's wrath."

"And did your father's anger ever keep you from returning?"

For a moment Rebecca regained her equanimity, and she turned to the captain to search his face for the part of his soul that he kept so well hidden. She knew it was there, just as surely as she knew she kept a part of her own carefully hidden.

"Did your father's anger ever keep you from what you wanted, Captain?" She saw the shadow once more fall across his face. He was withdrawing once more into bitterness, into cynicism. She was not surprised at his answer when it came.

"No one keeps me from what I want, Miss Cunningham. No one." It was spoken softly, yet it frightened her.

"I think it is time we eat, Captain. I must be returning home shortly. I have other commitments this evening."

Brad made no reply other than to begin his meal. As he studied her and made polite conversation, he became sure of one thing. He wanted her.

5

"You're a damned fool, girl, if you ask me!"

"Well, I'm not asking you, Jacob! And if you don't keep your voice down you'll have the whole group so frightened that they will become far more of a danger to me than the slave hunters or Captain Taylor. They'll become so skittish that they'll panic."

"They'll not panic, girl. They've come too far on their own. They've shown a pile of courage just to make it this far. You know that, Miss Rebecca, so why do you say such things?" Jacob's anger was well founded.

"I'm sorry, Jacob. You're right, of course." Rebecca felt genuine remorse for her remarks. The huddled figures before her had endured far more hardship in the weeks and months it had taken them to reach Detroit than she would ever know in her entire life. She, as well as Jacob, knew that the Underground Railroad did little compared to what an escaped slave had to do for himself. Most of these people had traveled by night and hidden by day, using only their ingenuity and a little bit of luck to get them to the Ohio River, and some form of help from Levi Coffin and the beginnings of the "railroad" in Cincinnati.

She tried to deny that her short temper of late had anything to do with Brad Taylor. She also tried to deny that she was as angry at herself as she was with the unflappable captain. It was easier to place the blame on him, which she proceeded to do with unwarranted fury. He really was a bastard, she told herself in less-than-ladylike language. He was utterly charming, and utterly without soul. He probably would sell his own mother into slavery if it would benefit his career. He was the antithesis of everything that mattered. He was an insensitive, arrogant opportunist.

Only after this internal diatribe did she let the doubts surface. Had she been a fool to think she could manipulate him? In the past she had always managed her relationships very easily.

"If we're to do this, we best be about it." Jacob's voice pulled her back to the matter at hand.

"Have they been told what to expect?"

"Yes, they know what is expected of them. I'd not worry about them, Miss. It's you who's been too dreamy-headed lately."

"You know me better than that. I would never endanger them. And what do you mean, dreamy-headed?" Jacob's remarks upset her more than she dared admit.

Jacob, to her consternation, merely shrugged and walked away.

The fog was heavy. It had started to roll in when she left home two hours ago. Now it hung over everything, giving beast and building an unearthly air. As she and the fugitives crept quietly toward the wharf, Rebecca kept alert. She listened for Jacob's approach in the black boat, keenly aware that the increased military patrols posed additional threats tonight. If her sources were correct, they would have only twenty minutes to board and clear the dock. The fog offered both help and hindrance. It would protect them from discovery, but it also would make navigating the river more difficult.

It was with a great deal of relief that she made out the dark shadow of the *Deliverance* as it silently approached the dock they had chosen near the railroad yard.

"Did you have any trouble?" The whispered question rolled over the water to Jacob.

His grim expression gave her reply before he voiced it. "I could barely make out the bow, let alone the shore. It was the good Lord's hand that guided me this night, girl. I'll take no credit for it."

Rebecca felt a pang of guilt for having insisted they make the trip tonight. She had been restless, and it had been more for her benefit than any other that they were going out on the water in this dismal weather. They had been forced to move farther downriver to avoid the patrols, and the winds were too calm for her liking. They would be lucky to reach Amherstburg by dawn.

With their passengers safely on board, she and Jacob quickly rigged the remaining lines. As the sloop pulled slowly away from the dock, Rebecca sighed audibly. She had been more tense than usual. She watched what little light the city offered at this late hour being swallowed up by the dense white blanket that now lay tight to the water.

She was grateful that Jacob had insisted on accompanying her tonight. He had been more concerned about the weather than she, and this irritated her. She was getting careless. From now on she would have to be more alert.

She heard it first: the soft lapping of water against another object. She could barely make out Jacob as he stood watch ahead of the jib, but she sensed his sudden fear. Then there were voices, barely above a whisper. The exchanges were curt. Was it the military? Jacob nodded toward the sails, but Rebecca shook her head. It would do no good to try and lower them. The noise it would make might be their undoing. She prayed that the blackness of their sails, which had always served them well, would not stand out in the ghostly white fog.

Suddenly she heard the sound of metal against metal, and fear ran through her. She knew that sound; it was one she had heard before. It was the sound of an iron hull, and it could mean only one thing—somewhere out there in the fog, not more than five hundred feet from them, lurked the gunboat, *Michigan.* Over four times the size of the *Deliverance,* she was rigged as a barkentine, but that was not what made Rebecca's heart pound. It was the two paddle wheels with newly designed long stroke, low pressure engines that could mean their demise. With no wind, the *Michigan* could easily overtake them. There was no sound of engines, though. The *Michigan* must be under sail as well. It obviously did not want its presence known.

Both boats were practically at a standstill in the water. The winds had slacked off, almost nonexistent now. Rebecca silently prayed that no sudden wind change would cause the rigging of the *Deliverance* to betray them.

"Damn it, Captain, this is sure to see us grounded before long. You couldn't see your own mother if she were nose to nose with you. No one in his right mind would be out here tonight."

The irritated voice was so close that it startled Rebecca. The response was deep and resonant.

"He's out here. I feel it."

That voice! Rebecca knew it. Her heart raced, but not simply in fear.

"Well, he may be out here, Captain Taylor, but he's got the devil's own luck with this fog."

Brad begrudgingly acknowledged the truth of this statement. Whoever he was, this Angel of Passage did have the devil's own luck. Brad had been in Detroit over two months, and was no closer to capturing his elusive prey than when he had arrived. When one of his paid informants had brought word of a major movement of escaped slaves set for tonight, he had felt confident that he would capture the elusive figure.

As he stood by the rail, searching the eerie fog for any movement, he felt once more the frustrations that had disturbed him these past two months. Returning to Detroit had been a mistake. At every turn, the city pulled at his gut and raked his soul until it was raw. It was a constant reminder of everything he had chosen to forget, everything, he told himself, that no longer mattered.

But it did still matter. He had realized that yesterday when he found himself, against his will, at the cemetery. He had been drawn, as if by some unseen hand, to the pain. The grave marker was in place. He had paid for it years ago but had never seen it. As he stood with the warmth of the May sun to his back, he had felt chilled. The granite marker said so little about the woman who lay there. AMELIA TAYLOR B. JULY 21,1812 D. DEC. 21, 1850. It said nothing of the pain, nothing of the degradation, nothing of the abuse. It told little of the love she had felt for her son, little of the despair she had felt at being unable to protect him. He had felt once more the rage he thought he had subdued. It was there again just below the surface, painful, as if it would force his skin to explode and leave him one throbbing mass of raw flesh—vulnerable. That was the one thing he swore he would never be again, vulnerable. Vulnerable people were stupid people, powerless people. Vulnerable people allowed themselves to be used. His mother had been vulnerable. His mother had allowed herself to be used, and it had gotten her nothing but pain, excruciating physical and emotional pain. No, he would never allow himself to care about anything or anyone other than himself. Caring left you vulnerable.

His thoughts turned once more to his adversary. Caring is what would make this Angel of Passage vulnerable, and his vulnerability would mean his capture.

Rebecca heard the engines of the *Michigan* start. It was with relief that she realized the iron paddle wheeler was now some distance from them. Captain Taylor's influence seemed limitless. The *Michigan* was normally stationed in Lake Erie and rarely ventured up to Detroit. Her capture must have become a top priority, she thought grimly.

She and Jacob remained alert until the engines of the *Michigan* were only a distant murmur. Then they set out, keeping the *Deliverance* tight to the Canadian shore. The fog and the lack of wind slowed their progress to the point that Rebecca became concerned about returning before daybreak. It was almost four before they reached the big island of Beau Blois, which marked their approach to Amherstburg. Ben and Hannah were still waiting when they pulled up to the small dock. Relief shone on their faces as they rushed to help the weary passengers off.

Ben and Hannah Finney knew firsthand the courage and ingenuity of the men, women, and children in Rebecca's care. It was only five years ago that they too had hidden in Seymour Finney's stable, too cold and tired to believe they were so close to freedom. They had crossed the river in the winter on foot and, in gratitude to the last man who had shown them kindness, had chosen for their surname that of old Seymour Finney.

As Hannah hurried the figures up to the house, Ben turned to Rebecca and Jacob. "You'd best leave the *Deliverance* here with Jacob, Miss Rebecca. You'll have the devil's own time gettin' back before dawn. I'll have Elijah take you upriver and row you across to your own dock. Even then, you'll have to hurry."

George Cunningham sat alone in his study as the first rays of the May sun crept over the horizon, trying to pierce the sodden blanket of thick fog that lay waiting for warmth to dissipate it.

The study was large and tastefully furnished. Located in the back of the large house, its beveled glass windows would normally have afforded him a view all the way to the river. But this morning, he could not even make out the stables fifty feet behind the house. A movement caught his attention, startling him out of his somber fatigue. It was a dark shadow amid the white fog. As the seconds passed, the shape materialized into a cloaked figure. George Cunningham waited for the figure to approach the house before he turned and left the room.

"You're home." The voice jolted Rebecca as she entered the hall from the kitchen. She quickly threw the cowl back and pulled the cape tighter around her trouser-clad figure.

"Father! What on earth are you doing up at this ungodly hour?"

"I might ask you the same thing."

There was a long pause as Rebecca struggled to think of a reasonable explanation. "I couldn't sleep. I decided to take a walk to the river. You know how soothing I find it." Her father was a sound sleeper, so sound that it had been something of a family joke. The fact that he was awake was a sign that something was not right. She could see it in the deep lines etched in his face.

"You will be caught one day." The sadness in his voice tore at her heart.

"Caught? Whatever are you talking about, Father? Caught taking a walk to the river? Is taking a walk in your own yard now a crime?"

George Cunningham gently moved apart the hands that clutched the black cape. He took only a cursory glance at her masculine garb before looking back up. With eyes glistening with unshed tears, he searched her face.

"Oh, Father, don't . . . please, don't . . ." She felt

compelled to embrace him, comfort him, even though tears of pain were welling up in her own eyes. Before she could act, she felt his strong arms encircle her as if she were once more a child.

"I'm so afraid for you."

"You knew? You've known all along?" She pulled back to study his face, blinking away her own tears.

"Yes, I've known."

"But why have you said nothing?"

He took both her hands in his. "Come, we must talk."

Once inside the study, he quietly shut the massive oak door behind them. Pouring himself a brandy, he raised a questioning eyebrow to Rebecca. She nodded, and he poured a second.

"I am not a doddering fool, Rebecca, regardless of what you may think."

"Oh, Father."

"No, let me finish. Did you think I would miss your comings and goings? You may be an enigma to the citizens of Detroit, but to your father you are no puzzle at all. I blame myself, you know."

"No, there is no one to blame. It is not something to be reproached for, what I'm doing."

"I didn't mean to say that. Your intentions are good, your motives well-founded. I have no quarrel with that. It is the method you have chosen to help. It is far too dangerous."

"But this is what I have to offer. It is what I am good at. I can sail as well as any man, and they desperately need safe transport for these people."

George Cunningham looked out the window. With his back to Rebecca, he spoke again, his voice choking with emotion. "You are so like her, you know.

She was forever fighting other people's battles. She was vibrant and passionate and not easily deterred once she made up her mind. My God, she could be so stubborn and strong-willed! She was far more forgiving and compassionate than I, you know. I thought I would die when she died. I didn't think I could go on, but I had you—a daughter to live for. I watched you grow and flourish and change into a woman, a woman so like your mother that sometimes I feel the pain again as if the loss were only yesterday."

He turned to her. "I couldn't live through another loss, Rebecca. I am too old, too worn down. I'm sorry if that disappoints you. The young are very idealistic. I have lived in fear for you every day of the last two years. I have said nothing, because I know what you do is right, and it needs to be done if this nation is to come to grips with this unconscionable evil. But I am selfish. I wish for someone else to do it. Is that so bad?"

Rebecca crossed the room to him, her heart nearly breaking. She embraced him. "No, it is not so bad. It is a most precious gift to be loved so. You have done something for the cause far riskier than I, Father. I risk only my life. You've risked your heart. You are much braver than I. I will not take unnecessary risks, I promise."

They stood in the quiet embrace until her father pulled away.

"You'd best get some sleep. I'll be upstairs shortly. I need a few moments." She turned and headed toward the door. His voice stopped her before she opened it.

"I am proud of you, Rebecca."

"I know."

* * *

"I told ya, Captain. Them niggers took in a whole passel of them early this morning, maybe twelve, fourteen. Brought 'em across by boat. Wasn't a thing my friend could do once they reached the other side, leastwise not without risking his own neck, if ya know what I mean. Sorry ya didn't get 'em, but a deal's a deal." The man stood with his palm outstretched. Brad unlocked his top drawer and removed a small satchel. He counted out some bills and threw them on the desk.

"Why, thanks, Captain. Much obliged." Pock snatched the bills and headed for the door. "Better luck next time!" he snickered over his shoulder.

Brad flung the satchel down on the desk. He had been right. The Angel of Passage had been on the water last night, and so near that Brad would have seen him, had it not been for the damned fog. If he believed in divine intervention, he would swear it had been at work last night.

6

"You are risking too much, Rebecca! I don't care what you say, you will be discovered. He is not a dullard. Quite the contrary, he is very astute."

"And his sources are impeccable, Rachel. He knows what we are going to do before we do it. That's what makes it so perfect. He himself will be our informant. Don't you see the irony in it?"

"All I see is the danger. He is very good at what he does. Do you really think he will just volunteer information to you?"

"It may take some time, but I think it can be done."

"It may take more than time, my friend, and I don't know if you realize the price that may have to be paid."

Rebecca's deep blush told Rachel that she understood.

"You will not be able to dally with him like your other admirers. He does not seem the type to be led on and then refused. I warn you, I can tell he is a hard man."

Rebecca shifted uncomfortably under the keen gaze of the woman who was both friend and surrogate mother to her. Rachel's concerns seemed unwarranted, though. Rebecca could easily manipulate Captain Taylor. After all, she'd always been able to handle men in the past. How different could this one be?

Brad had just stepped out of the Finney Hotel when he heard his name being called. He turned to see young Joey Whiton running toward him.

"Whoa, boy, slow down. Where's the fire?" There was affection in his voice. As the boy got closer, though, an almost uncontrollable anger welled up in Brad. Livid red welts were visible above the boy's wrist, where his arm protruded from his too-small shirt. It was not difficult to imagine how far up the arm they went. Who could do something like that to a child? He need not have asked himself the question. He knew exactly what kind of man would beat his own son.

"Mr. Finney said I was to give this to you right away, Captain Taylor." The boy looked up admiringly at the tall, uniformed officer.

"Thank you, Joey."

Brad studied the welts on the boy's arm. "You look like you've been run over by a train, lad."

The boy lowered his head. "Yessir."

"I would be more careful, if I were you, to stay out of its path in the future. I know a great deal about the damage trains can do, myself."

Joey looked up again. His eyes sought confirmation of what he had just heard.

Brad crouched down to speak to the boy more intimately. "I've been run over by a train or two in my life. Fact is, I got run over quite regularly." Joey's eyes widened.

He put his hand on the boy's shoulder. "Promise me one thing, Joey. Promise me you'll never let that train get the better of you."

Joey nodded. Brad had to force himself to remove his hand from the boy and stand. He pulled a quarter out of his pants and tucked it in the boy's shirt pocket. "Do you remember what I told you last time?"

"Yessir, Captain." A smile materialized on the child's face. "I remember. And thank you, sir."

Brad stood for a long time, watching the boy zigzag his way around the pedestrians who strolled along Woodward Avenue. He couldn't shake the unaccountable feeling of desolation the encounter had left with him.

Almost as an afterthought, he opened the note in his hand. It was from Rebecca Cunningham. He had not seen much of her in the last few weeks. He had meant to pursue the relationship, but his search for information on the Angel of Passage had taken up more of his time than he had anticipated.

Now, he realized as he read the invitation to a picnic, she was coming to him.

Several days later, on the first day of June, 1860, Brad knocked on the door of the Cunningham home. It was already hot and promised to get hotter. He could feel perspiration soaking the back of his linen shirt. As he waited for a response, he removed his jacket and slung it over his shoulder. He was not in uniform. He wore his shirt collar open to offset the heat, and buff-colored trousers tucked into high black military boots.

Rebecca steadied herself and opened the door. The man who stood patiently waiting took her by surprise. Gone was the crisp army captain, gone the disciplined enforcer. In his place stood, at least in appearance, a warmer, more human man. Rebecca found herself noticing the most insignificant details—the damp tendril of dark hair that fell across his brow, the black curls just below the hollow at his throat, the fresh smell of soap.

"Miss Cunningham." A warm smile softened his face, and for a moment Rebecca almost forgot what she was about.

"Captain." It took no effort at all to return his smile. "I am so happy you could make it. It is the servants' day off, and Father has gone to the office, so I'm afraid I will need your help." She turned and headed toward the back of the house. She wore a simple cotton dress in a pale shade of lavender. It was sprinkled profusely with small purple flowers—violets, Brad imagined—and lacked almost any other ornamentation except for the ribbon closures down the front. The neckline was gently gathered, framing her graceful neck. She seemed much more vulnerable when dressed this simply, much more touchable. Her heavy mane of honey-colored hair had been confined to a snood. This was a shame, Brad thought as he followed her into the kitchen.

"I had the cook prepare us a lunch before she left.

She's excellent, and I'm sure you'll enjoy it."

"I'm sure I will."

The simple statement, lacking in artifice, caused Rebecca to look over her shoulder at him. She found him studying her as she moved about, gathering the last of the things and placing them in the big sturdy basket that sat on the large kitchen table.

"Well, Captain, it's time you went to work." She indicated the laden basket and headed for the door that led to the stables.

Brad was only mildly surprised when she reached the stables and continued beyond them. He found it pleasurable just to watch her. She moved with grace, the slender curves of her hips swaying slightly with her gait. He felt himself grow hard with the contemplation of her body and attempted to distract himself by wondering where they were going. It wasn't until they reached the water that he began to understand. He smiled as she moved out onto the dock and sat at a small bench that had been constructed along one side.

"Go ahead and set the basket in the cabin." She indicated the sloop. "But make sure it's secured."

"Aye, aye, captain." Brad executed a mock salute. When he returned from his task, it was to his continuing amazement to see that Rebecca had removed her hose and shoes. She leapt into the boat, and for the first time he noticed that the skirt of the dress had been artfully designed to allow such an activity. It was split, much like a riding skirt, and the waist was gathered in such a manner that only an exaggerated movement would display its ingenuity.

Rebecca turned at his laughter.

"You are a source of constant amazement, Miss Cunningham."

Rebecca gave him a puzzled look before she looked down at her skirt and realized what had provoked his laughter.

"Yes, isn't it wonderful? Rachel designed it for me. She thought it much more suitable to these kinds of activities than the other things I might choose."

"It sounds as if the woman knows you quite well."

"She is a dear friend, and a wonderfully talented seamstress. She has become almost a second mother to me."

"I shall have to complement her on her resourcefulness, should I meet her someday."

Rebecca's demeanor suddenly became more reticent.

"I doubt you shall ever meet her, Captain. She does not move in the same social circles that you do." Her tone mimicked perfectly the cynicism he had displayed weeks ago, when he had answered similarly. "You see, Captain, Rachel is a Negro."

For a moment Rebecca thought she might actually have succeeded in embarrassing the normally unflappable Captain, but the moment passed, and she would never be sure.

"Well, Captain, I shall need your help if we are to be on our way."

"I'm not without experience on ships."

"I've no doubt, Captain." She recalled the fog and the deep voice that had floated across the water.

"Don't you think it's time you called me Brad? I fear two captains on one boat may be confusing."

She balked inwardly at the intimacy of addressing him by his first name but nodded her acquiescence.

There was little social conversation over the next minutes as Rebecca issued orders and moved the sloop out from the dock and into the river. Brad marvelled at her expertise. He would never have guessed it of her. She headed the boat toward the Canadian shore before tacking northeast. Even though they were headed against the current, the brisk southwestern wind filled the sails, and they made good speed. Within a half hour, they were abreast of Hog Island.

Brad sat back and studied the woman at the tiller. She had tied on a large straw hat, something of a concession to the sun, which had grown still hotter. The hat seemed incongruous, though, too constraining, like the snood. He was tempted to remove both but contented himself with enjoying the water and the breeze—and the view. The wind forced her thin dress to conform to her figure, outlining her firm derriere and slender waist.

His gaze returned to her face, and he saw in it her exhilaration.

"You're really quite good at this, you know."

"I don't need you to tell me that, Captain. Does it surprise you?"

"Everything about you is a pleasant surprise, *Rebecca.*" His emphasis on her given name came as a gentle reminder to their agreement.

"And you . . ." she hesitated, ". . . Brad, do you have any surprises?"

He laughed. "If I do, they would be surprises to me as well."

"Perhaps they will be." She paused. "Why are you here?"

"I thought I was here for a picnic. Am I mistaken?"

Rebecca was irritated by his intentional misunderstanding. "In Detroit. Why are you here in Detroit? Surely what we do in the provinces can't be of that great importance in Washington."

"I thought your resourcefulness had already determined why I'm in Detroit. Do I need to elaborate?"

"You need to justify why you pursue innocent people who have never done anyone harm and whom you threaten with imprisonment."

"Surely you're not speaking of the Angel of Passage."

Rebecca was caught off guard. Did he know something? He seemed to be gauging her reaction. She tried to shake off the ominous feeling that had enveloped her.

"No, I was referring to the Negroes, whom you would see back in slavery."

"There are others who will see to the slaves."

"Then what is it, Captain, that keeps you here?"

"I thought we both already understood that, Rebecca." There was a long pause. The intensity of his gaze made her uncomfortable. "*You* keep me here."

For one terrifying moment, Rebecca feared she had been discovered. She paled so dramatically, Brad's expression showed concern.

"Are you all right? I didn't know my attentions were so horrible to contemplate."

It was still another moment before Rebecca's heartbeat slowed down. "No, of course not, Brad." She forced herself to smile.

"For a moment I wasn't so sure."

Rebecca's mind was racing. He had made her lose control. She would have to be more cautious in the future.

She welcomed the distraction of having to tack to clear the channel into Lake St. Clair. "You'd better prepare to come about. We'll sail out into the lake awhile before we stop for lunch."

The next hour or so was spent in pleasant enough conversation. Once they had entered the lake, Rebecca had headed northeast. She moved to sit high on the starboard side, across from Brad. He entertained her with his talk of the comings and goings in Washington of late, and Rebecca was content to bide her time.

She failed to realize how engrossed she had become until a change in the light caught her attention. Looking up to the sails, she noticed the wind had slacked off. She pivoted in her seat to look in the direction they had just come. "Damn!" The word was barely more than a whisper, but it did not escape Brad.

"Something wrong?"

"Those clouds are what is wrong. I'm afraid your amusing stories have put us up for a soaking."

"I've been wet before." Brad looked puzzled by her worried expression. "Is there something else you should tell me?"

"I don't like the feel of it. The winds have fallen off completely. I'm afraid this is going to be a serious storm. The lake is exceedingly shallow, and high winds will turn it dangerous quickly. We'd best hurry back."

As she prepared to come about, she wondered what experience Captain Taylor did, in fact, have with small boats. She prayed it was considerable.

She coaxed the sloop, which was now almost becalmed. She had just about given up hope of bringing it around when a breeze filled the sails with just enough air to complete the tack. Facing into the wind, Rebecca realized the difficult task ahead of them. Black clouds had devoured the sun. Despite the fact that it was about noon, there was an eerie twilight feel in the air. The blue water was suddenly dark gray and frothy with whitecaps. The increasing waves beat against the boat, impeding its progress.

Rebecca berated herself for her laxity. She knew this lake, and she knew its dangers. How could she have been so unobservant? Why had she allowed herself to be so cajoled by a man she shouldn't even like? Now they would have a devil of a time beating into the increasing wind.

She ordered Brad to trim the sails, and she pulled the boat still tighter to the wind. She was steering a potentially dangerous course. Any change in the wind's direction, however slight, might capsize them.

"You'd better sit topside. With the wind this unpredictable, we will have to be ready to move. Do you understand?" A sudden gust caught her hat, blowing it out onto the lake, where it floundered for a moment before being sucked under. The sails strained in the strong winds.

"I understand," came the response, shouted now above the noise of the increasing gale. She looked ahead and saw the rain. It was a solid sheet of water approaching them with frightening speed. The wind whipped the shallow waters into a fury. Within a matter of minutes, the waves had risen to four feet. The small sloop rose and fell. Each time it fell, the wind fought with the sails, trying to catch the back sides. Rebecca was struggling to hold the boat on course.

"Do you want me to take the wheel?" he shouted.

"No, but I'm afraid we'll have to take down the mainsail. Running with just the jib will slow us down, but it will avoid our being capsized."

No sooner had Rebecca spoken when the rain hit. It was like being stung in the face by a swarm of bees. The drops were unnaturally cold, icy almost. Rebecca shivered, as much out of fear as from the frigid rain.

"We've got to get the mainsail down, now!" She shouted to Brad, who was already moving toward the clew. She watched as he released the mainsheet in preparation for taking the mainsail down. Once the sheet was released the boom shook wildly in the wind. As Brad made his way forward past the swinging boom toward the halyard, Rebecca realized that, with his inexperience, he would never get the sail down alone.

Turning the boat away from its tight tack, Rebecca grabbed the rope and hook behind her and fastened it to the wheel. It should allow her the time she needed to help with the sail. She crawled forward as the boat became more unsteady with the play in the wheel. Brad was still struggling with the halyard when she reached the mast. She positioned herself forward of it and awaited the release of the sail. Fortunately, her feet were bare, giving her a good grip on the slippery deck. She was soaked to the skin.

Brad was too. His hair was dripping, and his shirt clung to his torso. As he released the sail, the boat moved into a valley. The swell, combined with the slack in the wheel, forced the bow into the wind, allowing the mainsail to be caught from behind. As

Rebecca struggled to lower the sail, she saw the boom swing across the boat. Even as she screamed, she knew that Brad could not react in time. She saw his surprise for a split second, and then he was hit.

7

Rebecca threw herself on the deck and allowed the sail to fall on its own. Brad lay further back, dazed and in imminent danger of slipping off the wildly swaying boat. She crawled toward the stern, fighting both the enveloping sail on top of her and the bobbing boat to reach him.

She could see he was struggling to maintain consciousness. As she reached out to grab his shirt, he lost the struggle. She quickly moved between him and the four-inch railing that went around the deck. Wedging herself between it and Brad's unconscious body, she pushed and dragged him toward the rear. The mainsail was in the water behind her and she could feel the pull as it filled with water. The weight of their bodies and the water-filled sail made Rebecca's task that much harder. The boat was in danger of capsizing on top of them. She moaned when she finally pushed Brad off the deck into the cockpit. She quickly checked the wheel and saw that the line was still holding.

She had to release the mainsail, or they would go

over. She struggled back along the topside of the deck, releasing the lines that held the sail. When the last was released, the boat righted itself and bobbed frantically in the wind, the jib wildly luffing. She moved to trim the jib. As she did, she felt the boat regain its course and steady itself. She crawled back aft and took the wheel.

Her dress clung to her. Her hair lay in long wet tendrils across her face. She blinked, trying to see in the continuing rain. She occasionally looked down at Brad, who lay on the bottom of the boat. She could do nothing for him now. She sent a fervent prayer that he was not seriously hurt, and then nearly laughed aloud at the irony of her prayer. She no longer knew whether the water she blinked from her eyes was rain or tears.

It was almost an hour before she saw land. Brad had not stirred. The worst of the storm had passed overhead, but the water still roiled. She was exhausted. Her arms ached, and she shivered uncontrollably. As she guided the boat toward shore, she concerned herself with not running aground. It would not be an easy task alone, in the rough water. The jib was too far forward for her to control easily. Once more, she had to use the hook on the wheel. She had chosen the best place she could to land. The lake bottom fell off quickly here. It would allow her to guide the boat quite close to shore without the keel striking bottom. As the sloop moved under its own guidance, Rebecca went forward to release the jib. When they were within twenty feet of shore, she was able to drop anchor. Quickly she lowered the jib and returned to check on Brad.

He had begun to stir in her absence, which greatly

relieved her, but he had also started to shiver. The temperature had dropped at least twenty degrees in the wake of the storm, and his sodden shirt and pants clung to him, chilling him. She would have to do something.

Grasping him beneath his arms, she dragged him down into the cabin. She winced as his body was jarred by the steps. In her arms, against the wetness of her breasts, she could feel his warmth. She steadied his head with her cheek, and the smell of him drew her thoughts away from the recent struggle and toward other things.

She was acutely aware of the muscular hardness of his arms and chest as she struggled to get him onto the berth. At this moment she was grateful for her own size and strength. Without it, they both would probably be dead. She searched below the berth for a blanket and then began to strip him of his wet clothes. She sought a second blanket and used it as a towel to dry him as she went along. At first her hands moved quickly and methodically. Then, without realizing it, her actions slowed almost to a caress. She moved her hands across his muscled chest and down the line of his flat belly, marvelling at the soft, curly masses of dark hair that drew her still further down. She began to unbutton his pants, and her hands shook. She peeled down the wet layer of fabric, leaving only his knitted woolen underwear, which clung to his solid thighs. The wet wool filled her nostrils with a familiar smell as her senses became intimately aware of more unfamiliar territory barely covered by the damp garment.

She felt herself reacting to him, and her mind bridled at the intensity of her reaction. Still, she could not take her eyes off him, off his finely muscled chest and arms, off his face—very still, and for once devoid of any sarcasm, without any of the barriers he used to protect himself. Finally, she forced herself to cover him. She had begun to shake too violently, herself. Whether from cold or something else, she dared not think.

She turned away and moved to the opposite side of the cramped quarters, where she began to strip off her own sodden clothes. This act, in such close proximity to Brad's unconscious form, was almost too much for her to bear. Her nipples were erect and firm as the rain-soaked garments passed over them. When she had stripped off the last of her clothes, she wrapped herself in the damp blanket and went over to examine the welt that had formed on Brad's left temple. She moved her hand to push back his wet hair.

She jumped when he touched her. His eyes were still closed, and yet his hand captured hers and pulled it against his chest.

"If this is the river Styx, you are a boatman far more to my liking than any other." His voice was overpoweringly resonant in the small space. He slowly opened his eyes. His other hand found its way to her back, where only the thin blanket protected her nakedness.

She couldn't move. She heard her voice, hoarse and barely above a whisper. "How long have you been conscious?"

"Long enough." His hand moved up along the curve of her waist, upward, slowly upward, tantalizingly slow, until it reached her bare shoulders. Still she could not move. His hand moved up her neck to cradle her cheek. His thumb played over her lips, caressing each in turn. She felt herself reacting to the gentleness of his touch. She should move away, but she couldn't.

"You are far more beautiful this way than in all your finery."

She stared at him, mesmerized by his words, by the intimate timbre of his voice, by his touch. She craved more, even as somewhere inside her a dire warning sounded.

The back of his hand glided down her neck, then turned to caress her bare shoulder once more, causing her to shiver anew.

"You feel soft, Rebecca, soft and warm."

She was in torture.

"I want you, Rebecca."

His hand moved to the middle of her back where its insistence drew her to him. It continued up her back, commanding compliance. It guided her to him, her mouth to his, hungry and seeking.

He kissed her deeply and passionately, until she was finally shocked into movement. She pulled away from his probing tongue, from his desire. She moved back across the cabin, still alive with feelings she never knew she had.

His eyes followed her, sensing her confusion. "I want you, Rebecca Cunningham," he spoke slowly, as if to make her understand, "and I will have you. If not now, later."

She had been offered a reprieve. She bent and quickly gathered the wet clothing they had shed. She hurried up to the deck, where the brilliant rays of the returning sun branded her a traitor.

She sat shaking, aware of the perspiration that

coated her tingling skin. But it was the wetness between her clenched thighs that still betrayed her. She wanted him as much as he wanted her. She trembled at the thought of what almost happened. Yet what appalled her most was the fact that, even as she despised her lack of control, she continued to revel in the sensations he had stirred in her.

Rachel had been right. Passion did not answer to reason. It frightened her as nothing ever had. He was her enemy, and yet he could stir in her such intense feelings that she was left powerless. She had become a traitor to herself. She would have to learn to live with that, but she vowed on her life that he would never force her to betray those who depended on her.

Rebecca spread the soaked clothes out on the deck. She re-dressed in her chemise and pantaloons, despite their wetness, and wrapped the damp blanket around herself as further armor. She lay back on the deck and tried to rationalize what had occurred. It had to be something she could deal with, something over which she would have some control. She would have to stay in control, to avoid jeopardizing the others. As the minutes passed and the sun slowly warmed her, she felt herself regain some of her composure.

Down below, Brad attempted to sit up, but the throbbing in his head began almost immediately. He lay back and waited. He could hear her moving about on deck. He was pretty sure the storm had cleared. Sunlight filtered through the open door of the cabin. He moved his hand up to check the side of his head that had received the blow. The swelling was tender to his touch.

His erection was uncomfortable, but it would not ebb. The sounds coming from above kept alive the memory of her, almost naked, before him, and with the memory came the need to have her. What had scared her off? he wondered. There was passion in her eyes, but there was something else as well.

For a moment he thought he had seen fear, but fear of what? Perhaps he was wrong in his assessment of her. Perhaps she was not as experienced as he had assumed. He would have to go more slowly. He closed his eyes and strove to block out the whisper of her movement above him.

"Are you hungry?"

"Yes." His manner was more subdued now.

"Can you sit up?"

"That remains to be seen." He moved his legs over the side of the berth and slowly came to a sitting position, pulling the blanket tightly around him.

"I've spread our clothes to dry. It shouldn't be much longer."

He nodded.

"Do you feel that you could make it up on deck?"

He rose, and when she saw him sway she moved to steady him, allowing him to lean on her. She helped him navigate the narrow steps to the deck. Once he was seated, she returned below to get the basket.

When she came back, she saw he was smiling.

"Is something amusing, Captain?"

He did not miss the fact that she had reverted to her former manner of address. "I'm afraid, Miss Cunningham, that were anyone to join us for lunch, you would be unmistakably compromised." His eyes took in her scant wardrobe.

"And you find that amusing?" There was challenge in her voice.

"No, but I would find myself bearing the stigma reluctantly in light of our mutual lack of fulfillment."

"What makes you so sure it is mutual?"

"Experience."

She turned from him as a telltale blush threatened her self-control. "We need to eat if we are to get back by dinner. I don't wish to face another storm. The mainsail is lost, and the jib torn."

"You have no extra sails on board?"

Rebecca thought of the black sails carefully hidden in the bow. "No, Captain. We shall have to make do."

They ate in silence, and although the food was excellent, neither ate with any relish.

Brad's headache had grown worse in the heat of the sun, and he was relieved when Rebecca ordered him below to rest after they had eaten. He lay in the cool semidarkness of the cabin and puzzled over the woman who, after hurriedly re-dressing, now pulled anchor.

Although his dry clothes lay across from him on the opposite berth, he had not put them on. There was something exceedingly sensual about lying almost naked in the dark, listening to the sounds of the water against the boat and contemplating the woman above.

It had been too long since he'd had a woman, and Rebecca Cunningham was unlike any woman he had ever had. She lived her life with a strength of purpose he had never seen in a woman before. He was determined to pursue the relationship, despite her seeming reluctance.

* * *

He must have fallen asleep. The sun no longer streamed into the cabin, and it appeared to be almost dusk. Slowly, he rose from the berth, stiff and sore from the bruises he had received in the accident. His headache had lessened, although it returned in full force when he bent over. He struggled into his clothes, the task complicated by the movement of the boat.

When he came up top, it was to find Rebecca at the wheel, legs folded beneath her, looking drawn and tired.

She looked up as he appeared. "Are you feeling better?"

"Yes, thank you."

"We're almost home."

Brad turned to look off the bow where the city of Detroit lay basking in the receding sunlight.

"If you feel up to taking the helm, I might be able to improve our progress."

He stepped over beside her as she relinquished the wheel and watched her move across the deck toward the jib. Her footing was sure, and she did not hesitate, even as the sloop bobbed and rolled. There was a confidence about her, and he found himself drawn to her as never before.

She finished her task and moved back toward him. Her hair had dried, and the wind played with it, tossing golden strands of it across her face. She tossed her head to rid herself of their distraction.

He sat mesmerized, wanting to feel the fullness of her hair entwined in his fingers, to smooth it away from her brow. The gentle breeze behind her toyed with her light cotton dress, molding it to her long legs. He saw her shiver, and the thought of warming her with his body burned itself into his brain. He was unable to dislodge it. He had to have her. It would free him from this unfamiliar feeling of being driven by forces outside himself.

"You're cold. Let me get you a blanket."

"I assure you it's not necessary, Captain."

"But it is the least I can do in return. I haven't thanked you yet for saving my life. I am in your debt."

She shrugged.

He returned below, only to find the blankets still damp and chill from their previous use. He searched beneath the berths before moving on to the bow. He opened the door to the storage area. There were several blankets within easy reach. As he removed them, his eye was drawn to some large canvas bags lying at the far end. They would normally not have caught his attention, for it was common enough to carry extra sails on board. What puzzled him was that she had denied having any.

He heard a man's voice above. Still pondering his discovery, he closed the door to the storage compartment and left the cabin.

"We're fine, Jacob," Rebecca called to the huge black man standing at the foot of the Cunningham dock. The man's face showed concern. He fixed his gaze on Brad's emerging figure, and all emotion drained, leaving an expressionless mask.

"I'm afraid the sails are a loss," Rebecca went on. "We'll have to order some new ones. I don't think there is any other damage."

Jacob gave the black boat a cursory glance as he helped dock it, then returned to study Rebecca, worry once more evident on his face.

"Could you see that Captain Taylor gets safely back to his quarters?" Rebecca asked. "He took a nasty bump on the head."

She turned to Brad, her face impassive. "Good-bye, Captain."

Brad was coolly dismissed.

8

"I'm tellin' ya, Capt'n, there's somethin' afoot. Them niggers been meetin' right and left. Soon's I can figure the whys and such I'll let ya know."

Brad nodded to Pock, and the little man turned and headed for the door, with a twisted smile on his face. "Don't worry, Capt'n, we'll catch that nigger-lovin' bastard yet."

Brad didn't think it was possible to dislike the man any more than he had at first, but, with each of their meetings, Brad's aversion had grown until it had become disgust. What great ironic perversion had put this distasteful man on his side of the law? Brad wondered. He had more respect for the Angel of Passage than this poor excuse for a man.

This thought gave him pause. It was true, he had developed a grudging admiration for the dark apparition. Here was a man much like himself, single-minded, devoted to one purpose. To dedicate such effort with no benefit in sight for himself was unfathomable to Brad, who worked only to further his career.

That was why he had never concerned himself with the politics of slavery; he had seen nothing to be gained personally from taking sides. Taking a position might, in fact, have hindered his career, depending on which way the political winds in Washington were blowing. He was content to remain apart from the issue, treating it as a matter of law, not principle. Detroit had somehow managed to make him uncomfortable with this simple approach, and it angered him. Discomfort was not an emotion he was familiar with.

Neither, he thought painfully, were the feelings he harbored for Rebecca Cunningham. He had avoided her these past weeks, giving her time, hoping to further his chances in the long run, but she had been constantly in his thoughts. The look of her, the touch of her that day in the boat, haunted his dreams and distracted his days. It was as if she had bewitched him, and he, with all his experience, had allowed himself to be entrapped. One moment she was all proper reserve and practiced social grace, and the next, guileless sensuality.

Damn! He had given her enough time to play her little game. He would not be toyed with. He wanted her, and she knew it. She would have to make up her mind, or he would make it up for her.

The din in the meeting room quieted when George Fox's gavel hit the podium. The large group of abolitionists was gathering to discuss the upcoming election. The talk would revolve around the fledgling Republican party and its candidate, Abraham Lincoln. There was much concern over whether this Illinois lawyer was committed to the abolition of slavery. The word from the Chicago convention had been unclear.

There was talk of wheeling and dealing. Some said Mr. Lincoln's campaign manager had promised too much to too many people. Lincoln himself had left a somewhat puzzling trail of speeches. That he was not the abolitionists' ideal candidate was an accepted fact. But whether he should be supported as the lesser of evils was the subject at hand.

Brad had entered the room as inconspicuously as possible and leaned against the back wall. He had not worn his uniform. Even in uniform, he doubted that he would be thrown out. However much they might suspect his motives, the meeting itself was legal and open to all.

He scanned the room. He knew George Fox to be a leading Quaker citizen of Detroit. The Quakers' commitment to outlawing slavery was well known. He saw other familiar faces, black and white. George DeBaptiste was sitting in the front row. Further back he saw Seymour Finney. Somehow that did not surprise him. As he turned to survey the remainder of the crowd, he was surprised by the sight of Rebecca Cunningham.

He lost track of what the speaker was saying as he studied her. She spoke quietly to the dignified black woman who sat next to her. Rebecca had placed her hand over the black woman's and was urgently discussing something with her. The black woman shook her head as if to disagree. Was this woman Rachel? Brad wondered. He remembered Rebecca's mention of her on the day of the ill-fated sail.

So Rebecca Cunningham publicly proclaimed herself an ardent abolitionist. This was an interesting turn of events. It added a certain new dimension to this multifaceted woman.

He tore his attention from the two women and looked around the room once again, wondering which of the men among the assembly was the notorious Angel of Passage. No doubt he was here.

He had already eliminated several prominent suspects, having checked on their whereabouts the nights he had seen the stygian figure. There were many still to pursue, however. He hoped to catch the man in the act. It would give him great personal pleasure.

The meeting was drawing to a close when Brad turned his attention once more to Rebecca. As the final gavel came down, she rose and crossed the room to DeBaptiste and a man Brad recognized as William Lambert. They entered into a heated discussion, in which her urgent entreaties were met by forceful disagreement from the two black men. Brad could see disappointment and frustration on her face. She still hadn't noticed him when she finally approached the door to leave.

"Miss Cunningham, what an unexpected surprise," he said as he followed her out.

Rebecca was startled but quickly recovered. "No more surprising than your presence here, Captain. But then again, one can readily guess your purpose in coming."

"As long as we find ourselves together, regardless of the reason, may I escort you home?"

"I'm not going immediately home, Captain. And I don't believe I'm in need of an escort."

She had begun to descend the outer stairs of the building, and he doggedly kept pace with her. She stopped and turned to face him. "I see, Captain Taylor, that subtlety escapes you. I wish you to leave me. I assure you I can take care of myself very well."

"You can, indeed, Miss Cunningham." With a small bow, Brad accepted his defeat and turned to go.

Rebecca studied the broad back of the departing figure. She felt relief, but other more confusing feelings came back with an urgency that frightened her. She banned any thoughts of Captain Taylor from her mind as she tried to concentrate on the problem at hand.

As she turned on East Larned, she failed to notice the man who followed her.

She knocked on the beautifully carved door of a house. George DeBaptiste opened the door and stood aside for her to enter. When he finally spoke, it was in a smooth, cultured voice. In 1846, after leaving his post as valet to President Harrison, DeBaptiste had settled in Detroit. He had successfully established himself, first as a clothier and then as the owner of an excursion steamer. He later added to these occupations caterer and restaurateur.

"I will not say this again, Rebecca. You will not be involved in this move. Jacob tells me this Captain Taylor has intensified his search for you. If word leaks out that we have merchandise to be transported, you will be the one he is looking for. There are others who are competent and just as eager to help as you."

Rebecca bristled at his reprimand. "But I feel that I have brought the captain's wrath down on us, and I should be the one to take the risk."

"Even at the risk of other people's lives, Rebecca? Use your head. There are other ways you could help.

Distract the captain, if you will. He seems to have taken an inordinate interest in you. Have dinner with him Tuesday next, when we are on the water. That way you might further turn any possible suspicion away from yourself, and distract him from his purpose."

Rebecca lowered her head and nodded. She turned to leave.

"Rebecca, you know how invaluable you and the *Deliverance* are to the railroad. I would not want to lose you."

She turned and smiled warmly. "You won't, George."

The slovenly man who hid across the street marked her departure with a lustful snort. "Well, Capt'n, ain't we found ourself one perty little nigger-lovin' ass."

Brad stood looking out the window of his office in the military depot on Griswold. A sharp knock broke into his thoughts.

"Come in."

"Howdy, Capt'n." Pock entered the room like the devil's own shadow.

Brad didn't bother to turn. The thought of facing his informant's pinched face and leering smile was less than appealing.

"Got news, Capt'n. The word is there's a big shipment of them blackies sometime soon. Maybe next week."

"I need to know when. Exactly when."

"Yessir, Capt'n. I'm workin' on it. You can count on me to have the best information a good beatin' can produce." He chuckled. "Soon's I can get ya more I will, but it may be a last-minute thing, ya know. Them black boys don't give away nothin'. Ya gotta see 'em on the move, so to speak. If you get my drift."

"Yes, I get your drift. Let me know when you get additional information, whatever the hour."

"Yessir, Capt'n. An', Capt'n, I got another choice bit, seein' as where your interests lie."

Brad could sense his lecherous smile even without seeing it.

"I followed that Cunningham woman after the meetin', and I saw the nigger-lovin' bitch go into DeBaptiste's. Don't suppose she's a whorin' nigger-lovin' bitch, now, do ya?" He snorted and guffawed at his own humor until he found himself nearly suspended off the floor by his shirt front. The remainder of his laughter was strangled in his throat.

Pock was now eye-to-eye with the captain. It seemed he had touched a soft spot. He would be sure to file this tidbit away for future use, he thought as he was thrown almost the width of the room, landing on his butt in a corner.

Brad's angry voice echoed in the small room. "I'd be careful about voicing your theories, if I were you. I pay you for facts, not speculation."

The captain certainly was riled by his comment. In this matter, Pock decided he had the upper hand.

"An' you, Capt'n, I'd be careful about who you're throwin' around."

"Is that a threat?"

"No, Capt'n." The man smiled, showing his yellow teeth. "Jist a warnin'."

* * *

"Rachel, I need a new dress, a dinner dress for next week—Tuesday."

Rachel studied her friend. Rebecca stood in the doorway of Rachel's home with her back to the light. It was difficult to make out her face in detail, but the tone of her voice was unsettling.

"You received an unexpected dinner invitation?"

"No." Rebecca entered the room and immediately began to study some fabric samples laid out beside the door. "I'm extending one."

"To whom?"

"To Captain Taylor."

There was a long pause.

"Why?"

Rebecca spun around, anguish on her face. "I couldn't convince them to let me go. You know that, don't you?"

"Yes." Rachel's quiet answer contrasted with Rebecca's accusation.

"It's not fair."

"You sound like a spoiled child."

"No, Rachel, you don't understand. I'm so frightened for them. He's after me, not them. I've increased the danger for them. Can't you understand? Will no one understand? It's my responsibility."

"It is not your responsibility any more than it is everyone else's, from slave to slave holder. We all must take on the responsibility of seeing this evil end. Seymour Finney and my Jacob were running slaves when you were still in the cradle, Rebecca. Are you too proud to let someone else—someone who endangers the passengers less—take charge this once?"

"Why do you always accuse me of being proud?"

"Because sometimes you confuse what is good for

you with what is good for the cause."

Rebecca thought of her dinner with Brad Taylor and blushed, as much from guilt as from the reprimand.

"You never answered me, Rebecca. Why are you having dinner with Captain Taylor?"

"George DeBaptiste suggested it as a way to distract him next Tuesday, the night Jacob and Seymour will be moving passengers. He also said it might be useful in deflecting any suspicions the captain might have about me." Rebecca felt better after delivering this defense.

"Does he have any suspicions?"

"No. Why should he?"

"Does George know how you feel about Captain Taylor?"

"Whatever are you talking about, Rachel?" Rebecca continued to study the fabrics meticulously, unable to face her friend.

"Jacob told me about the storm."

"We were caught in one of those terrible summer storms that whip the lake into a fury."

"Jacob said you looked frightened when you returned. You've been caught in storms before. What else happened while you were out on the lake?"

"Nothing, absolutely nothing! Why are you badgering me so?"

Rachel could see the high color on Rebecca's neck and felt her heart constrained by fear. "Don't, Rebecca."

"Don't what?"

"Don't let yourself get involved with him."

"It's purely for the cause, Rachel. If I cannot help transfer the slaves, I will do what I can, and I can act as a diversion. Now about that dress. I thought maybe we could use the amber taffeta you showed me last month . . ."

"Rebecca!" It was a reprimand.

Rebecca turned. There was genuine anguish in her eyes. "How could I care for the captain? It would be betraying everything I've stood for, everything I've worked for these past two years. He's been sent here solely to stop us. To stop me! He cares little about the injustices that motivate us, the immorality of slavery. He sees only the law, the law that I personally break each time I go out under those black sails.

"And as for his feelings toward me, he would as soon jail me as make love to me. He cares nothing for me. Nothing! And I care nothing for him!"

There were tears in Rebecca's eyes, and the ensuing silence hung heavily between the two women.

"I pray to God that you are right, Rebecca." Rachel's voice was full of sorrow. She lowered her head and returned to her sewing. "You said you needed a new dress . . ."

Tuesday, July 4, 1860, dawned warm and humid. Rebecca stretched and groaned. She had been up late last night, helping make the final preparations to move the dozen or so slaves that were hiding in Seymour Finney's barn. Jacob and Seymour would row them in two boats straight across the river. The men were counting on the day's celebrations to provide an adequate distraction. Many of the soldiers would be on leave following the noon parade, and it was safely assumed that long before nightfall they would have succumbed to the sweet enticements of either liquor or women.

It was already late morning now. Rebecca hurried to dress, hoping to catch her father still at breakfast.

She donned the white batiste dress that Rachel had fashioned. The elegantly pleated bodice fit her perfectly. She had abandoned her hooped crinoline for an old-fashioned Swiss petticoat that had once been her mother's. The softer shape and lack of steel hoops assured her of more comfort on this hot day.

The dress had been created for the occasion. It was adorned with red, white, and blue ribbons. The ribbons finished the high collar and the hem, as well as the full sleeves, which were gently gathered at her wrists. She pulled her hair back from her face and gathered it in a ribbon, leaving the thick golden mane to trail down her back. As she headed for the stairs she picked up a gay straw hat, also trailing patriotic-colored ribbons down the back.

"Good morning, Rebecca."

"Good morning, Father." She crossed the dining room and placed a warm kiss on his cheek.

"You look particularly festive this morning."

"Do you like it?" She twirled slowly for her father, hat in hand.

"Yes. It reminds me of when you were a child."

She laughed. "I'd forgotten that I had a dress like this as a girl. It's very similar, isn't it?"

"Yes, very." George Cunningham's smile held a tinge of sadness.

"You look very dashing yourself."

He laughed heartily. "Dashing, is it. Well, I'd be hard pressed to match the beaus you'll be attracting, my dear."

"Father!"

"Which reminds me, Rebecca. Lewis Cass and his wife have invited us for dinner tonight. Kingsley Bingham has been invited as well."

"I can't, Father. Not tonight." She colored slightly.

"You have another engagement?"

"Yes, I'm having dinner with someone."

"Anyone I know?" He smiled at her secrecy.

"Why, yes, it's Captain Taylor." She said it as lightly as she could, but her father still paled. She had not told him of the sailing incident. She wished now she had not told him anything about this evening.

It was a moment before he regained his composure.

"You had better eat something. It will be awhile before you eat again." His voice was controlled, devoid of its earlier vitality and humor. She knew she had hurt him.

Rebecca stood anxiously beside her father in the official reviewing stands in front of City Hall on Cadillac Square. All the excitement and confidence she had felt earlier seemed to have disappeared with the morning breeze. Her father had made no comment whatsoever to her about her dinner plans, but she knew that he was deeply worried. She had convinced herself that there was nothing to worry about. Her disappointment at not participating in this evening's "railroad" activities had been replaced by a new resolve to play her role of diversion flawlessly. She told herself her nervousness was solely the result of her father's concern.

"I'm going up to sit with Joseph Campau, Rebecca. Will you join us?"

"Yes, Father, in a minute."

"Is something wrong?"

"No, of course not." She turned to her father. She could sense his distrust. "I promised Joey Whiton, Seymour's stable boy, that he could sit with me in the stands. I just haven't seen him yet. Go ahead, Father. I'll be there shortly."

That was only part of the truth. As she searched the crowd for signs of Joey, she also searched for any sign of the captain's wide blue shoulders.

"There you are, Miss. Sorry I'm late." Joey Whiton had approached her from behind.

"No, Joey, you're not late, not yet. The parade has just begun, and if we hurry I'm sure we'll still find a seat."

They started to climb up the pine structure. About halfway up, Rebecca spotted a place to sit.

"Here, Joey." She took his shoulder to halt his progress. As she did, she felt him wince. She looked down and gasped when she saw a red imprint of her thumb appear on the back of his thin shirt.

"Joey, you're hurt!"

"No, Miss, it's nothing." He moved quickly to sit.

"Let me look at it."

"Please, Miss Cunningham. It's nothing for you to worry yourself with. It's just Pa, he wanted me to do somethin' for him. I guess I just didn't do it good."

"You mean your father beat you?"

Joey shrugged. "He was real sore. He was countin' on me. It's his right, you know. He can whip me if he wants."

"What are you talking about?" Rebecca was outraged. "He has no right to whip you!"

"Please, Miss."

"Leave it be." A forceful male voice rumbled from behind her, eliciting a wide smile on Joey's face.

She did not have to turn to identify the voice's owner. Every fiber of her being identified it for her.

"Leave it be, Rebecca." This time the words came as a quiet entreaty whispered in her ear.

"Captain Taylor!" It took her a moment to recover. His nearness was unsettling. "What an unexpected surprise. I anticipated you would be down with Major Harcourt and the others."

"No, I'm afraid Major Harcourt was just as happy I declined his invitation to participate in the festivities."

"No doubt you have better things with which to occupy yourself, Captain."

"Better . . . and much lovelier things than the major's concerns, I assure you."

She heard Joey giggle beside her.

"As you can see, Captain, I already have an escort for the afternoon."

The boy blushed deeply in embarrassment. "If it pleases you, Miss Cunningham, I sure would like the captain to stay."

Rebecca was surprised at the boy's request. She turned back to Brad.

"Perhaps my charms are valued only by the young. Much like a pixie seen only by children and the true of heart."

The thought of Brad Taylor as a pixie was so ludicrous that Rebecca found herself smiling against her will.

"Now that is a smile worth waiting for." He reached out, and she held her breath. Instead of touching her, he played with the patriotic ribbons that bedecked her hat and ran down the length of her hair. His hand hovering close to her flesh left a trail of heat. If she moved her head ever so slightly, his hand would brush her cheek. She did not move, though. She was resolved.

"Although I may not be a pixie, you, Miss Cunningham, are an enchanting vision of innocence this day." His look was anything but innocent as his voice deepened. "And never has innocence seemed so attractive."

The parade had begun. It was with relief that Rebecca turned her attention to the proceedings. There was a frenetic feel about the celebration, which gave it an almost eerie quality. It was as if the city had chosen to forget, for the day, all the strife and turmoil. Their spirited effort to forget only underscored, for Rebecca, the ever-growing probability of war. With several Southern states threatening to secede should Lincoln be elected, the chances of a peaceful resolution of the slavery issue seemed more and more remote.

"You don't look at all happy. I hope my presence hasn't dampened your mood."

For once she could answer honestly. "No, Captain, it's not you who have disturbed me."

"No?"

"I'm afraid. Afraid for them." She indicated the soldiers who were passing in review. "And for all us. There will be war, won't there?" She sought from him a different answer than the one that would confirm her fears.

She looked so tormented. For the first time, he was struck by the depth of her feelings. Rebecca Cunningham's passions went beyond the flesh, and he admired that. This was not a woman to be shielded from reality. He knew she required honesty and would accept nothing less. "Yes, I'm afraid it is coming," he finally replied.

He seemed to have suddenly deprived her of what little hope she may have harbored. He found himself wanting to hold her, to comfort her, but he knew it would not change things.

The thought of a civil war was appalling, and yet he knew better than she that it was more and more inevitable. For the first time, he admitted to himself that his mission in Detroit, even if successful, would do little to change the course of events leading the country to war.

"Oh, look, Miss!" A steam calliope had caught Joey's attention.

Rebecca turned back from the captain and forced a smile.

The picnic that followed the parade was a huge success. The crowds were boisterous and happy as they filled Grand Circus Park. After many years of neglect, the boggy area had been filled in, new trees planted, and the whole area had been fenced. Now the lush green acreage bustled with activity.

Joey enviously watched the various competitions, laughing uncontrollably at the antics surrounding the sack race. Now a three-legged race was about to begin.

"I think it is time we showed this group our mettle, eh, Joey?" The small boy looked up at Brad, who had already begun to remove his blue uniform jacket. Handing his jacket to Rebecca with a smile, he led the excited boy over to the starting line.

In her arms Rebecca could feel the warmth of Brad's body still retained by his coat. The blue wool gave off an enticing male aroma, a combination of sweat, cigar smoke, and something else that seemed unique to Brad. What was it that caused her heart to race? She clenched the coat tightly to her and concentrated on the two male figures who had become so important to her.

Joey and Brad were talking eagerly as they each placed a leg in the potato sack. Rebecca could hear the raucous encouragement of the crowd, and then the gunshot that marked the beginning of the race.

She watched with fascination as Brad and Joey flew down the course. Brad had encircled Joey's thin shoulders with his strong arm, and after an initial hesitation put out a burst of energy that carried them down the field to victory. When they crossed the finish line, he swooped the child up and dangled him by his feet. Joey's inverted face was alive with laughter even as his fists pummeled the captain's knees for release. Finally Brad released the red-faced boy, placing him right side up on the grass. They collected their ribbons and headed back toward Rebecca.

Rebecca smiled at the adulation in young Joey's eyes as he looked up at Brad. She studied Brad. Could she be wrong, she wondered?

When they reached her, she took the boy's flushed face in her hands and kissed his cheek. The boy was too excited by the moment to be embarrassed by this unforeseen event, but he did look toward the captain to see if Brad too would receive the tender reward.

Brad's face had become serious as he watched Rebecca. If Joey had been older and more experienced, he would have sensed the tension that had arisen between the two adults. Brad raised an eyebrow.

Rebecca hesitated, then reached up to place a delicate kiss on his cheek as well. As she did, her breast brushed his shirt front, sending a wave of desire through her. He had seemed so vulnerable just moments before. Now she felt him tense with passion, and that frightened her as much as it excited her.

Brad broke the moment by pulling a penny from his pants pocket. "I believe you've earned a lemonade, partner." The lad eagerly took the coin and ran off in the direction of the lemonade stand.

There was strained silence for a few moments, before Rebecca finally spoke. "That was kind of you, Captain."

"No, it was really rather selfish."

"What do you mean?"

"I knew a boy once, much like Joey. He lived in fear and pain most of the time. There was nothing I could do back then for that boy. I was as helpless to change things for him as Joey is now. This time, perhaps I can help, if only a little."

He reached out to smooth a tendril of Rebecca's escaped hair back behind her ear. Before he withdrew his hand, he paused for a moment to caress her cheek.

"I am not completely the beast you would paint me, Rebecca." His thumb brushed a delicate path along her cheekbone. "Not completely."

She shivered, despite the heat.

"I have to go, but I look forward to tonight." He took his jacket from her arms, slipped it on, and buttoned it. Then he executed a slight bow and left.

Rebecca felt deserted. She couldn't explain it, but somehow he had left with a small part of her. Lord knew she had not given it willingly but it was his nonetheless.

10

"I tell ya, Capt'n, there's a big move on t'night. I just can't tell ya where. My source, he weren't too talkative today, despite my persuasions."

Brad had returned to the garrison and the unpleasant task of facing Pock. The man smelled of liquor, stale urine, and sweat. He paced the room as agitated as a coon on the scent, with a predatory glint in his eyes. He certainly seemed to find pleasure in his job. Once again, Brad regretted the need to use the man.

"I'll be having dinner at the Russell House tonight. After dinner I'll return here to await further news. Bring me word when you know more."

"Sure thing, Capt'n. We'll catch them sly bastards. You can bet your soul on it."

After the meeting with Pock, Brad returned to his room at the Finney Hotel. As he changed for dinner, Pock's words haunted him. Somehow, he felt his soul was part of some wager. Why or how, he didn't know, but things were no longer as simple as they once had been.

There was Rebecca Cunningham, for one. Her invitation had come as somewhat of a surprise after the aborted picnic sail. He had known many women, from whores to the elite of Washington, but this woman remained an enigma. One moment she was beguiling and almost brazen, the next totally ingenuous. He felt himself, against his will, inexplicably drawn to her, which made him feel uncomfortable and vulnerable. He wondered if she was aware of that fact. He wondered if she knew that she had already successfully seduced him.

The Russell House was ablaze with light as the Cunningham carriage pulled into Cadillac Square. The bricks that covered the square were rosy with the last rays of the setting sun. The laughter of people returning from the earlier festivities rang in the warm summer air. Rebecca descended from the carriage and stood for a moment, watching the animated crowd. A movement caught her eye, and she looked up toward the red orb passing out of view behind City Hall. The night watchman was preparing to lower the large flag that flew atop the building. The sun that only moments earlier had seemed benign, now tainted the flag with a deep red stain. Rebecca turned away quickly.

"Good evening, Miss Cunningham." William Chittenden, the proprietor of Russell House, the finest hotel in the city, greeted Rebecca at the door to the dining room.

"I'm meeting someone, Mr. Chittenden. Perhaps he has already arrived."

"Yes, Captain Taylor arrived a few moments ago. I have taken the liberty of seating him at a quiet corner table as you requested." He indicated the far corner of the elegant gaslit room.

"Thank you, Mr. Chittenden. I have another request of you."

"Of course, Miss."

"I want the bill put on my personal account, please. Captain Taylor is my guest this evening."

"Yes, Miss, as you wish."

William Chittenden was far too tactful to comment on the unusual request.

Brad had ordered a sherry and was staring into its smoky depths when he heard the rustle of taffeta. He looked up to see a golden vision approaching.

Rebecca Cunningham was aglow in an amber gown that mimicked exactly the color of her hair. She looked like some perfectly wrought gilt icon. Her white shoulders were offset by a low neckline which came to a seductive vee between her breasts. Her golden mane of hair was lifted off her brow and fastened with a golden coronet that boasted airy ostrich plumes. A few loose tendrils caressed her bare neck and shoulders.

Above her slender waist, her bosom moved in a steady rhythm, only slightly heightened by the moment. Across her arms lay a sheer golden shawl. Her slender hands were enclosed in white kid gloves.

Brad stood slowly. He bent low over her hand and then rose to study her eyes, looking for some clue as to which side of Rebecca Cunningham he would be treated to this evening. He found none.

"Miss Cunningham, you look ravishing."

"Thank you, Brad."

He was amused by her use of his given name. "Well, Rebecca, we are on better terms?"

"I didn't know we had been on poor terms." She smiled seductively, and he decided not to argue the point.

"Did you enjoy yourself this afternoon?" he asked.

"I always enjoy myself among friends. Did you enjoy the afternoon?"

"It was one of the more enjoyable days I've spent since arriving here. Thank you."

"Perhaps we need to get you away from your somber activities more often." Her voice was deep, resonant with an undercurrent of something beyond concern.

Throughout dinner, Brad tried to account for the sudden change in Rebecca. She was utterly charming. There were none of the acerbic comments that had marked all their earlier encounters. Despite his suspicions, he allowed himself to relax at the prospect of what the evening might hold.

As dinner progressed, Rebecca kept him thoroughly entertained with stories of her extensive travels and the local gossip. This was the Rebecca Cunningham he had seen that first night at the party—serene, self-confident, witty, and charming. He wondered what had happened to the other Rebecca, the one who had stood almost naked before him, tremulous and vulnerable.

Rebecca reminded herself she had promised to keep the captain occupied until well after moonrise. Seymour and Jacob would have to be off the water by that time if they were to avoid discovery. There was a long evening yet ahead, as the moon was not to rise until shortly after two.

She tried to concentrate on these things, since to do otherwise was to court disaster. Her heart had jumped at the sight of Brad sitting in the soft light of the table. It had taken several moments to compose herself and strengthen her resolve before she approached the table. She found him quite charming during dinner. He was bright, and witty. As long as she avoided subjects of obvious controversy, he was a delightful dinner companion.

She studied him now as, elbows on the table, he toyed with the remnants of his drink in the brandy snifter, twirling the aromatic contents thoughtfully. His dark hair was slightly damp from the heat, and it curled softly against the blue serge of his uniform collar.

She could smell him. Before she met him, she had thought of men as smelling of smoke generally, but in the air around Brad there was an almost palpable male odor. She couldn't identify it as a single scent. It was certainly a bit of brandy, and there was a slight bit of cologne, but the overall effect went beyond individual scents. It was very appealing, uniquely masculine, and uniquely his.

His hands as they held the glass were surprisingly slender for a man of his size. There was a grace about them and a delicacy as he cradled the snifter. She remembered their soft touch, their gentle caress.

She felt herself confused as her will seemed to suddenly take second place to her feelings. She warned herself to stay single-minded, and yet, even as she did, she felt her body betraying her. She could not suppress the need she felt, the craving to feel his touch again. Worse yet, to touch him, to stroke his brow and brush away the damp ringlets there. God help her!

He slowly looked up. His eyes met hers, and she was lost. Their black depths mirrored her own passion. The two of them sat motionless and wordless for what seemed like a long time.

It was fear of the emotions that entangled them that finally stirred Rebecca to speak, to break the hold he had on her.

"Would you like another drink?"

Brad smiled. "If I didn't know better, Miss Cunningham, I would think that you were trying to ply me with liquor."

She smiled in return. "If I didn't know better, Captain Taylor, I would be startled that you were even aware of that tactic."

"Touché." He smiled and held up what remained of his brandy. "A toast . . . to a very beautiful woman . . . who never ceases to amaze me."

Having finished off his drink, he helped her with her chair and offered his arm. The handsome couple raised more than one eyebrow as they passed through the dining room, for there was an unmistakable electricity between the abolitionist and the army captain.

"Would you like me to take you home?"

"No, I thought perhaps we might walk for a while. Have you seen Major McKinstry's public gardens, Captain?"

Rebecca indicated Monroe Street, and they strolled toward the lights and music that marked the favorite spot of many Detroiters. The band still played in celebration of the Fourth, and the theater was just letting out. Several young couples sought refuge and some degree of privacy along the walks laid out among the trees. Brad and Rebecca stood for some moments in front of the small pavilion as the band played, "Roll on silver moon, guide the traveler on his way." When the band struck up a livelier tune, Brad guided Rebecca away from the crowds.

Neither had said a word since they had left the hotel. Rebecca was afraid to speak, afraid her voice would betray her. She was helpless to direct the situation. She was faltering. She desperately fought to keep hold of the one thing she must do, keep the captain with her until moonrise. She shivered.

"You're cold." He turned toward her to help her with her shawl, but when he touched the warm flesh of her arms he hesitated, then slowly pulled her toward him. His hands moved up her arms to caress her neck and finally cradle her face in his hands.

"I want you, Rebecca. I want you more than any woman I've ever known. You have bewitched me."

He kissed her. At first it was the barest brush of his lips against hers, but his lips returned to explore the corners of her mouth before seeking it fully and hungrily.

She was lost, completely and utterly lost. She felt his tongue probe gently, and she opened herself to him. At that moment she did not care who he was or what he was. She knew only one thing, he had not lied about his need, and she could no longer hide the truth about her own.

He moved his head away to look at her, and she found herself reaching out to him—caressing his cheek, brushing a stray tendril from his brow, and finally guiding his lips back toward hers.

She didn't know how long they explored each other. He kissed her shoulders and the hollow at the base of her throat. She could smell him and feel the softness of his hair against her cheek. She touched his lips with her fingertips only to have one seductively teased by his tongue and drawn into his mouth. He kissed her again, this time less gently and more demanding. When he finally moved away it was to take her firmly by the elbow.

They were leaving the park. He was hailing a carriage. She knew where they were going. He did not touch her now, he did not have to. There was no other way. She had to keep him occupied. "He will not be toyed with," Rachel had said. Yes, she had led him on. It was the only way. But she did not know that for sure. She was making excuses. Yes, she had always made excuses. She wanted him.

The secluded back door to the Finney Hotel was quiet in the darkness. There was no soul in sight to save her from herself. For a second she thought that if someone saw them, she would be saved. She would have to preserve her reputation.

But secretly she knew she needed no one else to stop what was about to happen. She needed only herself. However much her head reasoned with her heart, she knew she would not stop it.

Brad opened the door to his room and moved behind her into the darkness. She turned to him for direction and found herself once more in his feverish embrace. His hands moved expertly to unbutton the back of her dress and release the tapes to her hoop. He eased the dress off her shoulders and it collapsed with the hoop in a graceful pool at her feet. Those same dexterous fingers untied her corset and eased it off to reveal her soft breasts.

As the cool air found her nakedness, she thought

again she should stop him, but her sanity fled when his mouth found the tip of her breast. She gasped. His tongue trailed a silky path down her midriff, lower and lower, taking with it her pantaloons. Then they were at her feet, and his mouth was pressed against her soft golden curls.

He rose and, finding her mouth once more, lifted her from the amber folds and carried her to the bed.

The only light was that of a gaslight outside. It sent a narrow glowing path through the open window. She watched in fascination as he began to undress. Her body trembled in anticipation as first his broad chest and then his heavily muscled thighs . . . and then she was lost. God help her, she was lost. He moved toward the bed torturously slowly. His eyes never left hers.

"Capt'n! Hey, Capt'n, are ya in there?" The pounding on the door shook the room and sent Rebecca into a panic. She clutched for something to cover her nakedness, but there was nothing.

Brad issued her a warning with his eyes as he pulled on his pants. He opened the door a crack, and the light spilled in, across one wall and to the bureau mirror. Rebecca could see the pock-faced man whose pounding had interrupted them and prayed that he could not see her.

"Them black boys are movin', Capt'n. They left the wharf, must be two hours ago now. I been lookin' for ya all 'round town. Too bad ya weren't at the garrison, like ya said." He spat on the floor before adding, "Chances are we lost 'em by now."

Brad said something to the man that Rebecca could not hear and then shut the door. In the darkness again, she could not tell if he had moved. Her eyes had not readjusted to the blackness. Then she heard the rustle of taffeta. He appeared suddenly in the light of the window.

Gone from his eyes was the softness she had seen before. There was still lust, but it was tempered by something else, something which frightened her.

"There is a name for a woman who sells herself for a price, Rebecca, my love. I'm sure you're familiar with it." He hurled her clothes at her. "Get dressed and get out."

11

In the blackness of the wharves along Atwater, Brad cursed. Not only had he missed the slave transfer again, but she had played him for a fool, and he had more than obliged her.

The others had gone. He had dismissed them when it became obvious that whatever movement there had been tonight was long over. The moon had just risen. It sparkled on the black water that lapped against the pier where he stood.

The quietness was broken occasionally by raucous laughter from the bars and taverns behind him. The area was a subcellar for the underworld of Detroit. Every con man, every lowlife, any sailor without a ship could find a snug harbor in the darkened streets east of Brush Street. Saloons, whorehouses, and cheap hotels were filled to capacity with the dregs of society. The atmosphere was particularly charged, even at this late hour, by the day's celebrations.

Brad's insides churned. He told himself it was anger at being distracted from his job, but it was more than that. She had gotten to him. He had allowed her to see a small part of himself that no one saw, and she had betrayed him.

She was a slut, a whore. It did not matter why she had made herself available to him. She probably thought herself noble, sacrificing herself to the enemy so that some black slaves she didn't know could live out their lives in free poverty. She was lucky he didn't arrest her for obstructing justice. Rebecca Cunningham jailed—wouldn't that be the talk of the town.

On that satisfying note he turned and headed for the nearest saloon.

Rebecca still trembled from the blow of his words. He might as well have hit her, the pain could not be worse than what she felt now.

She let herself in the servants' entrance at her home. Her gown was still in disarray from her hurried efforts to re-dress. Her hair had come loose from the coronet and lay tangled around her face.

"My God! Rebecca, what happened?" Rachel rushed to her friend, anxiously searching for any physical harm that might have befallen her.

Rebecca looked up. Her eyes were glassy with unshed tears. She bit her lip, hoping the pain would bring her out of the bad dream.

"Nothing, Rachel. Absolutely nothing!"

She tried to hold herself together, but it was useless. In the loving arms of her friend, she could no longer contain her pain.

Everything had seemed so simple. Now she was totally confused. Why had his words hurt so much? Why had the look of hatred in his eyes sent her soul into despair? He was nothing to her. He stood for everything she despised. So why did it hurt so much?

Her trembling worsened, and she felt sick and suddenly very tired. "I want to go to bed," she said.

Rachel helped her up the stairs to her room. She tenderly helped her undress, as if Rebecca were once again a child, and tucked her tightly into bed to ward off whatever it was that caused the haunted look in Rebecca's eyes.

"They are home safely, Rebecca."

Rebecca looked confused.

"Jacob and Seymour. They are back. Everything went smoothly. They wanted me to thank you for keeping Captain Taylor distracted. At one point they were afraid they had been discovered, but nothing came of it. They were grateful the captain was otherwise engaged." Rachel studied her friend closely, trying to gauge the impact of her words.

Rebecca curled up on her side. "Thank you, Rachel. Good night."

The smoky room in the saloon was still crowded, despite the first rays of dawn filtering through the open door. Brad stared into his empty glass. He had lost count hours ago. It did not matter. The drinks had done little to deaden the pain.

He could still remember her smile, feel her warmth, taste her lips. He still wanted her, craved her, needed her. But now she was more than just an object of his lust. Foolishly, he had let her become something more. She haunted him. He couldn't erase from his mind the look in her eyes when he ordered her out.

He had hurt her. That was good. She deserved to

be hurt as she had hurt him. Then why had the look in her eyes compounded his pain? She couldn't have been so naive as to not know what she was doing. Of course she knew! She had been playing a game the whole time. Two could play the game as easily as one.

"Heh, Capt'n! Heard you missed them niggers yet again." A large man, who had been loudly maintaining his presence in the saloon most of the night, staggered toward Brad's table. "Washington sends us one of its best, and he can't find shit up his ass. Ain't that right, Capt'n? Them niggers must be learnin' real quick to outsmart such a fancy man, wouldn't you say?" He leaned over to deliver this last bit so close to Brad's face that his foul breath turned Brad's stomach.

Brad stood, bringing the table with him and slamming it into the man's face. The man reeled with the impact, staggering back several steps before regaining his equilibrium. His friends at the bar watched with a certain morbid interest. They were content, for the moment, to let their companion fight his own battle.

The big man retaliated by charging Brad. Brad dodged the unsteady move of his inebriated assailant, but not without causing his own head to swim. Why, he thought with disgust, had the liquor waited until now to show its effects?

Once more the lout charged. This time Brad's movement slowed, and he was unable to avoid the man's bearlike hug. Brad drove his knee up into the man's groin, and the man doubled over in pain. Brad hammered his fists down on the back of the man's head, leaving him a crumpled mass on the floor. He steadied himself and turned to go, but it seemed it was not going to be that easy. He was facing a wall of men, each coming to the defense of their fallen comrade. Now it would be like running the gauntlet. Brad swore under his breath and moved toward the door.

When he awoke he was in his room at the Finney Hotel. His face felt raw. One eye was swollen almost shut. He lay still for a moment, trying to determine the extent of his injuries. When he tried to move, he groaned with the pain of at least one broken rib and fell back on the pillow.

That's when he smelled it, the faint odor that brought back a flood of memories of the night before. It was jasmine. Jasmine, the scent he would forever associate with Rebecca Cunningham. His mind wasn't playing tricks on him. She had been here, naked on his bed, tantalizing and perfidious.

Her treachery was so sensual it could have driven a man mad. It seemed she had succeeded. It must have been madness last night that drove him to the actions that left him so badly battered.

He hadn't done anything so foolish since he was a boy, since he had once tried to defend his mother from one of his father's drunken attacks. He had not thought of the incident in many years. He couldn't have been more than six. His father had bellowed a curse and hurled him against the wall, and he had lost consciousness.

When he had awakened, his mother had been gently crooning to him, her own face battered and blackened with bruises. He had gained a piece of wisdom that day that he had lived by since. It had taken twenty years and a woman for him to forget it.

He made no further attempt to rise. Exhausted physically and emotionally, he closed his eyes once more and slept.

Rebecca felt the warmth of the sun touch her cheek. It meant it was late. She opened her eyes to the familiar surroundings of her room. Everything was the same. She rose and, pulling her robe around her, walked to the window. She stared at the river, her river, and wondered if she would ever again find solace there.

She was a whore. That's what he had said. He was right. She had sold herself for a price, but certainly the price of freedom for twelve other human beings mattered. Surely God would understand that.

Or would He? Would He know that those slaves hadn't been foremost in her mind last night? She had been thinking only of herself. Rachel was right, she was selfish. She had conveniently confused her own needs with those of the movement.

It wouldn't happen again, she resolved once more, but even as she did, a tear trailed down her cheek, a solitary acknowledgment of what she had lost last night. She had lost her innocence, not literally, but lost it just the same. She had wanted Brad so much that she thought she would never rid herself of the pain she felt now. She had wanted him, this man who hid so much pain just below the surface.

Why did he draw her? Why did she, even after

last night's hateful words, want to comfort him, to tell him that he was safe with her?

For a moment last night she had thought he cared about her, too, but the moment was lost. There was no way to confirm that, even for a moment, she had meant anything to him.

She sobbed quietly with the realization that now she would never know. Shaking her head to rid herself of such useless thoughts, she turned from the window and started to dress.

12

The late August moon hung low in the sky, its full beauty gradually revealed in streaks by the long fingers of fleeing black clouds. Its luminous presence, which Rebecca might otherwise have admired, posed a danger tonight. Why had the heavy clouds that had obscured the sun all day chosen this moment to withdraw? She pulled the cowl of the cape farther forward and moved toward Seymour Finney's stable.

"Jacob, is everyone ready?"

"Yes, we're ready, Miss Rebecca."

Rebecca looked over the disparate group. To one side stood a young couple, the man's hand clasping the woman's shoulder. Their complexions were both warm and fair, and they were dressed well. They looked like anything but fleeing slaves.

They had accomplished the trip north by posing as a planter's younger brother and his wife. All had gone well until they reached Detroit, where their owner had traced them. Now the owner sat in the Finney Hotel, damning the young couple who dared pose as white. Meanwhile, they waited, like baggage, to be moved to freedom. Still they clung to their dignity. They were literate and well spoken. Rebecca could not say as much about their owner. She bridled at the injustice that had allowed these two lives to be determined by the blood of their mothers and grandmothers, who had been raped by white men.

Her gaze moved back to the center of the room, where a large man stood, with skin black as the night and a defiant look in his eyes. He had been apprenticed to a blacksmith and had refused to be returned to the cruelty of his owner. He had resisted the overseer sent for him, knocking the man senseless and then fleeing on foot. His sole guide north had been the north star. Now, months later, his determination was still unwavering, his journey nearly over.

Behind the lone man was a family of six. Rebecca could only guess from the looks on their faces the amount of courage they had needed to reach this last milepost. Now they waited anxiously, too exhausted and still far too wary to rejoice.

It was toward this family that Rebecca moved. As she approached a boy of no more than five, her appearance drove the child into his mother's skirts. Rebecca crouched and the child burrowed deeper, his eyes wide with fright. Slowly Rebecca moved the black cowl back, revealing first her feminine features and then her magnificent golden hair. The child peeked out from behind the folds of the skirt.

"Will you come with me?" Rebecca extended her gloved hand.

The child looked up at his mother, who held a sleeping baby. The mother nodded, but still the child hesitated.

"You will help me guide the others."

The child studied the strange woman who was dressed like a man.

"I need your help."

Slowly the child extracted himself from his mother's skirt and went to Rebecca. His small black hand took hers securely with the resolve of someone far older than his years. Rebecca pulled the cowl back over her hair and nodded toward Jacob as she headed for the door.

"The word is tonight, Capt'n."

"Where?"

"Even with persuasion, the lad wasn't sayin'. Don't think he rightly knows."

Brad did not miss Pock's reference to his undisclosed source as "lad," but he banished any thought of its implication from his mind. It did not concern him. He had more important things with which to concern himself.

It looked like the Angel of Passage might once more be in his grasp.

He went directly to Major Harcourt's office.

"Major, I need to handpick some men for special duty tonight."

"But that's highly irregular, Captain. What is it exactly that you need them for?"

"I don't think I need to reiterate my job and right to command, Major. Now, if you will but issue the order."

Major Harcourt stared at the young captain, knowing full well the uselessness of any protest. He sensed something different about him. Was it the slightest hesitancy?

Whatever it was, he knew he would not be privy to the captain's innermost thoughts. He reluctantly wrote out the order the captain requested.

Captain Taylor departed with the signed paper, leaving Major Harcourt to wonder if what he sensed had any connection to the rumors he had heard about the handsome captain and Rebecca Cunningham.

The August air was cooling in anticipation of autumn. The leaves of the maples had already begun their crimson journey into death. In the dark alley, the stillness was broken only by the scattering of rats, disturbed in their nightly quest for food. The ribaldry of taverns and saloons echoed in the distance.

Rebecca led the group toward Randolph Street and its gaslights. Suddenly she signaled them to stop. She had heard something, or had she?

Moving still farther back into the shadows, she listened. She had not imagined it. It was the thin metallic and leather sound of several harnesses. They were close. What struck her as odd was the lack of human voices accompanying the sound. The men who frequented this section of the city did not usually move quietly.

Her worst fears were realized when she heard the clipped orders of a barely distinguishable voice. It was a military patrol. Why tonight? Had someone gotten wind of the move?

The men and horses moved down Randolph toward the water. When the small patrol moved out of the darkness and into the light, her heart skipped a beat. It was him! He was not more than thirty feet away.

She had not seen him since that night in his room. Avoiding him made it easier to hate him. The patrol had stopped under the gaslight, and she could see him clearly now. She felt she couldn't breathe. She could not prevent the memories that rushed in to take control of her mind and her heart.

She could hear his voice, deep and controlled, and she remembered his laughter that night—she remembered him toying with his brandy snifter, toasting her, and she remembered him naked, his eyes dark with passion, driving everything else out of her mind.

She had to turn away to break the spell, and when she looked down she saw the small black hand that clutched hers.

She signaled Jacob to move the others still farther back. The baby whimpered in her mother's arms, and Rebecca prayed they had not been discovered. The patrol had just begun to move toward the river, and their clatter drowned out the baby's cries. Only Brad hesitated for a moment, as if trying to listen. Then he followed the others.

Rebecca and Jacob moved their group into an old warehouse to wait until the patrol was safely out of sight and earshot.

Brad had dismissed the noise he heard as that of a stray cat, but he continued to listen closely for any sound that might offer him a clue as to the whereabouts of his nemesis. When he reached the river, he sent two men in each direction to search the wharves. He dismounted and proceeded out on the wooden pier at the foot of Randolph. There were two schooners, one docked on either side of the pier. He recognized them as the ships that plied the Great Lakes, moving between Detroit and Chicago.

Normally he would have turned to go, but tonight he was deep in thought. He walked out past the schooners. As he did, the moon made a brief appearance from behind the clouds. He caught sight of a mast at the end of the pier. Suddenly he was alert. He moved forward cautiously. She was a small sloop, tied fast to the end of the pier. She rode well below the level at which he was standing. He doubted he would have seen her, but for the moon's timely appearance.

The sleek craft was black and eerily familiar. Her sails had been partially rigged, then carefully tied down. The sails were black! Brad hesitated before he walked toward the bow to check her name. The sound of his boots kept a steady rhythm, a counterpoint to his racing heartbeat. He bent low to read the name: *Tremont II.* The letters were painted in gold on the plaque that adorned the boat's stern.

He felt instant release from the torment he had briefly experienced, but this was quickly followed by puzzlement. He studied the small craft more carefully, taking in as much detail as he could in the darkness. He could not be sure.

"Captain! Captain! There's a brawl over at the Woodbridge Tavern. They've asked for our help."

One of his men had returned. Reluctantly, Brad left the small boat, but not without posting the man as a guard.

"Get me if you see anything unusual, anything at all. Do you understand?"

"Yes, sir."

Rebecca moved out of the darkness to stand on the pier. It took only a moment for her to be seen.

"Hey, you there!" The soldier ran toward her shadowy figure. Still she did not move.

The soldier pulled his gun. "Stay where you are!"

She saw fear and recognition on his face and smiled to herself within the concealing hood. Then she darted into the shadows, and the soldier followed. She slid around the corner just as Jacob wielded the small cudgel and sent the young corporal into oblivion.

Quickly, they gagged and tied the man and hauled his trussed body behind some crates. Rebecca returned to the warehouse while Jacob readied the *Deliverance.* Within a matter of minutes, they were away from the pier, their cargo stored safely below.

"Jacob, as soon as we've delivered our passengers, I want to head to our own dock. I fear the captain may not have been fooled by our name change and will come searching for the *Deliverance.* I want the black sails removed from the boat completely. Hide them with you and Rachel, along with the name plate. With any luck, our friends at the tavern should keep Captain Taylor occupied for the next hour or so, and then he will have to question his guard at the pier. I wish I could see his face when he learns that the Angel of Passage has once more escaped him."

It was almost daybreak when George Cunningham was awakened by a pounding that reverberated through the house. He hurried down the stairs, throwing on his silk robe. He reached the door and opened it cautiously. Surprise registered on his face at the sight of a mounted group of soldiers. On the step stood Captain Taylor.

"I'm sorry to disturb you at this late hour, sir, but there has been some illegal activity tonight. I would like your permission to search your riverfront for anything suspicious."

"Surely you don't suspect my involvement, Captain?"

"It is merely a formality. Someone may have used your property without your knowledge."

George Cunningham did not hide his concern well, and Brad sensed there was something amiss. He pushed a little harder.

"I would hate to have to report that you were reluctant to aid us. That might be poorly interpreted by others."

George Cunningham looked back toward the stairs, as if willing something to happen. Brad followed his gaze, but no one appeared.

"My daughter is sleeping, Captain. I'm sure you can understand my concern. I don't want her disturbed because of this foolishness."

"We have no intention of disturbing anyone, except perhaps any lawbreakers about, Mr. Cunningham."

"Who is it you are searching for, Captain, and what have they done to keep you out at this late hour?"

The older man was stalling, and not too skillfully.

"We have information that the Angel of Passage has been about his work. A boat was seen at the Randolph Pier, a black sailboat with black sails."

If there had been better light in the doorway, Brad would have seen George Cunningham's face turn deathly white.

"Search if you must, Captain, though the likelihood of finding anything of interest seems dim. I would not want to be thought of as obstructing justice." He put undue emphasis on the word justice.

Brad was about to leave when a familiar voice halted him.

"Yes, let him search, Father." Rebecca Cunningham stood on the landing, her silk peignoir moving sensuously around her slim figure. "If the captain believes we are criminals, let him satisfy his curiosity."

Brad nodded, acknowledging her presence. He studied George Cunningham out of the corner of his eye. The man seemed unduly relieved by his daughter's presence.

"It was not an accusation, Miss Cunningham."

Brad had tried to forget how beautiful she was, but now the picture of her naked and willing on his bed came back, unbidden. It was only slightly more torturous than the picture before him. Her hair fell over her shoulders and caressed her breasts. She had pulled the silk wrapper tightly around her in her hurry, and it revealed the curve of her hip and the flatness of her belly. He could see the impression of her taut nipples through the thin fabric.

"It should take only a few minutes. Then we will be gone."

"I insist, Captain. By all means conduct your search. We wouldn't want to be held in suspicion. What was the crime? You said it was helping some poor black child to freedom, I believe." She delivered this last in an unmistakably scathing tone.

Brad looked back up at her and their eyes locked—hers taunting and confident, his cold and silent.

Without another word, he returned to the small

patrol. He led the way around to the stables, where he ordered his men to wait while he went down the river.

He did not know what he expected to find. The possibility that the black sloop at the Randolph Street pier might have been the *Deliverance* ate at him. Was Rebecca Cunningham somehow allowing herself to be used? Had she permitted her boat to be used by this Angel of Passage? If she had, she was playing a very dangerous game. Didn't the foolish woman realize she could be imprisoned for any role she might play, however minor?

He approached the dock tense with strange, mixed emotions. It was with more relief than he would be willing to admit that he saw the shadowy presence of the boat. She was securely docked, her name clearly visible in the moonlight: *Deliverance.* The sails were not visible. He could safely assume now that the boat was not the one he had seen. He turned and began to retrace his steps to the stable.

In the moonlight, Rebecca could see the metallic reflections of his buttons and insignia, but she could not see his face. She wished she could. She had imagined that she would get a great deal of satisfaction from seeing his disappointment, but actually she was feeling anything but satisfied.

She needed to see his face, needed to see if it still reflected disdain. She could withstand his hatred but not that belittling look.

She wished she could scream out to him that it was *she* whom he sought so diligently, she who had outwitted him time and time again. Yet, deep inside her, she knew there would be no satisfaction in it. It was her pride that sought revenge, but her heart sought understanding.

What she had rationalized as simply a physical attraction for him had deepened. She had seen his pain, had felt his touch. He was not cold, she knew that now. She needed his admiration and his respect as much as she wanted his passion. It was as if she was no longer whole. He had kidnapped a part of her, taken it against her will. She needed to retrieve it. Yet to do so she risked losing even more of herself to this man.

It was a risk she was willing to take.

13

The Russell House glowed in the brisk September night. The air was now filled with the smell of autumn—the faint odor of growing decay, the smoky tang left from burned cornstalks, the musky odor of mold now permanently damp in the cooler weather.

The air was also alive with palpable excitement. The beautifully printed program said it all: The Governor of Michigan and the Mayor of Detroit were hosting a ball to honor Detroit's distinguished visitor, Edward, Prince of Wales.

The oldest son of Queen Victoria had arrived from Windsor earlier that day aboard a private train car. He had spent a good part of the last several weeks touring Canada, and his stop in Detroit was the beginning of a tour of the United States which would take him as far west as Chicago before he returned to the east coast.

Only nineteen years old, he was already considered

a bon vivant, and he moved in an exclusive circle. Many curious citizens had gathered outside the hotel to see the cream of Detroit society and the dark, heavy-set young man who would someday be King of England.

"Good evening, Captain Taylor." William Chittenden was basking in the glory of the moment. His hotel's reputation certainly would rise a notch or two from the unmistakable honor of hosting the future King of England.

Brad smiled at his slightly pompous manner before handing the man his invitation and entering the ballroom.

The crowd was particularly elegant tonight. The men all wore formal evening clothes, and the women had taken great pains to overcome any hint that Detroit was a backwoods town. Intending to prove they were not ignorant of the latest trends and fashions, they had meticulously copied the latest gowns from the house of Worth in England. The demand for imported silks and satins in the last several months had tripled. No doubt George Cunningham's shipping business was profiting nicely from this little visit.

Brad's interest in the Prince of Wales was nil. He had accepted the invitation purely as a source of further information, hoping for a slip of someone's tongue to give him the clue he needed to complete his task.

Yet as he studied the colorful crowd, he tried to deny what he was really searching for. When he finally determined she was not present, he felt a certain disappointment. He had counted on her being here. After all, she had said months ago it was the social event of the year. He should not care whether she came or not, and yet he did.

He soon realized that his own presence had created an undercurrent of whispered conversation. He saw people surreptitiously glance his way before they turned in urgent discussion with others. He cared little what they thought but decided, nonetheless, to make himself less conspicuous. He moved toward Major Harcourt, who stood with Mayor Patton against one wall of the elaborately decorated ballroom.

The room had been festooned with the flags of both countries, as well as red, white, and blue bunting. Towering floral arrangements of mums and other blooms Brad did not recognize were placed strategically around the floor. It was next to one of these that the mayor and Major Harcourt stood.

"What do you think of the city tonight, Captain?" Mayor Patton glowed with pride. "I think this matches anything Washington could put on."

Brad did not feel like dampening the mayor's enthusiasm. "Yes, it is very impressive, Mr. Patton." He saw the man smile in satisfaction. "No doubt the event will be talked about for years."

"Yes, yes, indeed. To think we are lucky enough to see this day. How much longer do you expect your posting to Detroit to continue, Captain Taylor?"

"That remains to be seen."

"I understand you have had some difficulty completing your assignment. I should think Washington would have better uses for a fine officer like yourself. Perhaps you will be called back shortly."

"I doubt that will happen, Mayor. There are those who consider my task here very important. I only wish the citizens of Detroit took it seriously."

"But we do, Captain. We do."

"That has not been my impression, Mayor Patton." He had grown tired of the vacuous conversation. Both he and the mayor knew the reality of the situation, and to speak of it lightly seemed hypocritical.

Major Harcourt spoke up. "You have a good showing, Mayor. Almost everyone seems to have accepted your invitation. But I have not seen George Cunningham and Rebecca. They were planning on attending, were they not?"

"There was some concern on George's part that Rebecca might not be feeling well enough to attend."

The fact that Brad might not see her tonight irritated him for some reason. Suddenly, both his companions' faces lit up. They smiled as Major Harcourt spoke with a certain admiration. "Here they are now. Rebecca's condition must have improved."

Brad doubted that Rebecca's condition was anything more than cowardice. Still, he could not bring himself to turn around to face the entrance to the ballroom. The more urgently he wanted to, the more determined he became.

"I do believe Rebecca has outdone herself tonight. Not even the Prince of Wales could find fault with such elegance," Patton said.

Brad turned, unable to feign indifference any longer.

She stood on a landing, a step or two above the dance floor, and was smiling warmly at the governor, who had just greeted her. She stood out from every other woman in the room. Her dress was the epitome of simplicity, but the color was a startling choice.

It was black. The deep lushness of the watered silk

acted as a richly rubbed frame, setting off her creamy arms and shoulders. Brad's eyes moved upward. She was even more breathtaking than that first night he had seen her. Her complexion glowed in the soft light of the gaslamps, and her hair . . . Brad recalled how it had felt that night to hold the great, sweet-smelling masses in his hands. He remembered the softness of her skin against the roughness of his hands, the sweetness of her lips tormenting his.

He knew now why she still haunted him, why his need for her had only grown in these past weeks. From clear across the room, she held a power over him. She aroused him like no other woman he had ever known. He sought to justify the attraction in purely physical terms. To delve deeper, to contemplate that the power she held over him might be more than physical was to risk too much.

He was tired of her game of cat-and-mouse. Tonight he would call her bluff and see if she was prepared to satisfy the cravings she intentionally stirred in him. If she was willing to sell herself, this time he would pay the price.

Rebecca had resolved not to be intimidated by Captain Taylor. She shrugged off her doubts about putting herself in such close proximity to the one man who could make her inexplicably lose all self-control. She could not, however, ease the tension that had built within her all day. Even now, she dared not look around the ballroom. She heard herself charming the governor, assuring him how lovely everything was, skillfully impressing him with her wit and charm.

All the while, she could almost sense his presence.

Was he staring at her? She could practically feel him. She opened her black lace fan. She had made a mistake, she knew now, but it was too late. She looked up as casually as she could and saw only him. He was staring at her, and she could not escape the intensity of his gaze.

Lord, but he was handsome. His dress uniform set off his wide shoulders and narrow hips. His dark hair curled teasingly over his collar. She remembered the feel of those black curls, slipping through her fingers. Suddenly, she could smell him again, musky and male. She could feel his arms crushing her, his mouth demanding hers. She felt her body begin to betray her, and she knew she was in great danger. She turned to plead faintness to her father, but it was too late. Descending the staircase behind them was the Prince of Wales.

She took her father's arm, and they moved to one side to allow the Prince and his entourage passage. She tried in vain to distract herself. She studied the young man whose presence in Detroit had created such a stir.

The Prince of Wales was not a particularly handsome man. He tended toward heaviness, no doubt as a result of his rich style of living. His features were friendly and soft. Perhaps this is what appealed to the women. He was reputed to be quite the ladies' man. She wondered if the women who were attracted to him felt as out of control as she did in the captain's presence. The prince came abreast of her, and she curtsied. She was startled when she realized he had stopped.

She looked up to find him smiling down at her in blatant admiration. Governor Bingham quickly made the introduction. "Your Highness, may I present Miss Rebecca Cunningham, daughter of one of our leading businessmen."

"Miss Cunningham." He bowed slightly. "It is, indeed, a pleasure. If you are any indication of the beauty of the ladies of Detroit, then I shall truly enjoy my stay here."

"I hope I will be able to add pleasure to your brief visit," she replied.

The prince laughed. "If you would accompany me through the formalities of the introductions, I would then be assured of the pleasure of you as a lovely partner for the first dance. I fear, if I do not claim you now, I will have to beat off a score of men for another opportunity."

"I am yours, Your Highness." She smiled.

Brad studied the little interchange. She had already charmed the man. She was very adept at that, as skillful as any whore he had seen. Perhaps she had already made plans to conquer this bit of nobility. No doubt it would be a special feather in her hat to have slept with the future King of England.

He watched as they moved through the crowd. The governor remained doggedly at their heels, making the appropriate introductions. Brad realized too late that he had chosen poorly when he had joined the mayor and Major Harcourt. The governor was guiding the prince toward them. Rebecca continued to entertain the prince with vivacious banter as they crossed the ballroom. The prince laughed deeply.

Brad felt a sudden antipathy toward this man who held her arm so familiarly. He would have turned and left if propriety hadn't demanded that he stay. There was a rising urge in him to shake her. Was she intentionally tormenting him? His body involuntarily reacted to her proximity. She was a conniving little vixen who needed to be taught a lesson, he decided.

"You already know Mayor Patton, Your Highness."

"You have outdone yourself, Mayor." The prince gestured to the room. "I am deeply flattered."

John Patton beamed.

"May I introduce the head of the military garrison here in Detroit, Major Edward Harcourt, and . . . I'm sorry . . ." The governor faltered at putting a name to Brad.

"Captain Bradford Taylor, Your Highness." The feminine voice grated on Brad's already sensitive nerves.

Rebecca continued. "He is on special assignment from Washington to track down the most vile of criminals here in our fair city." She smiled sweetly.

Brad's insides roiled. What the hell was she doing? Her voice was laced with sarcasm, even the prince had sensed it. He looked to Brad with barely concealed curiosity.

"I fear Miss Cunningham and I do not share the same view on certain controversial issues." She had put Brad on the defensive, and he resented it. "It seems we will have to discuss them further to reach some understanding."

"I always find it dangerous to disagree with beautiful women, Captain Taylor."

"I am beginning to understand that, Your Highness."

"Now, I believe, it is time to dance. Miss Cunningham, if I may have the honor."

"It is my honor, Your Highness." Rebecca curtsied

deeply, and Brad could not help but notice her white breasts, teasingly revealed by the low-cut gown, as they descended to give him a luxurious view.

He then watched silently as the prince led Rebecca out onto the ballroom floor. It soon became evident that they were both accomplished dancers. They waltzed as one, intimately connected by the music. Brad had never considered himself a jealous man, but as he watched the future King of England with this woman, he felt the silent torment possessiveness brings with it.

The prince held Rebecca confidently in his arms, one hand pressing the small of her back, the other hand clasping hers familiarly. Brad was resentful of the sensual looks Rebecca showered on her partner. Regardless of his original plans, he knew he would have to leave. If he remained, he might well do something foolish, something he might later regret.

"Major Harcourt." Brad nodded his departure. "Mayor Patton, enjoy your evening."

"Surely you are not leaving, Captain." Major Harcourt was surprised. "You don't want to disappoint the ladies who have spent the better part of the last two months preparing for this event. We will never hear the end of it, Captain."

"Come, Captain, let's take a moment from the activities. A man sometimes needs nothing more than a good cigar to regain his courage." Mayor Patton had taken Brad's arm and began to lead him toward a set of doors that opened onto a patio. Brad's attempts to extricate himself were met by good-natured encouragement. He would have to postpone his departure for the moment.

Rebecca felt as if her face would crack from all her

smiling. She was exhilarated tonight. She liked to think it was from the earnest attention of the Prince of Wales, but she knew better. It was the sweet smell of revenge that excited her—at least that was part of it. The prince's attentions had nothing to do with it, beyond providing the means of her retaliation.

She had moved through the waltz with the feel of Brad's eyes on her every move. She had gained satisfaction every time she made the prince laugh. The fact that she was the envy of every woman at the ball meant less to her than the fact that Brad was watching.

She was a beautiful, witty, elegant woman, eagerly sought by many men. She did not need him to complete herself. In fact, he was the farthest thing from the kind of man she desired. He was crude and insensitive, and he hadn't the faintest notion of who she was, of what she valued in life. The whole series of events leading up to tonight had been unfortunate. After tonight, she would even the score, and it would be over. She need never have any more contact with the man.

14

When the prince left her to attend to social obligations, Rebecca felt relieved. She scanned the room, but Brad was nowhere to be seen. Her heart sank. She circled the room, greeting the other guests warmly, until she found Major Harcourt near the entrance to the ballroom.

"Major Harcourt, you look particularly handsome tonight."

"Why, thank you, Rebecca, my dear. But there is no need to flatter me. There are far younger and more desirable men for you to charm."

"Nonsense, Major."

"I do believe that the ladies will all be disappointed that Captain Taylor has left. There always seems to be a shortage of eligible men, particularly those as dashing as the captain."

"You say the captain left?" She suddenly felt abandoned.

"Yes, he was eager to leave, even before you had finished the first dance with the prince."

"I should be getting back to Father, but I will be saving a dance for you." She smiled kindly at the portly man.

The major colored slightly, delighted with her attentions.

Rebecca did not return to her father. She was too agitated to be in his company, or in anyone's company, for that matter. She slid out the doors to the patio into the inviting fall air, trying to collect herself. It had been even warmer than she realized in the ballroom, and she shivered now at the abrupt change in temperature. The light from the ballroom fell in a single path from the doors, leaving the corners of the slate patio dark. Even the beautiful full moon failed to intrude into these private spaces.

She walked away from the light, deep in thought, trying to make sense of the evening's events and her jumbled feelings. She was angry and frustrated. Why, she couldn't explain. She worked a small chip of slate with the toe of her black satin slipper, then kicked it vigorously. She was shaking now with more than the cool night air. She felt tears welling up in her eyes. She bit her lip. What was happening to her? She felt a tear start on its salty trip down her cheek. She was helpless to stop it and the one that followed it.

Then she smelled something in the night air. It couldn't be, but it was. There was no mistaking the odor of cigar smoke tinged with cologne and something else, something very familiar. Her body tensed even before she felt his warm hands settle on her naked shoulders, even before she felt his familiar warmth against her cool back.

His hands moved down her arms, caressing them gently. She hesitated, torn by her conflicting feelings.

She felt his breath on her neck, felt his soft kiss.

She could resist no longer. She surrendered to the pure ecstasy of the feelings he aroused in her. She leaned back into him, into the rough texture of his serge jacket against her bare back, into his strength. His hands moved to grasp her waist urgently before they rose again, this time up across her midriff to cradle her breasts. His thumbs moved as lightly as a warm breeze over the creamy flesh pushed up by the dress.

She said not a word. Words seemed to make no sense. She was tired—tired of thinking, tired of rationalizing, tired of everything but his touch. His hands returned to her shoulders. He turned her slowly. She felt the tender touch of his palms as they cradled her face. His thumbs brushed away her tears. He kissed first one eye, then the other. He brushed her lips, and she could taste the salt of her tears on his warm lips.

"Rebecca," he whispered in her ear before he warmed it with his breath, his lips, his tongue. "Rebecca."

Each time he repeated her name he felt his need grow. He had not intended this to happen. He should have been gone by now. What was it that had forced him to keep his lonely vigil in the darkness? Was it the chance that she might come out? Had he wished her here in his arms, her warm flesh beneath his hands, the smell of jasmine enticing him to even more foolishness?

He trailed kisses down her neck, breathing deeply of her heady smell. It was like exotic incense, opium to his mind, to his senses, heightening them to an excruciating level where pain combined with unspeakable pleasure. He had never intended to be gentle with her, and yet he found the sensations so exquisite that he dared not tarnish them with anything less.

He would have her. Now. Tonight. He suckled at the creamy flesh above her gown as if to release it from its confines. He barely restrained himself from pushing the gown down off her arms. He could stand it no longer. He firmly moved her out the gate that led to Cadillac Square. He kept his arm encircled around her waist as if to prevent her escape, but she offered no resistance. She was silent and compliant. He dared not question why. He dared not think of that other time, of the bitter words he had flung at her. He would have her this time.

He hailed a carriage among the many that awaited the departure of guests and helped her in. When they were alone, out of the sight of intruding eyes, he took her in his arms and kissed her deeply, achingly. She responded with a passion that matched his own. Its intensity frightened him. It was unlike any past experience. It was as if he were an inexperienced youth again, feeling, for the first time, the powerful urges of manhood.

His appetite was voracious. He could not get enough of her. He wanted to strip her naked and allow his hands and his mouth to explore every inch of her. He remembered her beauty as she had lain on his bed that night. He loosened her hair, and it fell in great luscious waves across her shoulders. He caught it in his hands and buried his face in it before lifting his head to her lips again.

He did not hear the horses' hooves as they moved down Woodward. He did not feel the sway of the carriage. He had ordered it on impulse to the place where he was compelled to take her. He would complete the circle and rid himself of her unwanted mastery over him.

Rebecca could no longer think; she could only feel. She wanted to release herself from the material confines that kept her body from his. When the carriage stopped, it brought back the intrusion of the outside world. She was in total disarray. Where had he taken her? She could not be seen this way, not with him. She was ashamed enough by her need, she did not wish to proclaim it to the world.

She looked to him for guidance. He took her arm, opened the door, and helped her down. He kept her protectively behind him while he paid the driver. The look on the man's face said he need not have bothered to shield her.

She was dazed. This made no sense. She was standing in front of her own home. Surely he was not going to abandon her again, kiss her chastely and leave her on her doorstep! He could not do that, not now, not with all the aching need inside her, so raw that she could not live if he left her. She felt his arm around her waist, and it urged her on, not to the door but to the back, to the river!

Still, neither one spoke. When he reached the dock, he turned her toward him and kissed her hungrily. He moved down her neck, across her tingling breasts, until he knelt before her with his head against her belly. She heard the taffeta of her dress rustle as he gathered great masses of it. His hands were moving to release the stays of her hoops. When he had accomplished this he rose again to begin the exquisite task of removing her dress. His mouth explored her shoulders and found the soft hollow at the base of her neck, while his fingers worked expertly to release the back of the dress.

She lost track of time. It seemed only moments. It seemed an eternity. She felt the dress release and he pushed it urgently from her shoulders. He lifted her from the mass of fabric and turned to the black sloop, *Deliverance.* How ironic, she wondered in a brief moment of sanity, that this was to be her deliverance from the passions that haunted her. Or would it deliver her to them?

He stepped onto the deck and lifted her down beside him. The full moon cast them in an almost magical radiance. He removed his jacket and then gently released her hair from the last of the pins that bound it. He combed through it with his fingers, caressing her cheeks as his warm hands passed them. Then he moved to release the corset that still confined her aching breasts. The air was cool, yet she did not feel it.

She felt hot with his touch, mesmerized by his passion. At this moment, she could not prevent him from doing anything he wished. He knelt to slip her corset and camisole down over her slender hips. He moved his hands back up over her waist to cradle each creamy orb before he drew her toward him to take first one breast and then the other into his mouth, teasing their tips with his tongue.

When he withdrew, she still leaned into him, cradling his head against her belly, feeling the silky softness of his hair teasing her flesh. He turned once more to tantalize her navel before he slowly eased her white linen pantalets down, trailing their path with reverent kisses. She gasped when he found the golden curls that sheltered her maidenhood.

She was naked, and yet she knew no embarrassment. She watched him remove first one boot, then the other. He began to unfasten the buttons that barely withstood the pressure of his manhood. Free of his pants, he removed the loose-fitting woolen undergarment that did little to conceal his need. Then he stood naked before her.

It was as if this were some ancient ritual, some primitive rite of passage. His eyes made his need plain, his request urgent. She surveyed his broad shoulders and heavily muscled arms and chest, and felt no timidity as she admired his taut belly and slender waist. She remembered the feel of dark curls beneath her fingers. Now she saw the intensity of his need for her. She felt a warm wetness between her legs that came from deep within her. She slowly looked up. Her need was as great as his.

Brad held out his hand, and she came forward. He led her down into the cabin. When he took her in his arms and felt the warmth of her body along his, he felt the agony of unbearable pleasure. His mouth sought hers hungrily, his hands grasped her buttocks, pressing her against him. Gone was any gentleness. He was past that, half-insane with need. He lowered her to the narrow bunk and covered her with his body.

He opened her mouth with his and explored its tender recesses. He pressed himself between her legs, seeking the shelter of her warm, wet flesh. When he felt resistance, he withdrew.

Something deep inside him gave warning, but he paid no heed. He suckled her breasts, and moved once more down her belly, devouring everything he passed. He reached the golden curls, and his tongue sought the recesses that still resisted. He felt her start at his presence within her and then moan. He was lost. He desperately explored her, urged on by her moans of pleasure. Then he felt her hands cradling his head, their entreaty clear.

He moved up along her body. Rising up on his elbows he cradled her head between his hands and moved himself between her thighs, pressing upward for entrance, for release. He saw her wince. He saw her amazement at the feel of him within her. He moved within her and was forced to close his eyes with the force of the sheer pleasure of it.

He rose up on his hands and began the steady eternal rhythm of life. He felt her straining toward him, and he increased his thrusts. It could not be stopped, this neverending need. He felt the release. He felt the warm fluid fill her. She had this part of him, this part and much more. Had he truly given it against his will?

She cradled his head against her breasts. She could feel his breath in short pants, she could feel his heartbeat against her belly. She felt his vulnerability, and she felt protective of him. She stared at the ceiling, marvelling at what had just occurred, at the sensations he had aroused in her, at the overpowering animal urge she had felt.

How had this man managed to capture her soul when no other could? She felt a sudden fear. She would never again be free from this man. Was that a curse or a blessing? She shivered.

"You're cold. Let me get you something." His voice was hoarse. He moved slowly from atop her, and she shivered anew. He went to the small storage area in the bow and opened the door. He found the blanket he was searching for, but something else caught his eye. He bent again and retrieved the item, thoughtfully fingering it as he straightened.

It was a small piece of a sail, torn, long-forgotten—and black. The memory of the black sloop that night at the foot of Randolph wiped even the most recent sensual experiences from his mind. He searched for some legitimate explanation, but he had never seen a black sail until that night, on that sloop that so resembled the *Deliverance.*

He turned and tossed the blanket to Rebecca, still fingering the rough fibers of the canvas piece. He studied her. She had not yet noticed. When her eyes were finally drawn to the sailcloth, he had his answer.

Rebecca had sensed the change in him even before she saw it in his eyes. When she looked down to what he held in his hands, her heart sank. She willed her determination back.

He slowly took two steps back to her. She clutched the blanket around her body. She felt suddenly naked. He held out the ripped piece to her.

"I believe this is yours."

She began to deny it, desperately trying to give him a reasonable explanation, but he interrupted her.

"You play a very dangerous game, Rebecca. And dangerous games have tragic consequences. You and your friends would do well to remember that in the future."

"I don't know what you are talking about."

"Don't play the naive innocent with me, Rebecca. I believe we are long past that."

She blushed at his innuendo. She felt vulnerable sitting naked before him, and from that vulnerability came anger.

"You think you are impregnable, invincible. Everything is black and white for you. You care nothing for anyone but yourself. You are incapable of imagining the pain of having your children sold, your wife sent off. You are incapable of caring! Incapable of feeling! Incapable of loving!"

She was losing control. She would not give him the benefit of seeing her cry. She turned away from him, frightened of the emotions he had drawn to the surface, emotions that left her skin tingling.

She did not turn until he had left the cabin. She heard him dressing and felt the boat sway slightly when he stepped ashore. Finally, she lay back against the bunk. She was drained, emotionally and physically. She could feel his seed between her legs, slowly deserting her, just as surely she knew the man was deserting her as well.

15

Rebecca leaned her head back against the wall and closed her eyes. She was tired. The normally stirring voice of the speaker was distant, disembodied. It rang through the hall, creating a fervor of support for Lincoln's election, and yet to her it seemed as far away as that night on the *Deliverance.*

She was strangely apart from it all. It was she who was disembodied, passionless. Even though she knew her convictions were as strong as ever, the decisions were no longer simple, life was no longer black and white. It now contained great gray areas of doubt.

What had changed? A blush colored her cheeks. She was no longer a virgin. Somehow it went beyond that. She had given him her virginity, but he had taken much more.

"Rebecca." Rachel's concerned voice brought

Rebecca's eyes open. "Are you ill?"

"No, just tired, I think."

"You've been so quiet of late. So withdrawn. Is something wrong?"

"No, dear friend." Rebecca forced lightness into her voice and a smile to her lips. "I assure you, I am fine."

Rachel said nothing.

The crowd roared in approval of the speaker's stirring conclusion. Rebecca rose to go.

"Would you like a cup of tea?" Rachel was determined to get to the root of the problem. Rebecca had not been herself for over a month.

"Yes, that would be lovely."

The two women left the hall and headed for Rachel's cramped home that doubled as her dress shop.

"Miss Rebecca!" The chorus of small voices that welcomed Rebecca as she entered Rachel's home brought her out of her morbid reverie and back to the warmth of the world. The babble of the children and their excitement gave Rebecca the first pleasure she had known since that night. She smiled at the eager young faces.

Mary, at seven, was all decorum, but still so young that she lacked the guile to hide her pleasure at Rebecca's unexpected arrival. Ezra was a five-year-old bundle of energy. He tugged at Rebecca's cloak for attention. Little ten-month-old Charity sat on the colorful rag rug in front of the hearth and gurgled at all the excitement.

Rebecca laughed.

"That is a good sound, Miss Rebecca." Jacob entered the room from a second one that served as the family's sleeping quarters. He smiled at Rebecca.

"I'm sorry, Jacob, I guess I have been a bit of a sour puss lately." She addressed this as much to the children as to the large black man who had been her companion and mentor for so many years. "But I am promising right this minute that I will turn over a new leaf . . . starting . . . now!" She bent down and grabbed Ezra under the arms, tickling him furiously. The boy responded with a fit of laughing and thrashing that left the other two children laughing as well.

"No! Stop! Please!" Ezra's halfhearted pleas came out in spurts between lyrical bursts of childish laughter. Mary's giggles had joined the cheerful chorus, and Charity held her arms up imploringly.

Rebecca left the boy rolling on the floor as she approached the baby.

"So you want a tickle, too, little one? Well, you shall have your wish." She knelt and gently lay the baby back on the rug before she tickled the child's feet. The baby squealed in delight.

Rebecca rose and opened her arms to Mary. "No tickling, promise," she assured the girl as she moved into Rebecca's embrace. "And you, young lady. Have you been studying your letters? I shall test you before I leave."

The usually somber girl looked up with a smile. Her braided hair ringed her head like a coronet, and her eyes blazed with intelligence and wisdom far beyond her years. "I have been studying every free moment, you shall see."

"So I shall."

"Mary, put the kettle on," Rachel said. "I've promised Rebecca some tea before she heads home." The girl reluctantly separated herself from Rebecca's embrace. "Jacob, we will need some more flour if I am to bake that boysenberry pie you've been pestering me for. Why don't you take the children down to the store with you?" Rachel's eyes communicated far more than her lips. "Perhaps Mr. Farnsworth has some stick candy certain children might like."

"Oh, Papa! Can we go?" Mary and Ezra piped up in unison. Even little Charity, bouncing on Rebecca's lap, seemed to sense something was afoot. Rebecca handed her to Jacob, who swung the baby up to his wide shoulders, much to her delight. The foursome headed out the door in high spirits.

It was only after they left that Rachel moved toward the steaming kettle and prepared the tea. There was an uncomfortable silence between the two women.

"Do you think Mr. Lincoln will win?" It was Rachel who finally spoke.

"Yes, I believe he will. With the Democrats split, I think there is a good chance he will be elected."

"What will that mean, Rebecca? I am as frightened by the thought of his election as I am by the thought that he might be defeated."

"I don't know what it will mean, but surely we cannot go back to where we were."

"But he has promised us nothing! All the Republicans talk of is not allowing slavery in the new territories. They are all cowards when it comes to ridding this country of its terrors."

"We may find, Rachel, that if Mr. Lincoln is elected he will have no choice. If the Southern states who swear they will secede carry out their threat, there will be more than slavery at stake. The very existence of the Republic will be in jeopardy."

"Is that why you have been so somber lately?"

Rebecca suddenly felt uncomfortable, suspecting this was the subject Rachel really wanted to discuss. She was afraid she could not hold up under Rachel's scrutiny.

"Perhaps it has put a damper on my spirit. That must be what you sense. I will be my old self soon. Maybe when the election is over and things have worked themselves out."

From here the conversation moved on to less personal things, much to Rebecca's relief.

Rebecca pulled the black cloak closer around her. The night was frigid. The cold weather had come quickly and surely. Her horse whinnied with impatience and Rebecca turned to calm it.

"That's all right, girl. I don't blame you. I would rather be home and warm, too." Once the horse had calmed under her gentle strokes, she listened in the darkness.

The election had proved Rebecca's hunch correct: Abraham Lincoln had been elected President. The only immediate result was increased talk of secession in the South.

Seymour Finney's barn continued to harbor fugitives. By the middle of December, the river had frozen over. There were many who waited to be transported. In the preceding weeks, the river had been too clogged with ice to be crossed by boat, yet still too dangerous to manage on foot.

Tonight, finally, some of the slaves would be moved. Rebecca felt alive for the first time in a long time. Once again she had purpose.

The sky was without light. Neither moon nor stars would betray them. The sound of the horses' hooves penetrated the darkness long before any movement caught her eye. As the figures slowly emerged from the blackness, she felt a certain exhilaration.

"Were you followed?" she asked Jacob.

"No."

"I've seen no one. The cold has kept everyone indoors."

"I hope you're right, Miss Rebecca." Jacob's voice betrayed his concern.

Rebecca looked at the two horses he led. One carried a woman with a child of about six, the other a man.

"Do you see that light, just to the left?" she asked the mounted figures.

They nodded.

"If for any reason we are separated, or if I tell you to go on without me, you are to head for that light. The people there will know what to do. They are expecting you."

Once more the couple nodded.

Rebecca turned back to Jacob. "If all goes well, I should be back before midnight."

"Be careful."

"I don't believe anyone will be out tonight."

"Even so, the ice may not be completely frozen. Watch for thin ice. Do not hurry—it could cost you your life."

Rebecca nodded, remembering the conductor they had lost last year to the ice. His body had not been recovered until spring.

Rebecca mounted her horse and carefully made her way toward the open stretch of ice and snow that stood between them and their destination.

Snow had begun to fall heavily, and the wind had picked up, blowing the cold flakes into her eyes. She had to move cautiously as they descended the bank to the icy river. The snow would provide better footing for the horses, but it would also hide any thin ice.

She proceeded slowly, listening for any telltale cracking sounds. The horse moved reluctantly out into the open, where the wind whipped the snow into icy waves. She signaled the two who followed to stay close behind.

When they were about a third of the way across, she began to relax. She tried to protect herself against the cold by securing her wildly flapping cloak around her numb body. She had just looked behind to check on her charges when she heard it.

Horses' hooves, then a shout, a command to stop! She reined in to let the other two horses come abreast.

"To the light! Do not stop!" She slapped the rumps of the two other horses before she looked back to assess the situation. It was an army patrol.

"Halt! You! Stop there!" The words fought the

wind as the sounds of the hooves moved closer with alarming speed.

She wheeled her horse around. The island, she would lead them to the island. She knew it like the back of her hand. She could lose them there and give the fugitives time to reach shore. She bent low over the horse's neck and urged it to a gallop, praying that the horse could maintain its footing. Her cloak flew out behind her, and the cowl tore at the hairpins she had used to secure it. The shouting behind her reminded her of a fox hunt, only she was the fox. She heard a shot but was only vaguely aware of the whizz of the bullet as it passed close to her head.

She was forced to slow down at the southwestern tip of Hog Island, and another shot whistled by. Her horse almost slipped as it climbed up the sloping bank. Once securely on land, she headed for a familiar, heavily wooded area. There were already more than two inches of snow on the ground. She prayed that the lack of moon and the blowing snow would make her trail difficult to follow.

She worked with the horse, urging and cajoling it through the dense underbrush. There was a trail that led along the north side of the island. The river was at its narrowest there. If she could make it that far, she could make a dash for shore with some assurance of making it.

She heard some confusion as the platoon reached the woods. Someone was barking orders.

She knew the voice. It was him! A new shiver ran through her. Then the woods seemed to come alive. The cracking of twigs and branches and the panting of horses seemed to be coming from all directions. She could see the path ahead. She broke through to it and once more was able to move with some speed. There was a shout. The path had been discovered. Hoofbeats behind her confirmed that fact. She looked for an opening. She and the horse plunged down the bank to the river once more.

No more than twenty feet out, she heard it—the first sound of cracking ice. The currents in this narrow channel had kept the ice from freezing as thickly as in other places on the river. As she moved, the sharp reports from the ice warned her the thin layer might give way beneath her at any time. Fear sent her heartbeat into double time. She could not go back. She had no choice. She was no longer aware of anything but the ice.

She urged the horse to greater speed. To slow, to stop, could mean death. Then there was another shot. She heard the ice breaking and the frightened whinnies of a horse. It took her a moment to realize it was not her horse. She tried to make some sense of it. The patrol must have attempted to follow, and the weight of several horses on the already weakened ice had caused the break. Had he gone down? She dared not stop or turn to look. She heard a horse thrashing in the icy water and the curses of its rider. She was safe, at least from the patrol.

She must have been holding her breath, for when her horse's hooves hit the opposite bank, she heard herself gasp and then pant with exhaustion. She resisted the urge to stop, to turn and determine the identity and fate of the unlucky rider who still struggled in the deadly cold river. She urged the spent horse slowly up the incline. She would have to head to the road before turning toward home. A more direct route might leave telltale tracks.

Brad Taylor yelled orders to the men on shore to help the flailing man and horse. Once more, luck had worked against him. They would have to retrace their steps to return safely. The cloaked figure would have more than enough time to escape undetected. He had come so close this time.

He blew on his hands which were numb with the cold and stared off into the darkness. For the second time, he had seen the Angel of Passage. He tried to remember if the cloaked figure had given any clues to his identity. In the darkness there had been little to see beyond the trailing black cape. He wondered who this man was who held everyone's imagination and respect, who had everyone's protection, including Rebecca Cunningham's.

Surely they knew one another. Rebecca's involvement with the movement had been made clear that night aboard the *Deliverance,* the night he had found the black sailcloth. For a brief moment he wondered if their relationship went beyond friendship, this man and Rebecca. This thought was painful. He tried to dismiss it, and yet it ate at him. This Angel of Passage was the kind of man she would respect, the kind of man she could love. Yet she had slept with *him,* and he had been the first to make love to her. It made no sense. No slaves had been moved the night they had been on the *Deliverance.* Why had she sacrificed her virginity for nothing? Had there been a plan that had been aborted at the last moment? It became only more confusing. He knew he could not let it rest.

Jacob greeted her at the stable door. It was well past two. She did not have to say anything. He knew from the condition of her horse that something had gone wrong. He helped her down, holding her a moment until she steadied herself. He waited for her to speak.

"It was a patrol. Somehow they knew we were going to be there. We were barely abreast of Hog Island when I heard their shouts." She paused. "I fear there is a traitor among us, Jacob. He will have to be found. Until he is found, we are all in danger."

"How did you get away?"

"I headed for the island and crossed back. The ice was thin. It barely supported me. When the patrol attempted to cross, it gave way."

Jacob wrapped her shaking figure in a blanket.

"Jacob, take the horse. I don't want anyone to find it lathered and in our barn at this hour. Leave it at Seymour's. Its presence is not likely to be questioned there."

Jacob led the exhausted horse to the stable door before mounting it. "It was the hand of God that saved you, Miss Rebecca. That's for sure."

Rebecca smiled at the man. Thank God for Jacob. But who was feeding information to Captain Taylor? Who among them was the traitor? Pulling the blanket closer around her, she made her way slowly through the deepening snow to the house.

* * *

Brad returned his men to the garrison and dismissed them. He ordered a fresh horse. In the dark hours before dawn, he remounted. He rode out Jefferson Avenue on his bizarre personal quest. He could not even explain to himself what he was looking for. There were few tracks along Jefferson, and few of these were anywhere near fresh.

As he approached the Cunningham home, he slowed. He studied the blowing snow that covered the road and the driveway that led to the back of the house. There appeared to be tracks left fairly recently. They approached from still farther out of town, toward Hog Island, and entered the Cunningham driveway. Still others, perhaps left by the same horse, led from the back of the Cunningham home to Jefferson and toward town.

Brad moved his horse toward the back of the house. The snow had slacked off. When he reached the stables he dismounted. The snow was in disarray. A horse, a man, maybe two, had been here not long ago. He looked back toward the house. A light shone from a rear bedroom window. It had to be close to four, a peculiar hour to be up. Somehow this woman who haunted him was much more deeply implicated than ever. Her link to the Angel of Passage could no longer be overlooked. Who had been here earlier?

When he tried to make sense of it his thoughts grew dark. To contemplate the fact that she might be intimately involved with one of the men who had been here earlier left him open to disturbing feelings of betrayal and jealousy. He vowed she would not do that to him. She did not mean that much to him.

He remounted and headed back to the cold and the darkness, to his hotel room, and to the balm of sleep.

16

"It's beautiful, Father!"

"Yes, it is. Far more because of your doing than mine, I'm afraid."

George Cunningham stood back to admire the large spruce tree that had been set up in one corner of the ballroom. The evergreen had been gaily decorated with garlands. Its fragrant branches were heavy with the white candles whose brilliance would cheer the celebration.

"Merry Christmas, Father." Rebecca threw her arms around her father and stood for a moment in his embrace.

"Are you all right, Rebecca? You've been so quiet, almost melancholy. I've been worried."

Rebecca pulled back and smiled. "I'm fine. I'm just concerned, as everyone is, about South Carolina's secession. I don't think it will be the only one." She paused a moment before she asked the question on everyone's lips. "Do you think there will be war?"

"It is a horrible thing to contemplate, a war that would pit brother against brother, father against son. I would have to be a fool to deny the course that has been set. I don't see how we are to avoid war without abandoning the very things you have fought so hard for these past years. Some things have to be purchased at a very dear price. I'm afraid this may well be one of them."

The smile Rebecca had worked so hard to muster was gone. They stood in thoughtful silence for several moments before Rebecca walked to the large windows that looked out toward the river.

There had been a heavy snow the day before, and several inches of the glistening white crystals blanketed the ground and outbuildings. It was a pristine scene, seemingly untouched by man. The river was an icy ribbon, a demarkation line. Today it seemed a scornful barrier, keeping all the fear, all the tensions on her side of it. On the other side there would be no war. On the other side, in Canada, there was no slavery.

"It's so beautiful out, Father, so peaceful. It all seems so far away, and yet, I know you are right. I sometimes fear that the price we will have to pay will be so high, the victory will be hollow." She turned to her father. "Can you ever pay too high a price for something?"

"Each one must decide that for himself, my dear. There is no easy formula to guide you. Only your heart, only your soul, can judge the value of the thing you seek."

"Yes, I suppose you are right."

"But now, my dear, there is much yet to be done before our guests arrive. Go see how cook is progressing. Tell her that I sent Samuel into town some time ago to get the last of the things she needs. He should be back any time now."

Rebecca laughed. "Poor Bertie, every year she tries to outdo herself. I fear the poor woman will collapse one Christmas Eve. But then, if she did, she would miss the celebration, and she wouldn't let that happen. She enjoys it as much as or more than anyone." Rebecca found her spirits somewhat restored.

George Cunningham watched his daughter leave the room. He was worried about the change he saw in her. She had lost some of her spirit. What had happened? Only on the night she had been chased across the icy river had she been her old self. Later that night, in her room, he had scolded her once more for the risks she took. She had laughed and made light of it. There had been the old exuberance about her.

Aside from that night, her mood had continued to be somber. She seemed troubled. He didn't know why, but this mood change seemed to be linked to the night of the ball, to her departure with Captain Taylor.

George hoped he had not made a grave mistake in inviting the captain to their annual Christmas Eve open house. It seemed a risk worth taking. Rebecca had seemed to be hiding from someone or something lately. If she was hiding from the captain, he would have the answer tonight.

The knock on the door to her room startled Rebecca.

"Come in."

Rachel opened the door and stepped aside to let in Jacob, who was laden with boxes and parcels.

Rebecca's face lit up at the sight of her friends.

"Rachel, Jacob, Merry Christmas!" She rushed to embrace Rachel and place a kiss on Jacob's embarrassed cheek.

"Merry Christmas, Rebecca! I'm sorry we're so late delivering the dress, but Charity was ill the last several days, and it was only last night that I managed time to finish hemming the mantle." She nodded to Jacob, who eagerly took it as a sign of dismissal. As he left the room, Rachel smiled after him. "I'm afraid a lady's boudoir is not the most comfortable place for him."

"Is Charity all right, Rachel?"

"Yes, it was nothing serious. She is much better today. You are still coming over after the party, aren't you? The children would be sorely disappointed if you missed our annual hot milk and cookie celebration."

"Tell them I would not miss it for anything in the world."

"I shall. Now, you must tell me what you think of our creation." Rachel busied herself with the packages, shaking out their contents one after the other.

"Rachel, you have outdone yourself again. They are exquisite."

Rachel had completed her task. Before her on the bed lay a dress, mantle, matching bonnet, and muff. Rebecca moved toward the bed and picked up the dress. Holding it up to her, she moved toward the full-length mirror in one corner.

"Oh, Rachel, it's unbelievably lovely." The dress was velvet of a shade of red unlike anything Rebecca had ever seen—deep and lush, touched with a blush of violet. It resembled a breathtaking sunset. The neckline was cut wide and had been delicately trimmed with ermine. The waist was tightly fitted and moved to a deep V in front. The lush skirt fell, only to be gathered and draped between fabric roses, revealing a rose-colored silk underskirt.

The mantle was of the same velvet, lined with rose satin and trimmed luxuriously in the white ermine. The velvet bonnet and ermine muff gaily displayed black-tipped tails.

"Can you stay a moment and help me dress? I want you to see it on me before anyone else."

Rebecca began to remove her dressing gown. The late afternoon sun lay across the floor, warming the highly polished wood. A fire blazed in the grate, warding off any winter chill. Rebecca felt safe here. It was a harbor from the stormy thoughts that buffeted her of late. Here, with Rachel, she could block out the feelings that tormented her. She could block out Brad. She could keep distant the memory of that night and the sensuality of his touch, the feel of his mouth on her breasts, drawing life from her. She could forget the feel of his fullness within her, of her urgent need to abandon herself to him, to be swept away by his strength.

She could convince herself it was a fluke, a momentary lapse on her part. She could almost convince herself it would never happen again.

Rachel was just closing the last of the buttons on Rebecca's dress when a knock disturbed them.

George Cunningham entered the room, formally dressed and carrying a gift in his hands. He crossed the room to where his daughter stood.

"I wanted you to have this now, Rebecca, before the party. Merry Christmas, my dear."

Rebecca opened the jewelry box slowly. Inside lay a pearl and ruby necklace with matching drop earrings.

"Oh, Father, it's too much."

"It is a father's privilege to buy beautiful things for a beautiful daughter, is it not?"

Rebecca threw her arms around his neck and kissed his cheek. "Thank you, it's a wonderful gift. I don't deserve it."

"Nonsense, my dear." He held her at arm's length. "Let me see it on you." Rebecca fastened the earrings while Rachel worked the clasp of the necklace.

"There. They suit you well," the older woman said.

The necklace and earrings did suit her. The necklace lay tight around her throat, its delicate pearl strands emphasizing the luminescence of her bare skin. The rubies at the end of the pearl drop earrings moved seductively in and out of her hair.

"You look especially lovely this evening, Rebecca."

"Thank you, Father. I'll be down shortly."

"I think I'll go calm Bertie now. The guests should be arriving soon."

After her father had left, Rebecca smoothed the folds of the velvet gown. "Thank you, Rachel, the gown is as lovely as anything you've ever made. Please tell the children I will see them as soon as I can get away."

Rachel collected the tissue left from the dress and turned to go. At the door she turned and said, "Take care, Rebecca."

Rebecca felt her friend's unspoken concern. "I will." She smiled tremulously.

Rebecca turned back to her reflection in the mirror. She studied herself closely, looking for any outward indication of the emotions that had been taking such a toll on her. She could see none. Downstairs, the first guests would be arriving. She turned and slowly headed for the door.

George Cunningham raised his glass to the room full of friends and associates.

"A toast to our friends, this Christmas Eve. May the holidays be joyous and the new year full of new hope."

The dull murmur of "Amens" filled the Cunningham ballroom in response. Rebecca stood beside her father, glass raised. The evening had been pleasant. The party had been an annual event of the Cunningham family as long as Rebecca could remember. Amidst all the turmoil, there was something reassuring in tradition.

"Father, it's getting late, and I promised Rachel and the children I would stop by this evening. I'm going to tell Samuel to prepare the carriage. I do believe you will be able to manage without me." She gave him a wink and then placed a kiss on his cheek.

Brad slowly fastened the last of the highly polished brass buttons on his dress uniform. His thoughts were on Rebecca Cunningham. He was tense with anticipation of seeing her again. He wondered if it was she who had extended the invitation. It seemed unlikely after their last parting. But it was not the anger of that parting that stirred his loins now, but rather the passion of the coupling. It had not worked. Having her had not sated him. She angered him, frustrated him, and excited him as no other woman had.

She was unattainable. He had experienced her body, and yet it was her soul, her spirit, that still remained beyond his grasp. She despised his work. Did she despise him as well? She had used him, and he had begged for more. He was a fool.

He swore and threw his gloves down on the bureau before crossing the room to the window. He had been delayed by some business, and now the party would be almost over. It had started to snow again.

There was a hesitant knock on the door to his room. He turned, welcoming the distraction.

"Captain, I've your horse saddled and ready, sir."

Joey Whiton stood before him, his red hair liberally covered with the huge snowflakes. Brad noticed he worried his cap in his red, raw hands. The boy had wrapped rags around them to fend off the cold. At least he did not seem to have been beaten recently, Brad thought grimly.

"Thank you, Joey." Brad flipped a shiny quarter at the boy, whose stiff fingers barely managed its capture.

A bright smile crossed the boy's face. "Thank you, Captain." He turned and ran down the hall to the staircase, where he stopped. "And Merry Christmas, Sir."

"And to you, Joey . . . and to you," Brad whispered the words after the boy. He stood in the doorway for a long moment before re-entering the room.

He shrugged into his overcoat and walked over to the mantel which held an intricately carved railroad engine he had finished earlier that day. Picking up the locomotive, he inspected it thoughtfully before placing it in the pocket of his greatcoat. Then he picked up his gloves and left.

When he reached the lobby, he found Seymour Finney at the front desk.

"Mr. Finney, your stable boy . . ."

"Joey?"

"Yes. Is the lad still here?"

"No, Captain. I sent him home early, seeing that it's Christmas Eve."

"Where would that be, his home?"

"Down on Atwater, Captain. It's not much more than a shack, really. Next to the saloon at the corner of Bates."

"Thank you, Mr. Finney."

Seymour Finney's words halted him before he reached the door: "Captain, it's not the best of neighborhoods. I'd be careful venturing down there, even on Christmas Eve."

"I'll remember that, Mr. Finney. Thank you."

"Good evening, Captain. Merry Christmas."

"Good evening." Brad handed his coat to the servant who had greeted him at the Cunningham door.

"Mr. Cunningham and Miss Rebecca are in the ballroom."

"Thank you." Brad nodded his acknowledgment.

He was the last of the guests to arrive. In fact, some were already leaving.

"Merry Christmas, Captain Taylor," a departing guest said as he helped his wife with her coat.

Brad acknowledged the greeting and then moved toward the ballroom. He stopped at the entryway. The room was crowded with the city's notables. He saw George Cunningham against the far wall and made his way toward him, exchanging formal greetings with some of the other guests as he went.

George Cunningham was deep in conversation with another gentleman, but he excused himself when he saw Brad approaching.

"Captain Taylor, I'm glad your schedule allowed you to come." Brad sensed a certain hesitancy in the greeting.

"It is my pleasure. Your hospitality in this city is legendary, so it seems, and rightly so."

"Most kind of you to say so." There was an awkward moment before George Cunningham continued the conversation. "My daughter will, no doubt, be pleased you could join us. She has gone upstairs for the moment but should be returning shortly."

The older man seemed to be studying him, looking for some indication as to what her reaction would truly be. Brad wondered how much the father knew of his daughter's activities.

"Ah, here she is now." The older man quietly departed, leaving Brad alone to face Rebecca.

It was almost déjà vu. She stood smiling at the foot of the steps, but this time, when their eyes met, there was recognition, and her smile became artificial, her chatter with those around her forced. She excused herself and approached him. Her eyes were cold, chillingly cold.

"You are not welcome in this house, Captain."

"I think you should have had this conversation with your father before he extended me the invitation, Miss Cunningham. It seems he does not share your antipathy."

"Father need not know how low and vile you are, Captain. It is sufficient that I know. You are not welcome, and I request that you leave at once."

"Perhaps we should discuss this with your father, then." He took her arm, holding her a little too tightly. "Perhaps your father would be interested in knowing just what his daughter has sacrificed for the cause, particularly when it was sacrificed so willingly to the low and vile creature that I am." He smiled benevolently as he forcibly moved her toward her father. The feel of her skin, soft and malleable beneath his fingertips, and the smell of her so close, were even more wonderful than he remembered.

She jerked her arm away. "You would not dare!" she whispered fiercely.

"I am capable of almost anything, my dear Miss Cunningham. Are you not aware of that by now?" He continued to smile at her.

"You are worse than despicable. You have no soul, no heart. You are beneath despicable. If you will not leave, I will!"

With that, she turned on her heel and headed for the door. A servant was already there with her cloak and muff. Another stood dressed for the outdoors with a stack of brightly wrapped Christmas packages in his arms.

After she had gone out the door, Brad intercepted the servant who held the packages.

"I'll take those. There is no need for your services," he told the startled servant. "I have offered to accompany Miss Cunningham on her errands."

Rebecca had already entered the carriage when he approached. He opened the door and installed himself and the presents on the seat across from her.

"It seems, Miss Cunningham, I will have to redeem myself."

17

Rebecca was stunned. How could he! Hadn't she made her feelings perfectly clear? He studied her now, and she grew warm under his scrutiny, despite the chilly night air. Her flush brought back a rush of sensations. She could smell his cologne. The familiar scent sought her out, even though he remained smugly in place across from her. It was a heady combination that was his alone—his when she had held his head in her hands and kissed his hair, his when he had nibbled her neck and . . .

No! Refusing to give in to the memories, she looked away from him, out the window.

"It seems, Captain, you are not to be put off this evening."

"So it seems."

"Have you any idea, Sir, where you are headed?"

"The destination matters little. It is the pleasure of your company I seek."

"Is this some perverse pleasure you take in torturing me? I would have thought that after our last unpleasant parting, my company would be the last thing you would desire."

"My memory, at the moment, prefers to go back further than yours, Miss Cunningham, to much more pleasurable activities shared that evening."

She could feel her color intensify. The man had no conscience whatsoever. A gentleman would never have alluded to such a thing, certainly not to a lady. But then the captain was no gentleman, and she—perhaps she had abandoned all rights to be considered a lady the night she had given herself to him. She shook her head to clear it. She needed her wits back. Why was it she seemed to lose all rational thought whenever he was near?

"You may find that our destination this evening greatly diminishes your pleasure in my company, Captain."

"Nothing that I know of could do that."

"We shall see."

The house they stopped at was neat, yet sparse. The light that fell from the windows was brightly colored by the starched curtains that covered the small, single-paned openings. Rebecca knocked firmly on the door. The captain stood behind her, his arms laden with the brightly wrapped parcels.

"Miss Rebecca! Miss Rebecca! We've been waiting ever so long for you!" The smiling faces of the children gave way to eyes widened with surprise and fright as they recognized the figure in blue behind her.

Her heart went out to them. "Merry Christmas!" she said, forcing her smile wider. When they did not respond, she bent low and whispered for their ears only, "There is no reason to be afraid, my loves. I will see to that." Then she rose and smiled again.

This time there was a tentative response: "Merry Christmas, Miss Rebecca," and almost as an afterthought, "And to you, too, Sir."

"Well, you must let us in if you are ever going to see what is inside these very special packages."

The children took her cue. They remained distracted by the huge figure of the captain that followed her into the room. Rebecca shared their fear. She looked pleadingly at Jacob, who had stood and now seemed to physically challenge the captain's presence.

"You are not welcome here, Sir."

Jacob's somber voice sent a chill down Rebecca's spine.

She looked now toward Rachel. She pleaded with her friend, her eyes speaking more than her words. "He offered to help. He did not know where we were going."

She could not see Brad behind her, and she dared not turn. She damned herself for allowing him to accompany her. It seemed hours before Rachel spoke.

"It is Christmas. There should be no room in our hearts for animosity. Jacob, set the kettle on for our guests." The room remained deathly quiet. Then, without lowering his gaze, Jacob turned and did as Rachel bade.

"Come, sit down, Rebecca." Rachel motioned to the second chair at the small scrubbed pine table. "Captain, please set the parcels by the door. There is a peg there for your coat as well."

"Thank you." They were the first words he had spoken since their arrival. The tone gave no clue to his thoughts.

He approached Rebecca, who had unfastened her

cloak, and silently helped her with it before returning to the door and removing his own coat.

"Children, I believe you have some gifts of your own, do you not?" Rachel's words of encouragement sent the children off.

Seven-year-old Mary smiled tremulously and went to her small pallet beside the hearth, where she retrieved a carefully wrapped brown parcel. She placed it hesitantly in Rebecca's lap before glancing toward the captain.

"I get no hug with my present, Mary?" Rebecca asked softly with a smile.

The girl smiled then and moved close to embrace her. "Merry Christmas, Mary. Now I shall open my gift. What do you think it is, Ezra?" She addressed the small boy whose sparkling black eyes peeked around his sister.

He opened his mouth in answer, but his mother spoke. "Remember, it is to be a surprise, Ezra. Do not spoil Mary's gift." The boy placed a hand over his mouth to hold the secret tightly in place, and a giggle escaped.

Rebecca carefully unwrapped the brown paper, revealing a painstakingly executed needlepoint. "Why, Mary, it's beautiful. The stitches are as well formed as your mother's."

The young girl demurred. "It is not as good as Mother would do it."

"May I see?" The deep male voice startled the group. The captain's presence had almost been forgotten.

The girl's eyes showed hesitation. Rebecca sat up to her full height. "Show the captain, Mary. He may yet appreciate the sentiment as well as the workmanship." Her eyes dared him.

The girl took the gift from Rebecca's hands and delivered it to the captain. Then, to Rebecca's amazement, she stood before him almost defiantly while he read the delicately needlepointed words:

"Thou shalt not deliver unto his master the servant that has escaped from his master unto thee."
Deut.23:16

Rebecca studied his face while he read it. It had softened from earlier, and in the golden light of oil lamps it almost had warmth. She had seen him like this before. It was the side that he hid so well, without the usual defensiveness he harbored. When he looked back to Mary, there was genuine feeling in his eyes.

"It is a gift that Miss Cunningham no doubt will cherish. It is a fine piece of workmanship of which you should be truly proud. We should acknowledge our strengths as well as our weaknesses."

"It's my turn now!" Ezra's small voice interrupted the silence. He hurried over to his mat to retrieve his gift and then ceremoniously laid the item on Rebecca's velvet lap.

"Why, Ezra, it is a beautiful stone. Where did you find it?"

"I found it by the river when it was warm. I've kept it all this time. Do you see how it sparkles? I think it is gold."

"It does indeed sparkle. Look how beautiful it is when I hold it up to the light! Thank you, Ezra, and now for a hug."

The boy climbed onto her soft lap. His small black arms encircled her neck, and he squeezed with all his might.

"Merry Christmas, Ezra."

This task completed, the boy stretched out his hand to retrieve the small rock. Unbeckoned, he moved toward the captain, somberly presenting it for further assessment.

The captain took it, and after studying it for several moments he smiled. "I believe you have discovered a magical stone." The boy's eyes widened. "I have seen a stone like this once before. With that particular stone, if I placed it in my left hand like so . . ." He made a great show of placing the shiny rock in his left hand and making a fist around it. This accomplished, he reached behind the boy's ear with his right hand, producing the sparkling rock. "It would mysteriously jump to some other location."

The boy's eyes widened still further as the captain winked, entering into a small conspiracy with the child. The ebony face came alive with excitement. "Do it again. Can you do it again? Can you show me? It is magic, isn't it?"

"Yes, but only for very special people."

The boy's face fell.

"And I think you are one of those special people. But first, I believe there are some packages begging to be opened." He bent and took one of the gifts and handed it to a startled Rebecca. Her thoughts were in total disarray. The scene that had unfolded before had touched her, and yet she warned herself that she might be reading too much into it.

She began to distribute her presents. The captain moved across the small room and sat on the floor by the hearth, unbuttoning the top button of his blue jacket.

Even among the excited children, Rebecca found her gaze returning over and over to the captain.

Baby Charity had been sitting quietly on a rag rug before the hearth. Now that someone had joined her on the floor, she decided to share the company. Crawling over to the captain, she stood on shaky legs, one hand tightly holding his sleeve for support, the other fingering the shiny buttons of his jacket. When it was time for Charity's gift, all eyes turned to the twosome.

"I can help her with it, if you don't mind."

Rebecca speechlessly handed the gift to young Ezra, who scooted over to his sister and the captain with the package. With two young hands in eager accompaniment, Brad began to help the baby rip the wrapping. The baby squealed in delight as a little rag doll appeared. She clutched the doll in one hand but still seemed reluctant to release the blue serge of the captain's uniform.

Brad took a moment to point out the finer points of the doll to the girl and her eager brother before he stood, bringing Charity and the brightly colored doll up with him. The child seemed to have taken to Brad as easily as she had taken to her new doll.

"You seem to have chosen your gifts well, Rebecca." Brad turned from the girl in his arms to the woman who sat with a bewildered smile on her face. His face showed a warmth and depth of feeling she had never seen before.

"Captain, won't you join us now for some tea and cookies?" It was Rachel who extended the invitation.

The captain nodded. He set Charity down and made his way to the small table. Then, while the children played with their new toys, the adults discussed innocuous topics like the weather in an uncomfortable Christmas truce.

Rebecca finally ended the awkwardness. "We should be going, Rachel. It's getting late."

Rachel nodded, relief apparent on her face. Jacob had maintained a surly silence throughout the evening. They obviously would rest easier when their unwelcome visitor was safely gone. Rebecca smiled her understanding and embraced her friend.

The captain had already retrieved her mantle, and she welcomed its heavy weight as armor against the jumble of emotions in the small room. While Mary hung back, aware of the tension in the air, little Ezra approached Brad. "You can't go! You forgot to show me again."

"I'm afraid we have another stop yet to make tonight," Brad said, to Rebecca's surprise. "But I promise you"—he took a shiny penny from his pocket and placed it in his left fist—"on this magic penny"—he reached behind the boy's ear—"that I will show you the secret another day." He presented the amazed boy with the shiny copper coin. "Is it agreed, then?"

The boy nodded. "Yessir, Captain."

"Good!" He nodded toward Rachel and Jacob. "Thank you for your hospitality." He took Rebecca's arm and led her out the door to the waiting carriage.

At the carriage door, he stopped and turned Rebecca toward him.

"Will you accompany me, then, on a similar visit?"

She was too confused to speak. She merely nodded her assent.

"Thank you, Rebecca Cunningham." His smile warmed her. "Merry Christmas." He enfolded her in his arms and sought her lips. The warmth of his breath frosted the air as he drew near. He touched his lips gently at first, as if waiting for her objection. When none came, he broke off the kiss and moved away slightly to study her. She couldn't stop herself. Her gloved hand moved to the back of his head, and she drew his warmth back to her. This time, the kiss, while still tender, was more thorough. While his tongue sought the warm recesses of her mouth she found her other hand had come to join the first behind his head. It was he who finally broke off the kiss. When he had pulled slightly away she said, "Merry Christmas," her voice a breathy invitation.

"We had best be on our way." He turned and helped her into the carriage. Once she was settled he gave the driver instructions and sat down across from her again. She studied him now, as he searched his greatcoat for something. When he withdrew his hand it held a beautifully carved locomotive.

"It's beautiful. Did you make it?" Once more this man surprised her.

"Yes, it was something I learned to do as a child. It filled the voids." He offered no further explanation.

"Who is the lucky recipient?"

He smiled at her. "Patience, Miss Cunningham, patience."

18

Brad Taylor gently fingered the wooden locomotive. He did not know when the idea had come to him. He had picked up the piece of hard maple one day not far out of town. That day, it had offered no more than the opportunity to whittle, something he had done little of since childhood. In his youth, it had been an outlet for his anger and frustrations, and he had spent days releasing exquisite horses from their wooden bindings.

He had never given them to anyone. They were always destroyed. Watching the flames lick at their intelligent eyes and powerful limbs had been part of the ritual. He had created them, and the fire had ensured that they would never be harmed by anyone. It was his way of returning them, instead, to whence they had come.

Once he had saved a horse. It was a stallion, high on its haunches, defiant and beautiful. His father had found it. All these years later, he could still see the sadistic smile on his father's face when he had destroyed it before his son's eyes. The old man had known that destroying the animal would cause him more pain than a beating.

Brad couldn't even remember why his father had sought him out in anger that day. It had not mattered. That had been the end of it. From then on, he had lived only to escape the brutality of the man.

He looked up from the toy train. The carriage had traveled only a short distance, and yet the neighborhood had changed dramatically. He was more than familiar with the area around Atwater. He had not forgotten the beating he had taken that night in one of its taverns. The boardinghouses and saloons were full this time of year with those who plied the Great Lakes in milder weather.

While it was a disagreeable place even in the best of times, winter was particularly dangerous. Drink was the primary entertainment for the temporarily displaced seaman. Why, then, he asked himself, was he dragging Rebecca Cunningham down into this seamy and squalid environment?

He looked over to her. The darkness of the carriage was relieved occasionally by light from a gas street lamp. The light resonated in her hair, finding nuances in its golden tones. She seemed calm, or resigned, he did not know which. The ermine of her mantle lay softly against her cheek, and he longed to share in its gentle caress.

She turned to meet his gaze. Her eyes held a question, but she never spoke. Instead, she waited in silence for any explanation he might offer.

She was open, vulnerable. Such trust placed in him at this juncture unnerved him. His body longed for her warmth, her smooth soft skin. He did not deserve her trust. He would as soon ravish her as protect her. Did she not know that?

The carriage stopped at the corner.

"Stay. I'll be back shortly." With the train in hand, he descended from the carriage.

He stood for a moment, surveying his surroundings. The fact that it was Christmas Eve did not tame the wild revelry in the local drinking establishments. If anything, the occasion marked a more strident celebration among those without kith or kin.

Light glared from the windows of the Sailor's Ale, an interrogatory torch. Unrelenting in its harshness, it lit the faces of a passing couple. The woman was poorly dressed, and the neckline of her tattered costume had been adjusted to display more of her wares. Her face was years past her age, and her heavy makeup added a certain macabre quality to the vignette. She supported her partner, a seaman. His garbled words and groping hands left no doubt as to his expectations. Brad wondered if he would get his Christmas wish. More likely, he would awaken penniless in some back alley.

He walked past the saloon. In the bluish radiance of the new fallen snow he could see the skeletal outline of a shack. He would have thought it abandoned except for the dim light of a fire that shone through the window. Brad's hand tightened around the locomotive in his pocket. He had not known what to expect—certainly not the welcoming glow of candlelight and fir boughs—but the dwelling contrasted so sharply with the one he had just left that it unnerved him. It bore an uncanny resemblance to another house, in another time.

Fear touched him—fear of the powerful emotions he had carefully locked away. This had been a bad idea. He should never have come. He fought for control.

Then he felt Rebecca's warmth beside him. She had left the carriage to follow him quietly across the snow. She must have sensed his hesitancy, for she placed her slender gloved hand on his arm, and her touch gave him strength. He moved slowly forward.

At the door, he turned toward her. What he saw in her eyes shook him to his very soul. There was no question, no pity. She could not know what he was going through, and yet she did. What he saw in her eyes frightened him more than anything he had ever experienced. In her eyes he saw love—unqualified, unquestioning love. She raised her hand to his temple, drawing it in a tender caress down his cheek, and he turned and placed a passionate kiss in its palm. He clasped it to his lips in gratitude, unable or unwilling to release it for a long moment.

When he did, he still did not speak, nor did she. He knocked on the unsteady door. The sound of the knock reverberated in the cold night like a death rattle.

There was a shuffling movement and then a crack of dim light. A woman's fearful eyes peered through the slender opening. Her hair was dislodged from the bun in which it had been fastened, and a bluish bruise branded one side of her face.

"I'm looking for Joey Whiton. Is this his home?" Brad's voice sounded deeper than usual.

The woman nodded but did not open the door further. Panic registered on her face when she noticed his uniform.

He sought now to reassure her. "I am a friend. I

have come to drop something off for him."

She looked cautiously to the right. Joey's voice came from behind her. "It's all right, Ma. I'll take care of it."

The woman backed away, and Joey moved into the opening. Rebecca gasped, and her hand tightened on Brad's arm. Despite the fact that the light was behind him, there was no mistaking the brutal beating the child had taken. He kept his head down, but it was impossible to hide his condition. His face had caked and dried blood in various places, and his features were badly swollen.

"You shouldn't have come, Captain."

Brad's arm tensed under Rebecca's increasingly strong grasp. It was as if she was attempting to forestall the inevitable.

The sound of the door as it was forced open and banged against the wall echoed in the night. Brad was no longer in the present, but in the past. It was twenty long years ago, but it felt like yesterday. He knelt before the boy. "Who did this to you? Who?" His bellow caused a stirring in the corner of the room. A head, bent on the table in drunken stupor, slowly rose.

"You!"

"I'd move your blue ass out of my house if I was you, Capt'n. This ain't none of your damned business," Pock said with a sneer.

He stood up, taking an empty whiskey bottle with him, which he struck against the side of the table, sending shards flying across the room and leaving a jagged weapon in his hand.

"Like I said, Capt'n, you'd better leave now. Or else you might regret you ever came."

Rebecca froze in the doorway, unable to find a way to stop the impending violence. She shivered as Pock took note of her presence.

"I see you've taken to whorin' with the nigger's bitch."

He did not get a chance to say more. Brad was across the room in a single stride. His boot sent the small pine table flying, catching Pock with its force and driving him back into the wall. Pock somehow managed to keep hold of his homemade weapon. Quickly recovering his wits, and fully sober now, the wiry little man moved out on the attack. He slowly circled his prey, brandishing the crude weapon with a gleam in his eyes.

"I see you still want to be nosin' around in other people's business. You'll soon be regrettin' that urge. I been waitin' to take you down off your high and mighty . . ."

He lunged, making a broad sweep with the bottle toward Brad's side. Brad stepped aside but did not recover in time to prevent the attack that Pock waged from the rear. The bottle caught the back of his greatcoat, cutting through several layers until it found flesh. Brad brought his arm up under Pock's, sending the bottle flying. He completed his turn and brought his fist into the other man's face.

Pock flew across the room, hitting the wall so hard that several pans hanging on it hit the floor. He recovered far more quickly than seemed possible, this time finding the handle of an iron skillet. Once more he was circling the larger man.

Rebecca still stood in the doorway. Joey and the woman had moved to stand beside her. All eyes took in the scene unfolding before them.

Pock swung the heavy skillet at Brad, forcing him back toward the fireplace. Brad grabbed the poker, which was propped on the hearth. The small cabin rang with sound of metal on metal as the strange duel continued. Pock attacked again, and Brad managed to parry the blow with the metal poker. A second blow from the heavy skillet sent the poker flying. Pock was moving in, his heavy weapon sweeping menacingly closer to Brad's head each time. On one pass Brad attempted to catch the smaller man's arm. Instead, he felt the heavy iron pan catch his upper arm with frightening force. His arm was temporarily useless. Pock sneered.

"Never try to best me, Captain."

Brad studied the man, waiting for what might be his final chance to separate him from his weapon. Just then, an object came flying across the room, catching Pock in the back. It was all Brad needed. He flew at the distracted man, pinning him to the wall. His grasp tightened around Pock's wrist, forcing him to drop the pan.

He released the little man's left arm, freeing his own for the moment it took to deliver a powerful blow to the man's middle. He backed off as Pock doubled over in pain.

Pock was not finished, however. He rose from the crouch and came again at Brad. This time Brad caught him with a powerful fist to the jaw. The man collapsed. Brad stood above him, hatred visibly raging in him.

Rebecca saw the great struggle that was taking place. She moved over to Brad and placed a hand on his arm. It was only with her touch that he seemed to regain control.

She spoke quietly but firmly. "It's over. You'll kill him if you don't stop."

Slowly, he turned from Pock's prone figure. She led him to the door, never letting go of his arm. When they reached the door, he stopped her. He reached into his pocket and removed the intricately carved train. He offered it to the boy, who took it without a word.

"You should leave, you know." His voice was full of pain.

"I can't leave her. Don't you see?"

Yes, Brad did see. He knew the terrible trap of love.

19

Rebecca helped Brad to the carriage and ordered it to the Finney Hotel. He had refused to let her look at his back. Now he sat beside her in silence. As the minutes passed, she became increasingly concerned about him. With every jolt he grew more pale.

When they reached the hotel, she slid her arm behind him to offer some support and realized the reason for his pallor. The seat back was soaked in blood. He was still bleeding. She prayed the layers of clothing he wore had provided some protection, but she could not tell. She did not like the presence of so much blood. She struggled with him to the door of the hotel. Seymour Finney, sensing something amiss, approached.

"Seymour, please. I can't support him any longer."

The hotel owner rushed to her aid. "My God, Rebecca! What's happened?"

"The captain's been injured. He needs to be gotten to bed. I'll need bandaging and something to clean the wound."

Even with the two of them, it was difficult to get the semiconscious man up the stairs to his room. Rebecca ignored the unspoken question in Seymour Finney's eyes.

"There," she said, indicating the bed. "Hurry, Seymour. I don't know how badly he's been hurt."

Brad moaned as they settled him on the bed.

"Rebecca, surely this is not your concern. Let me send for your father and a doctor."

"Damn it, let me worry about what is my concern!" She stopped for a moment. She was close to hysteria, and she knew it. She turned away from her old friend and freed herself from the heavy mantle. Before she turned back, she took a deep breath. She fought to control her voice, her emotions. "There is no need for you to notify my father. It would only worry him. As for a doctor, let me check the wound first. If he needs the services of a doctor, I'll have you fetch Dr. Tanner."

After Seymour left, she turned to Brad. "We'll have to strip you of your overcoat and jacket." She remembered the other time, after the storm on Lake St. Clair, when she had undertaken this unfamiliar task on his unconscious form. Much had changed since then. Somehow, he had become an inextricable part of her life. She knew tonight that she never wanted him to leave it.

He winced as she began, too weak from loss of blood to be of much help. "I think being conscious will greatly add to my enjoyment of your task." So, he, too, was thinking of that other time.

He smiled briefly, before closing his eyes against the pain.

When he opened his eyes again, he studied her closely. "No need for such somberness. I assure you I am not going to die. It would deprive me of your company."

She looked down at him and smiled. "I feared we would not be so lucky, Captain." Suddenly her smile faded. She could feel the shaking start at her very core. She bit her lip, but it did not prevent the tears.

"Come here," he whispered.

She bent toward him and, with his thumb, he gently swept away the tears. This intimate task complete, he tenderly pulled her down so her head rested on his chest. She felt him wince with the weight.

"I'm sorry." His breath stirred the hairs on the back of her neck.

She sobbed now, her hands clutching the knit woolen undershirt that still covered his chest. She could not speak. She had no way of voicing the emotions his simple statement evoked in her.

She did not know how long they lay like this. She had stopped sobbing. They found some peaceful accord in the silence. She found herself listening to his heartbeat, strong and sure. It comforted her.

She heard Seymour's approach. He was carrying on an animated conversation with himself. She smiled at the irony. If her dear friend did not know what to make of this bizarre situation, he would be startled to learn that she was equally confused.

She rose, wiping her eyes on the back of her hand.

She caught a glimpse of herself in the bureau mirror. Her hair was in disarray, and her dress bore dark stains of a frightening redness, thankfully somewhat concealed by the ruby velvet. When Seymour burst through the door, he looked as concerned by her tears as by the captain's state.

"Are you all right?"

"Yes, Seymour, I'm fine. If you'll help the captain turn over and strip off his undershirt, we'll see what damage has been done."

The wound was not as bad as she had feared. It was long, an arc from his shoulder to below his shoulder blade. Although it was bleeding freely, it was not as deep as it might have been. Were it not for his topcoat, the glass would have cut heavily into muscle, causing permanent damage. It looked almost as if a surgeon's scalpel had made the incision. Only one piece of the jagged glass had met the flesh. He had been lucky.

"It appears to be clean and not too deep. I think I will be able to take care of it without a doctor. Thank you, Seymour."

She meant her statement to be a dismissal, and the older man did not mistake her tone. "Are you sure?"

She smiled at him reassuringly. "I'm sure, Seymour. You know I'm capable of handling it. Go spend the rest of this Christmas Eve with your family."

The man turned to go. Her voice stopped him at the door. "Tell Samuel to put the horses in your stable and find a warm place for himself downstairs. I may be a while. I'll notify him when I'm ready to leave."

Seymour Finney nodded and quietly closed the door behind him as he left.

"There was more to it than I saw, wasn't there?"

Rebecca worked on the wound, cleaning small pieces of fabric from it. She could feel him flinch as she worked. He had said nothing since Seymour had left. Now he lay face down, with his head in his folded arms. He seemed to have purposely turned his face away from her. She could only guess at his thoughts, guess at what explanation he might offer. She could not ask. What she wanted to hear had to come freely, for she was asking for far more than an explanation. She was asking him to reveal a painful part of his past and to strengthen the bond between them.

She continued to tend to him in silence. His breathing changed from a slow and even cadence to a ragged, strained movement. With her bandaging almost complete, she stopped and lay her hands on his back. She could feel the sudden upheavals in his chest. She dared not move. Then, as if he sensed her confusion, he spoke, his voice thick with emotion.

"You're right. There is much more to it. I would have killed him if you had not been there. I would have happily beaten him to death and then kept on long after." He paused, and she did not know if he would continue.

"One time, when I was a boy, I worked secretly through a long hot summer at a blacksmith's. The man was gruff and demanding. The work was difficult, but it had not mattered to me. I wanted to save enough to purchase a birthday gift for my mother. It was a hat, a frilly thing. She had seen it at the mercantile. She had nowhere to wear it, nothing to wear with it. But it became a symbol to her of a better life, an unattainable life. I was ten years old. I thought somehow that if I could buy it for her, it would change things.

"Her birthday was in September, the twentieth. The day was glorious. Warm but with a tinge of winter. I hurried down after school, singleminded. I knew the day was to be a memorable one. I had the clerk wrap the hat in blue paper, my mother's favorite color, and I headed home. I knew before I got to the door that he was there. I heard his drunken bellowing. I was undaunted. It was my mother's birthday. Surely he could not . . ."

His voice trailed off in hoarseness. Rebecca felt his chest heave. After a moment, he began again. "I stood in the doorway unnoticed for a long time, watching the familiar scene. My mother cowered in the corner while my father ranted. When they noticed me and the package, my father yelled at me to bring it to him. I ignored him, taking it instead to my mother. I set it in her hands and reached up to kiss her. 'Happy Birthday,' I said." Brad laughed painfully.

"My father bellowed again, this time at my mother. She brought it to him. He laughed when he saw what it was. He ridiculed her and then started to rip the hat apart. I flew at him, possessed. But it was no match. My mother tried to intervene. He struck her so hard her body flew like a rag doll into a table. I could hear the sound of bone breaking from where I lay bleeding. He refused to call a doctor. When her arm healed, it was useless. She was a cripple because of the hat. I had not been wrong. The day had been memorable. She lost what little hope she had that day." He choked on these last words.

Rebecca wanted to move from her chair beside the bed, wanted to take him in her arms and comfort him, but she was not sure that it was comfort that he wanted. She waited until his breathing returned to normal. He rolled onto his back. His face was wet, whether with sweat or tears she could not tell. It was suddenly too difficult to look at his drawn face.

She dropped her eyes and noticed that the upper part of his left arm was swollen where it had been hit. She went to the basin, wet a towel with cool water, and returned to sit beside him on the bed. She wrapped the towel around the arm.

"I wanted you to know." He smiled tenderly. "Despite what you think after this evening, I am not some ferocious animal."

"I never thought that."

"What did you think?"

She paused a long time before she spoke. "I thought you were lost."

"Lost?"

"I thought you were lost in pain, pain so severe it forced you to block out everything and everyone, just to cope with it."

His face clouded over.

She waited a moment before she spoke again. "Is there nothing we can do for Joey?"

"No doubt I've made matters worse." He moved his good arm up across his forehead.

"No, you've given him hope. You've shown him someone cares."

He removed his arm from his forehead and brought up his hand to caress her cheek. "Does the fact that someone cares change things, or does it only increase the agony of the inevitable?"

She shivered. Was that the truth? Was it impossible to change fate? Was it useless to try to avoid the inevitable? She was afraid of the answer, afraid of the fact that eventually she and Brad would reach the inevitable.

She was the Angel of Passage, and he was to be her captor. She knew now, in the deepest recesses of her being, that it would come to this final confrontation. Could what was between them withstand such an encounter? She turned her head to press a kiss into his palm and prayed fervently for them both.

"Merry Christmas, Rebecca Cunningham."

She smiled. "Merry Christmas, Bradford Taylor."

"Your father will be worried. You should go."

"Yes." She was reluctant to move.

"Is the carriage still below?"

She nodded. "Will you be all right?"

"It is nothing a little rest will not cure."

"If the wound starts to fester, have Seymour call Dr. Tanner."

He smiled at her. "Go, now."

Slowly, she rose and collected her mantle. When she reached the door, she paused.

"Good night," she said, and then was gone.

Seymour Finney had not abandoned his post at the front desk. Rebecca suspected it had much to do with her presence upstairs. After Samuel left to fetch the carriage, he spoke.

"Is he all right, Rebecca?"

"Yes, the wound wasn't as deep as I first thought. I was able to stop the bleeding. Will you call Dr. Tanner in the morning, Seymour? I'm afraid it may have to be stitched up."

"What happened, Rebecca?"

"It was an altercation of sorts down on Atwater."

"What in God's name was the man doing down there, and on Christmas Eve? I warned him."

The look on her face must have given him pause. "My God, Rebecca, you weren't with him?"

"Does it really matter?"

"I don't know. You would be the only one to answer that."

Seymour's probing was too much for her. She felt herself color.

"I know what I am about, Seymour. There is no need for concern."

"Do you truly know what you risk, Rebecca? You can't be so selfish as to risk others for some personal whim." His voice was a tense whisper.

"I don't know what you are talking about."

"I am not blind. I saw how you were with him. He has sworn to find you, to find all of us. Does that not concern you? That you are involved with a man who would as soon jail you as make love to you?"

"You have no right to say that!"

"I have every right. It is my life you risk as well. Mine and countless others. Think of it, Rebecca. Don't be selfish in this. The price you may have to pay will be a grave one."

"You do not understand. In this I risk no one but myself."

"Do not be so sure, Rebecca. Do not be so sure."

She turned and headed for the door. Seymour could not be right.

20

The last of the guests had left long ago. The house was dark except for the kitchen and the single lamp that shone in her father's bedroom. Rebecca instructed Samuel to take the carriage straight to the stables. She needed to walk the distance to the house to clear her thoughts.

Before her, the snow was unbroken. Her red velvet dress moved through it like a single drop of blood across a frosted pane. The air was clear and cold. Halfway to the house, she stopped to draw in a breath of its crispness. It seared her lungs, yet it failed to have the cleansing effect she had hoped for. She still felt buried in the avalanche of the evening's emotions, suffocating in its pleasures and passions.

She was gripped by a great fear. Perhaps Seymour was right. She, who always prided herself on being in control, was becoming a threat to them all, as great a threat as the man she loved.

The lamps in the kitchen had been left low. She

did not see the figure who sat in the corner of the darkened room. She was almost out of the room when a male voice stopped her.

"Rebecca." For the first time in her life, Jacob addressed her without his own chosen salutation, "Miss." When she finally made out his weathered black face in the dimness, she saw that it was filled with reproach.

"Were you with him?"

She nodded, unwilling to defend herself from his presumption that their time together had been spent on amorous pursuits.

"He will betray you in the end."

"No, Jacob, I don't believe that."

"Then you are a fool."

Jacob's bulky form moved to the window that looked out on the river. "We have a shipment to make."

"When?"

"There is to be a meeting, Monday next. It will be decided then, when and by whom."

"Where are they?"

"Rachel has care of them. There is a child, a babe. It is ill from the cold. They cannot be moved until the child is recovered, or . . . gone." He turned accusingly on her. "They had waited out in the cold for hours. Frightened to approach because *he* was there."

Rebecca blanched at the accusation. "Surely you're not saying that because of me the child is dying. You cannot be so unfair. I had no way of knowing they would be there, and no way of knowing the captain would be with me."

"We will never know, will we."

Rebecca dropped her head in exhaustion and turned to go.

"You will be at Webb's on Monday?" he asked her, a challenge in the question.

"Yes, I will be there."

She left him at the back door and climbed the stairs.

Her skirt was sodden now with melted snow, and its weight dragged her spirits down as well.

"Rebecca." Her father's voice startled her. He was standing in the open doorway to his room. He saw her disarray. "What's happened?"

"I'm unhurt, Father. Captain Taylor was injured in a fight, and I was delayed, helping him back to the hotel." Her hands had been pressed against the skirt of her dress. Now, as she lifted them, she saw they were imprinted with blood. She stood there, staring at them.

"Rebecca!" Getting no response, George Cunningham repeated her name. His voice was keen, a sharp reflection of the agony she felt.

"Oh, Father!" She did not have to say more. Her father rushed to her. Wrapping an arm around her, he led her into his room and lowered her into one of the large leather chairs beside the fireplace. A fire still burned in the grate, its eerie reflection all around her in the room. Its scarlet tongues seemed to lick the dark walls. Rebecca closed her eyes.

She felt the glass of brandy her father pushed into her hands. She drank most of it in a single swallow. When she opened her eyes, the flames were lower, restored to their place in the grate.

The silence between father and daughter moved

slowly from fear to comfort, and then to the awkwardness brought on by unspoken and unanswered questions. She couldn't bear to look at him. She was afraid she would see disappointment and disapproval.

Finally, it was her father who broke the uneasy silence. "Do you want to talk?"

"I don't even know where to begin."

"Why don't you just begin. Everything has a way of working itself out."

Why had she been afraid? Her father had never been judgmental. "I love him, Father, God help me, I love him. I didn't mean for it to happen. But it has. And there is no going back. I'm afraid, I'm afraid for everyone. For those I jeopardize. But most of all, very selfishly, I'm afraid for myself. There is no happy ending to this, Father. There cannot be."

For the first time in many years, George Cunningham felt the loss of his wife acutely. He was helpless to comfort his daughter. He could not be falsely reassuring. He knew that the events that would shape this passionate relationship between his daughter and the captain would pay little heed to his entreaties.

He moved to comfort his daughter in the only way he knew he could, by drawing her into a tender embrace. Then he guided her toward her bedroom and the rest she so desperately needed.

Brad opened his eyes slowly. He lay on his stomach. When he tried to move his arm, the pain in his back sent a sharp reminder of the previous night coursing from shoulder to ribs. The pain was real, familiar. He recalled the unfamiliar emotions of the night before. He moved the arm again, this time more slowly, testing it as he went. The swelling on his left forearm had diminished somewhat. He flexed his hand. It would be a while before he could use the arm without pain. He rolled carefully over to his back, wincing with pain.

When had his physical passion for this woman, who defied him at every opportunity, turned into something else? It was the very thing he had fought against his entire life, the one thing that would leave him vulnerable and hurt. He had loved her last night, love with all that it entailed—the care and the concern, the desire to protect and nurture. God help him! He even wanted to protect her from himself.

He turned his head to look out the small window. It was Christmas Day. He had never had happy thoughts of Christmas—until now.

George Cunningham responded reluctantly to the persistent knocking at the front door. His thoughts were elsewhere this morning. His daughter had yet to appear downstairs, and his concern for her had caused him to leave instructions with the servants that she was not to be disturbed.

In fact, most of the servants were preparing for family visits of their own. Bertie was bustling around the kitchen with the last of the cleanup from last night, showing him where he could find the cold supper she had prepared for him and Rebecca.

They always spent Christmas quietly, and he was puzzled as to who might be disturbing them.

"Good morning, sir."

George Cunningham couldn't have been more dumbfounded if the devil himself had appeared on his doorstep.

"Captain Taylor, what an unexpected surprise."

"May I come in?"

The older man stood back, torn between a lifetime of good manners and the sudden urge to throttle the man before him. He did notice the officer moved with some difficulty. Surely he must be in a great deal of pain. What had possessed the man to come out in the cold on Christmas Day? He did not wait long for an answer.

"Is your daughter available to speak with, sir?"

There was no need to prevaricate. "She is ill disposed this morning, Captain, and has not as yet risen."

The captain looked ill at ease. Perhaps it was the effect of the pain he was in, but the discomfort was most peculiar, George Cunningham decided.

The captain removed a small box from his pocket. "Would you see that she gets this when she awakes? Tell her it's a good memory."

"Yes, Captain. I'll see that she gets it."

When Brad turned to go, the older man found himself compelled to speak again. "I love my daughter more than life itself, Captain. I would not want to see her hurt."

"Neither would I."

There was some understanding in the captain's terse reply, some realization that, as Rebecca had said, it would not end happily. Cunningham found he could not hate this man. He knew through years of experience that circumstances often put one's actions at odds with one's feelings. It looked as if the captain had just discovered this little irony of life.

He stood in the doorway for a long time, watching Brad's slow progress back to his horse. He had seen enough men mount horses to know that the captain did so with a great deal of pain. He waited, deep in thought, until the captain was out of sight, and then he turned and walked wearily up the stairs toward his daughter's bedroom.

He knocked. Hearing no reply, he opened the door a crack to check on her. She was not in her bed. He walked into the room. It took him a moment to locate her. She sat in the alcove of a window, still in her nightgown. She had pulled her legs up toward her; her head rested on her knees. She was gazing out the window. Evidently, she had not heard him come in, for she had not stirred. He was hesitant to disturb her and was about to withdraw when she lifted her head and spoke.

"It was him."

It was not a question but a statement.

Her father nodded.

"Has he left?"

"Yes."

She slowly lowered her head again, as if the answers to her questions were of little significance.

"He left something for you. He said to tell you, 'It's a good memory.'" He held out the small parcel. When she made no move to take it, he set it on a small table by the door.

"Rebecca," he began, and then stopped. He did not know what to say.

"Thank you, Father."

"Bertie has left us a wonderful supper for later. Will you be down?"

Once again she lifted her head, this time with a little more life. She smiled at him. "Would I abandon my favorite fellow on Christmas?" She rose from the window seat and moved to embrace him. "Merry Christmas, Father." She pulled away then. "Give me but a few minutes, and I promise I will be down."

George Cunningham returned his daughter's smile. "Merry Christmas, Rebecca." For the first time in his life, he doubted he was her favorite fellow.

Rebecca refused to think of the small gift that lay on the table by the door. She chose instead to busy herself with her toilette.

She washed her face carefully to remove the paths the tears had made. Her hands still showed signs of the blood. With a washcloth, she scrubbed them. She glanced in the mirror. Her hair was in disarray. She methodically removed the hairpins that held the remnants of last night's elaborate coiffure. Taking her mother's silver hairbrush, she began to brush it. She did so indelicately, attacking the long golden tresses and their snarls with much vigor. She continued to stroke it long after the last tangles were gone.

When she was done she pulled it back more severely than usual. She felt the pull of each hair against her scalp and found satisfaction in the tightness of the bun into which she fastened it. She chose to wear a corset today, something she often overlooked. The bone stays cut into her flesh as she tightened the lacings beyond comfort. Then she chose a simple dress, a navy serge with a small black collar and turned back cuffs.

When she had completed her task, she surveyed the results in the mirror. She looked pale, with dark circles under her eyes. She saw herself, and yet the reflection in the mirror seemed no part of her. It was as if it had some life of its own, beyond the dull pain that was the only thing left of the tumultuous feelings of yesterday.

She smoothed the folds of the dress with long white fingers before she turned to leave the room. At the door, she saw the small box that lay innocently on the delicately crocheted doily. She stood for long moments, unable to leave but unable to touch the package.

Suddenly, with a wave of resolve, she picked up the small gift. She removed the twine and the plain brown paper and held her breath as she removed the top. She remembered her father's words, *He said to tell you it was a good memory.*

It was a child's toy, a soldier, no more than three inches high and carved out of hardwood. It had been painted once, and small chips of color attested to its age and wear. She turned it over in her hand. Down its smooth blue back had been carved the name of the young artisan who had brought a dream to life.

She didn't know how long she stood there. Finally, a tear fell onto the wooden toy, nestling itself in the crevices of the child's name. The simple scratchings soon became a living, moving thing, as the tears obscured her vision.

B. Taylor. A child's dream had become a man's reality. She let out a long ragged breath and tenderly lay the wooden soldier back in his box. Replacing the lid, she moved to the wardrobe. She sought out the least-used drawer and, moving the contents slightly, she placed the box as far back as she could, covering it with things she no longer had use for. She reclosed the wardrobe, and then turned and left the room.

21

Brad walked through the dirty, ankle-deep slush. January had been a peculiar month. It had started out frigid and then warmed up to almost fifty degrees in the past week. While it was warm, it was anything but cheerful. The sun had not been seen for over a week. The air was dense with moisture, and the snow seemed to be dissipating directly into the air. It took great effort to walk through its heaviness. By the time he reached his office, he was soaking wet.

"Ah, there y'are, Capt'n!"

Pock sat behind his desk, his mud-covered boots propped up on its previously spotless top.

"Get your feet off my desk and your ass out of my chair."

"Sure thing, Capt'n. Hope you're not holdin' any grudges on account of the other night, now." Pock moved cautiously, despite his conciliatory words. "Wouldn't want a little thing like the boy to come between a good workin' team, now, would we?" He ran the filthy forearm of his coat across the desk top, depositing as much dirt as it removed.

Brad was silent.

"Just to show there's no hard feelin's, I brung you a little tidbit. Seems there's to be a move some time soon. There may be children in the shipment. That'll slow 'em down real good. If this thaw continues, they're gonna have one heck of a time makin' it across, 'specially with you and me on their tails."

"Neither you nor I will be on their tails. I've suspended all operations until I receive further orders from Washington."

"You're not goin' soft on me now, Capt'n? That little nigger-lovin' bitch ain't got to you, has she? A man that lets a woman run his life is a fool, or maybe he's just a coward."

"Get out of my office, now. And listen well. If I hear that you or any of your little vigilante group has taken action against my direct orders, you'll live to regret it."

"Last I checked, Capt'n, I didn't sign my name to no army sign-up papers. I'm a free, law-abidin' citizen of this here United States. And as such, I mean to do my duty as an upstandin' citizen when I see the laws of this great land bein' broken."

Pock slowly moved around the desk and stopped when he reached the door. "There's not a thing you can do to stop me, Capt'n. You'd do best to remind yourself of that little fact. 'Cause maybe some day I'll catch your pretty little nigger-lover out there, and it sure would be nice to get a taste of what's made you go baby-ass soft."

"You touch her and you're a dead man!"

"We'll see, Capt'n, we'll see." Pock gave a sardonic little smile, and then he was gone.

Brad turned away from the door. The man was not stupid, but how far would he go for revenge? The thought of Rebecca in this man's hands, either figuratively or literally . . .

He clenched his fists. The knuckles turned white, every bone clearly delineated, before he relaxed them. He sat down to his desk and took out a sheet of paper.

"Corporal!"

"Yessir." The aide came in from an adjacent office.

"I want you to deliver this to Miss Rebecca Cunningham."

"Yessir."

He wrote a brief note and sealed it. "And on your way, I want you to send off a telegram. Take it down."

The aide produced a writing tablet.

"Colonel Samuel Cooper, War Department, Washington, D.C. Dear Sir. Stop. Request immediate reassignment. Stop. Effectiveness has been compromised. Stop. Captain Bradford Taylor. Detroit, Michigan. January 27, 1861."

"Send it off immediately, Corporal."

"Yessir."

"No, I can't do it!" Rebecca cried.

"Can't or won't do it? Rebecca?"

"Does it matter which?"

"Yes, it matters. It matters for the future and your usefulness to the movement. You have to decide, Rebecca. We will respect your decision. But you must choose."

"Why must I choose?"

"Captain Taylor is a threat to us all. We need to know where your feelings lie. You could jeopardize us all if your loyalties are mixed. We need to know. You may some day have to choose, Rebecca, and we need to know what your choice will be. Will it be this man or the movement?"

"How can you ask such a thing, William? Haven't I displayed my devotion, my commitment all these years? Why must I suddenly prove myself to you?"

William Lambert continued to speak in his soft, well-modulated voice. "Because you are only human like the rest of us, Rebecca. Sometimes the sacrifices we are asked to make are more than we can withstand. I need to know when we are asking too much. It is better then, safer then, to move on. To let you live your life and to go on with ours."

"I would never abandon you, never!" There were tears in her eyes. "How can you suggest such a thing? What we are doing is more important than a single life, than one person's wishes. I know that. I accept that." She paused and inhaled deeply. "I'll do what you ask. I'm sorry if I gave you cause for concern."

"Good. Let us know if you have any trouble setting it up. Jacob will be ready to move at nine. They cannot be delayed for long. The babe is still not completely well, and they must cross as quickly as possible. We will need two hours at the minimum, and as much more as you can gain for us."

"I understand. You will have more than enough time."

Rebecca sat in the carriage, chilled to the bone. The short ride from the meeting at William Webb's to Rachel's home had been a desolate one. For all her words of loyalty, she felt the fear of betrayal in her heart. It hid in the deepest recesses and whispered the unthinkable. What if she could not abandon him? What if her feelings betrayed her thoughts, her heart betrayed her will?

It would not happen, she resolved. It could not happen. She could not live with the consequences. She could live without him, but she could not live with herself if innocent people died because of her.

She could live without him, she could. Life had been full before he came. Why did she fear it would be empty after he left?

"Is Jacob here, Rachel?"

"He's out back. Come in and I'll fetch him."

"Here, let me take Charity." Rebecca took the baby from her mother. She looked down into the trusting face of the black child and knew what she must do. How could she ever have questioned it?

"Rebecca." Jacob's voice was guarded.

Rebecca felt pain again at the loss of Jacob's trust. "It's been decided as you wished, Jacob. I will distract the captain. You will move the family."

He nodded.

"How is the baby?" she asked.

"Come with me," Rachel said.

Rebecca handed Charity to Jacob and followed Rachel out the back door and around to the wash-room, a lean-to attached to the back of the house. Inside, Rachel dexterously removed several of the boards that it seemed to share with the back wall of the house. Moving through the narrow opening, she signaled Rebecca to follow.

The small space, about six feet by ten feet, had

been expertly designed to be undetectable from the outside. It was nestled behind the fireplace, gaining warmth from it. Here, five souls huddled for warmth. Their eyes were wide with fright at Rebecca's unexpected appearance, but Rachel mutely signaled reassurance. Rebecca knelt beside the young woman who cradled a child. She moved away the blankets to reveal a small face, no longer polished ebony or burnished walnut but gray, the color of a burned wood turned to ash. It slept fitfully, too weak to cry. Its breathing was labored, the raspy sound of its phlegm-filled lungs echoing in the tiny room. Rebecca turned to question Rachel, but Rachel's expression silenced her.

The two women found their way out and returned to the house.

"Should they be moved now? The baby still seems so ill."

"Jacob is afraid they will be discovered. They've been here over a month. The baby is as well as he's been, and the conditions here are not good. They need medical help and need to be able to move about. The baby may die yet if we cannot get them to Canada." She turned away from Rebecca to put a kettle on for tea. "Jacob says there may be an informer. That someone may be betraying our movements. Is it true?"

"There is some reason to think it might be so."

"Who could do such a thing!" Rachel's voice was impassioned. "Who could see these poor souls and then wish them imprisoned and returned to the life they left at such risk? What kind of human being could do that?"

Rebecca had no easy answer. She had not thought

of the traitor in a while. Her thoughts were in a jumble—of Christmas Eve and Joey Whiton, of the man who was his father, the man who had elicited such hatred from Brad Taylor, of Brad himself. Was there a connection among them? She paled at the possibilities.

"Are you all right, Rebecca?"

"Yes, yes, I'm fine." She turned now to Jacob, who sat quietly by the hearth with Charity on his knee. "Have you checked the river?"

Jacob nodded.

"You must be very careful on the far side. You know this thaw will have made it treacherous."

Again, Jacob nodded without a word.

"Make sure the family has a warm meal before you go. Will you take them first to Seymour's?" Why was she babbling on? Jacob knew these things better than she.

He waited for her to finish and then said, "We will wait at the barn until Seymour sends word that the captain is otherwise involved."

Finally, she touched upon the point that gnawed at her. "I wish I were the one going, not you. If anything were to go wrong, what would Rachel and the children do? I have no family dependent on me, no one but Father to mourn my loss."

"Don't talk so." He spoke deliberately, as if he had been giving the matter a lot of thought. "If anything were to happen to me, I entrust Rachel and the children to your care, Rebecca. Will you do that for me?"

"Of course." Her voice choked at the possibility that something might go wrong—that this man, who was both friend and husband of her best friend, might not return.

Rebecca saw some softening on his stern face

before he spoke again. "You, Rebecca, are of more use as a distraction for the captain." He smiled at her for the first time in many weeks. "It is something I'm afraid I would do poorly."

She smiled back, but her vision was blurred with tears. "No, I don't think you are quite the captain's type."

She heard his deep laugh, and for the first time in a long time she experienced a deep sense of peace and belonging. This was what she was about. This was what mattered more than anything else in the end—her friends, the movement, the freedom of so many innocent people. Until there was another solution, all they had was themselves, their strength, their loyalty. It would have to be enough.

Her father greeted her as she entered the house. "Is all well?"

"Yes, Father. You have gotten your wish. Jacob is to move the shipment tomorrow night, and I am to provide a distraction only."

"I can't say I am not relieved. You know how I worry."

She smiled. "Yes, I know how you worry." She kissed him on the cheek. "I will not be home tomorrow evening for dinner."

She felt her father sharpen his perusal. "What is the nature of the distraction you are to provide?"

"It seems I am to entertain Captain Taylor tomorrow night."

She felt him studying her every move.

"I know what I'm about, Father. I was just with Rachel and Jacob, and I saw the family that is to be moved. I will not put them in danger." She purposely held his eyes, communicating her determination. "If I have to make a choice, I know the right one."

His hand came up to caress her cheek, as he had done so often since her mother's death. "I've no doubt it will be the right choice for the movement, Rebecca, but I worry that it will not be an easy choice for you. I worry that you will bear the scars of the decision for many years to come."

"Is it so different from the scars so many of the escaped slaves bear on their backs?"

"No, perhaps not."

"I love you, Father."

"And I, you."

"I'll go change for supper."

"A letter was delivered earlier for you." He picked up the envelope from a table beside the door.

"Thank you."

Although the outside of the letter bore no clue as to its sender, there was something familiar about the strong script. She opened the envelope slowly as she walked up the stairs and unfolded its contents as she entered the room.

Dear Rebecca,

I feel things have been left awkwardly. I don't quite know yet what needs to be said, and yet it cannot be left unsaid. Will you have dinner with me? Tomorrow, eight o'clock, the Finney Hotel. If I do not hear from you I will assume you will be coming.

Until then I am yours faithfully,

Bradford Taylor

She tried to stop the pain that seared through her. It was fresh once again with simply the touch of the letter in her hand. She smiled ironically. It seemed that fate had made things easy for her—or had it?

22

She saw him before he saw her. He sat in a corner with a drink in his hand. It was the first time she had seen him since Christmas Eve. She studied his back for a moment and wondered how well his injuries had healed. She shouldn't have done this; it evoked too many memories. There was no place for memories tonight.

"Rebecca." He rose from his chair. She could never quell the feeling his size elicited. Each time she saw him she felt protected by his strength. She had never been one to need protection, and she wondered why it had such a tantalizing appeal now.

"Brad." She felt the softness of his lips against the back of her hand and tried to rid herself of the memory of those lips elsewhere on her body. She was resolved to accomplish her mission with little emotional involvement. It would not end well. She would be stupid to do otherwise.

"I was afraid you would not come."

"I don't generally turn down invitations. You need not have worried."

"Please, sit down. Would you like a sherry?" He summoned the waiter.

"No, thank you." She was afraid the liquor might lead her astray.

She felt him studying her. His manner seemed less aggressive than usual, almost tender. She had seen him this way with Joey Whiton.

He did not know where to begin. How did one go about ending something that had never really begun? How could he explain that for the first time in his life he had seen the possibility for warmth and tenderness? He had seen the strength that love can bring with it, and he knew as surely as anything he had ever known that it was not his to have. She was the one person he could not have.

God, he wanted her, and not just her body. He wanted her laughter, her wit, her devotion, her love. What insanity! Their lives were so divergent in ideology and wealth. It was a chasm not easily crossed in the best of times. With war imminent, the reality of their differences was even more apparent. Better to never begin than to risk being hurt. He had sworn he would never be hurt again.

Yet, already he was hurt, and he ached just looking at her. She was dressed conservatively, almost severely. Her dress of gray wool was buttoned high at the neck, where it was clasped by a brooch. He could not see the small indentation at the base of her throat where his lips had found shelter. But he remembered how he could feel the beat of her heart, how rapid it had been.

Tonight, her hair was pulled back tightly into a

snood. He remembered it free and loose in the wind aboard the sailboat. He had memorized its texture—smooth, dense, vibrant, as if it had a life of its own. He remembered the luxurious feel of it wrapped around his fingers.

He questioned the madness of simply walking away.

"I wanted to thank you for your nursing skills, Christmas Eve. Thanks to your efforts, Dr. Tanner says I will have little scarring. I think he was grateful that your ministrations saved him from being called out in the middle of the night."

"There is no need to thank me."

They were being so civil. What was she thinking? Why was she so reserved?

"Are you ready to order?"

She nodded.

He signaled the waiter. After the waiter had gone, she spoke.

"Is that what you implied had been left unsaid? I assure you, you need not have gone to such lengths to thank me. I'm sure anyone would have done the same under the circumstances."

"No, there's more than that. I wanted to apologize for putting you in such danger."

She studied her hands. He wanted her to look at him, but when she did there was accusation in her eyes.

"You knew that man? Joey's father?"

"I've had some dealings with him."

She studied him so closely he was forced to look down at the glass he once more cradled in his hands.

"You once said my choice of associates was poor. If that man is an indication of your acquaintances, I would hesitate to throw barbs if I were you."

He tightened the hold on his drink. She was right, of course. It stung, nonetheless, to be reminded.

"Perhaps you are right."

"Perhaps?"

"It's none of your concern."

"It's none of my concern? You force me to accompany you and watch you be beaten and stabbed within an inch of your life. I spend hours cleaning up the mess, and it is none of my concern? Everything you do is my concern!"

"Is that professionally or personally, Rebecca?" His voice was laced with irony.

She colored, and he found the blush exquisitely appealing.

"I don't know what you are talking about."

"I think you do."

"Why are we talking about this?"

"About what?"

She held him captive now with her intense gaze. Suddenly, it was she who took control of the conversation. "About what never will be, about what cannot be."

He saw her tears, and it was his undoing.

"Don't, Rebecca."

"Don't what?"

"It will do no good to speak of it."

"Why?" Her voice was strained. "Because if we do not speak of it you can be comfortable in denying it?"

"No."

"Yes. You are afraid. You have spent so long wallowing in self-pity and protecting yourself from being hurt that you forgot what it is to take risks. Risk is what makes us alive. Risk is what opens our lives to joy as well as pain. I pity you. Your safe and sheltered existence leaves you no room for passion, no room for anyone but yourself!"

She looked as if she would bolt. Panic struck him. He didn't want her to go. Not in her current state—not in any state.

He rose and stood before her, protecting her from the prying stares of others in the room. "I think we should find a more private place to finish this discussion."

"But dinner . . ."

"I'll take care of it."

He took her arm and guided her through the tables to the door. He spoke briefly to the waiter before wrapping her cloak around her and leading her out the front door.

She did not resist him as he moved her around the side of the building and into the alleyway to the familiar back door of the building. He did not trust himself to speak, to ask her acquiescence or even question the risk of once more taking her to his room so early in the evening, with so many people around. The danger of gossip seemed to pale in comparison to his need to have her alone.

She did not quite know what was happening, or perhaps she did and was justifying it in terms of keeping him occupied. No, that was not it at all. Their conversation had grown so intimate that it could not be finished in public, but how it would be finished remained to be seen.

She did not know if there was reason to resist, or, even if there was reason, if she chose to. In her anger, she had touched upon the passion she felt for this man, and it had overwhelmed her. How had he done this to her, caught her up into his very being so that anything that happened to him affected her so deeply.

It could not go on this way. The results would be cataclysmic, a passionate collision that would destroy them both. She had to think. She had to stop the path they were following.

He opened the door and led her into the semidarkened room. She stepped across the threshold into his arms.

He pushed the door closed and pressed her against it. She could feel him against her whole length. His head was haloed by the light of the single lamp, leaving his face in shadow. There was only his voice, deep with emotion and passion.

"You were right. I never intended to care about anyone other than myself. Then I met you. You have bewitched me, Rebecca Cunningham." She felt his lips touch hers softly and then pull back. "I don't know when I began to care for you instead of just wanting you. It was long before I loved you on the boat. I had denied it up until then. In having you, I only wanted more. Now I am insatiable."

Once more she felt his lips, this time trailing along her throat to the small hollow at its base. "I am lost, Rebecca, lost in you and with you. Lost in a time and place that has doomed us before we ever had a chance to begin." His hands gently cradled her face. He moved slightly, and the single lamp cast a soft shadow across his face.

She could see his eyes now as they glowed in the dim light. "I love you. Nothing that will come will ever change that. When you are old and gray and still beautiful, with your children and grandchildren gathered around you, you can tell them you were loved once passionately, deeply, totally. You can know that wherever I am, that is still the truth. For I do not think I could stop loving you if I tried."

It sounded like a good-bye. No, her soul screamed, not now. She was not ready. She had thought she would choose the time and place, and she could not do it here, not tonight. Oh Lord, not tonight. It was too soon. There had been only anger in her words tonight. She had spoken no words of love.

She took his hands and gently removed them from her. Then she drew his head toward her until she could feel his ragged breathing, and she kissed him.

Her kiss was deep, open-mouthed, passionate. It was not a good-bye kiss. It was a kiss that promised him everything he asked for, and more.

When she withdrew, she felt his fingers slowly working the buttons on the bodice of her dress, and she returned the favor, unfastening the buttons on his jacket with care, savoring each movement, burning each sensation into her memory for the eternity they would be apart.

She pushed open his jacket and lay her palms on his chest, feeling the accelerated beating of his heart. She moved her hands up to his neck and felt his pulse, his life, now inextricably intertwined with hers. No matter how far apart, no matter how long.

He was right. There would be no way to ever forget. She ran her fingertips over his lips, exploring them as if for the first time. He drew one into his mouth and suckled. She felt the pull down to the core of her being.

The moistness grew between her legs, but still she did not rush. The agonizing slowness would leave that much more of a memory. If he would haunt her the rest of her days, she wanted not a pale ghost but a vivid spirit. She wanted the memory to have a life of its own.

She felt his hands free her breasts. He bent low to caress them with his tongue, and she ran her lips across his hair, feeling it, smelling it. His efforts became too much of a distraction, and she began to lose all sensation but the most immediate one of him at her breast.

She raised her head, pressing it back against the door. When she could stand it no more, she guided his lips up once more to meet hers. He loosened the tapes of her skirt and crinoline and lifted her out of them. Then he lay her on the bed and stood beside her to remove his jacket and shirt. She saw the scar then, the unnaturally white crescent, carved into his flesh by hatred.

He sat on the edge of the bed, and she moved to kneel behind him. She followed the course of the wound with her tongue, tracing the path to below his shoulder blade. She felt him stiffen at first and then softly groan with pleasure at her exploration. She placed her hands over his, feeling their strength. She moved her hands up, over the finely muscled forearms and heavy biceps, across his shoulders.

He turned suddenly then. He was taut with desire, hard with the passion she had aroused in him. It was almost frightening in its intensity, and his excitement fired her own. She needed to touch and explore every part of him.

As he released her from the rest of her corset, she struggled with the buttons of his trousers, clumsy in her hurry and unfamiliar with the task. When he was done, he moved to finish what she had begun, finally releasing himself.

With his hands on her shoulders, he gently leaned her back onto the bed and covered her with his body. Then he began his urgent exploration down her neck, across her breasts, down to her navel, and beyond. To kiss and lick, to explore and give pleasure.

When she thought she could stand it no more, there was the soft, teasing intrusion of his tongue, and she cried out in pleasure and need.

"Brad! Please!"

He rose then and covered her once more with his body, supporting his weight with his forearms, cradling her head in his hands.

"I need you!" she pleaded.

Still he did not move. He watched her, waiting.

She sobbed then in frustration, in the agony of what should not be. And through the sound of her own sobs, she heard her words. "God help me, I love you!"

He entered her then, opening her to his need, losing himself in her. They moved as one, both anxious to satisfy their incompleteness, to make themselves whole in each other. When they were spent, she could not stop sobbing and he held her tightly against him, knowing full well he had no words to console her, no words to make the ending happy.

23

"Damned if I'm gonna let them niggers do as they like, rubbin' our faces in it. The capt'n may have gone soft on 'em, but the money on their head's the same. Those Southern boys will pay a pretty penny to get their niggers back."

Pock swaggered. The liquor he had been consuming fueled his bravado. Easy money, that's what it was. No pantywaist officer was gonna tell him he couldn't uphold the law. He was a law-abiding citizen. There was nothing to stop him from arresting them himself if he caught them in the act.

The boy had been harder to handle tonight, but he had finally beaten it out of him. There was gonna be a move, most likely tonight. Just the old black they called Jacob and a family. Kids would slow 'em down real good. It would be easy pickin'.

Pock guessed he'd just have to enter into a little private business.

"There's some good money to be made here, fellas. For them that don't mind freezin' their ass a bit. Hear there's some real valuable merchandise bein' moved 'cross the river tonight. Black merchandise, if you catch my meanin'. Might be worth a pretty penny to certain folk in the market for contraband goods. Anybody here ready for a little cold work and easy money?"

"You wouldn't be chasin' some livin', breathin' merchandise now, would you, Pock?" someone said above the murmurs in the bar. There was laughter.

"What's it to you? There's a law, you know, and it says they go back. Plain and simple. If a fella can make a little profit in the process of upholdin' the law, what's the harm, I say?"

There was sporadic agreement in the smoky room, but one dissident challenged him:

"You're a fool if you're goin' out on that ice tonight! The thaw will make it near impossible to tell the thin ice from the thick. You'll end up bein' pulled up downriver like a frozen carp. If I fancy to take a trip down the river, it sure ain't gonna be under the ice." There was some laughter at this remark.

"I ain't afraid of a little risk. Money makin' ain't supposed to be easy. And this here's a hell of a lot easier than most. Anybody who chooses to join me, meet me down by old Ander's warehouse. Guarantee it'll be one hell of a chase." With that, he downed the last of his drink and headed out into the darkness.

* * *

The night was cold. The ice had refrozen in patches. Jacob knew it instinctively. He had crossed its icy barrier too many times not to acknowledge the risk. It would be next to impossible to tell the depth of the ice over the areas of recently open water. The fact that there was no moon was a blessing and a curse.

He led the small group onto the ice, testing each foothold before placing his weight on it. The crossing would be dangerously slow. He carried the baby, heavily wrapped against the cold. Behind him came the couple, a frightened child with each.

For the first time in a long time, Jacob feared for his own family. He was not a believer in second sight, and yet, tonight it haunted him. Would he be like Moses in the desert? Doomed never to see the promised land, never to see the ultimate freedom for his people? The feeling was so strong that he found himself praying, not just for himself and those with him, but for the wife and children he would leave behind.

About a hundred feet out, he felt it. Thin ice from the increased current. They would have to move farther downriver, farther away from Hog Island and the currents it created. They would have to move parallel to the shore and try to find ice that would support them. Already, the group was tiring. The cold robbed them of energy, and the slow pace was torturous. Still, the wind had not picked up. If anything, it was uncannily quiet.

The only sound that disturbed the dark stillness was the ice. It groaned eerily as it shifted and refroze. The sound of its upheaval sent a chill down his spine. Still, he could not be distracted.

He studied the shoreline. For the moment, they seemed undetected, but as they moved farther downriver, the chance of discovery would increase.

He held the baby tighter and moved on. They were down to a point at the foot of Randolph Street before the ice seemed sufficiently thick to support their weight safely. He turned the small group once more away from the shore and headed out for the opposite bank. The ice was covered in places with great waves of snow that slowed their progress. Other places had been blown so smooth by the wind that they were forced to shuffle along to prevent slipping.

It was when their pace had slowed at one of these open places that he first saw them: a small group of men, almost ragtag in appearance, all on foot. Not army, he thought gratefully, yet a cause for concern. There could only be one reason why they were on the ice at this hour. He estimated their distance and then calculated the time he would need to see his charges all safely to shore. It would be close, especially with the children.

He stopped for a moment. Trying not to frighten the children, he signaled the man and woman with his head. They turned to follow his gaze. When they looked back, he knew they understood the situation. The father picked up the small boy whose hand he had held and nodded. They picked up their speed. Still, it was impossible to move fast enough to prevent the unencumbered men who pursued them from gaining.

He could already hear their laughter and ribald remarks. It was a game to them, a disgusting game in which innocent lives were the ante. He considered himself a God-fearing man, and yet he found it difficult not to curse these men. They were foul-mouthed, foul-smelling scum of the earth, and yet the law was on their side. Surely God had never intended this.

"What'd I tell you!" Pock's breath made a soft white cloud in the clear cold air. "Once we get ourselves those black bastards, we'll have enough to keep our bellies warm and filled with the good stuff for the rest of the winter."

He was drunk, as were the men with him.

"Forget the money. This here's a matter of upholdin' the law," one of them said.

"Not to mention the sport of it," added another with a laugh. He was joined in laughter by the others.

"We've got us a few coons to track tonight. Bet their skins'll pay plenty."

"Too bad we ain't got no dogs. My dogs woulda been real keen on this here hunt. They can smell a nigger halfway across the state."

"Damn, it's blasted cold out here. Let's do it. I want to find myself some warm ass to cozy up to tonight."

Brad lay awake long after Rebecca had fallen asleep. He should awake her, yet he was reluctant to do so. He had never felt so protective as now, with her nestled against him, seeking his warmth and comfort.

She had exhausted herself crying. Now was the time to let her go. Now, before things became more complicated than they already were. He should be receiving an answer to his request for reassignment soon.

The soft tap at the door would not normally have awakened him. As it was, he gently separated himself from Rebecca's sleeping form and pulled on his pants.

"Captain, sorry to bother you, but the major said you should know. There's been some trouble out on the ice tonight."

Jacob could tell the men had gained on them considerably. Their baiting words, once indistinct, were now clear. He had heard it all before.

He forced himself to concentrate on the opposite bank and what stood between them and it. They still had over a thousand feet to cover. He hoped that the men who chased them were unarmed, but it was unlikely. He prayed that at least they were anxious to capture them alive for the reward.

The first gunshot and the yip that followed it told him they were too drunk to realize that dead slaves were of no value.

The older children began to whimper. They sensed the fear. The gentle consolation of their parents lent an eerie counterpoint to the obscene shouts that spurred them all on. No other words were spoken. There was no despondency, only increased determination.

Another gunshot rang through the air, landing frighteningly close this time. Jacob signaled the parents to move ahead of him. The shore was not more than two hundred feet away. He studied the ice. It looked secure, and he prayed that it was.

But a few steps further, the telltale voice of the ice spoke again, sounding its betrayal.

"Keep moving. Whatever happens, keep moving."

Their pursuers could not be more than a hundred feet behind them. Only the moonless sky protected Jacob's small party. Their weight strained the ice, and it protested still further. Its creaking reminded him of the keening of a family for their dead.

They were so close now. By rights, their pursuers should have stopped midriver, at the border, but he knew that in their drunken blood lust, they would not give up the chase until fear of discovery stopped them at the Canadian shore.

Another shot rang out. He felt a searing pain pierce him. He stopped in realization and agony. The sensations in his right arm fled, leaving it a dangling, useless appendage. He struggled to catch his breath. The frigid air burned his lungs. He gasped in small pants, struggling to safeguard the baby he held in his good arm.

The shouts of the hunters rang in his ears, obscene in their glee.

"You got one! Harry got himself a 'coon!"

"Come on, fellas! This here's gonna be a good night for 'coon huntin'."

The cackles and cheers swirled in Jacob's head. He fought off the dizziness and nausea that threatened to overcome him. It was instinct that, amid all his pain, sensed the change in the groaning ice. He knew it was going to happen before it did. His shout caused the pair ahead to stop. A shot rang out almost simultaneously.

As the ice gave way, his body was jerked awkwardly by the impact of the second bullet. One leg slipped into the numbing water. The child! The child! He struggled to keep the babe above the frigid depths.

Suddenly, a black face loomed before his blurry sight. Flat on the ice with his arms extended, the father willed his child to him, and in the father's determination Jacob found strength. "Take him! Run! Don't stop!" His last words were buried beneath a final wail as the ice supporting Jacob's bleeding body gave way.

Rebecca awoke with a start, her eyes swollen and puffy from crying. She felt the cool night air against her back. She searched the dark, unfamiliar room. Fear pricked at her skin. Something was wrong.

She saw him then. He stood in the shadows to one side of the window. The glow of his thin cigar was more visible than his features. He wore his trousers, but his feet and chest were bare.

"Brad?"

He turned slowly toward her and stepped into the light streaming in from the lamppost. His face was a mask—unmoving, inscrutable.

"What's wrong? What happened?" She began to panic.

He deliberately snuffed out the cigar. Still, he did not move toward her. He turned instead to stare once more out the window. When he spoke, his voice was devoid of any warmth, of any involvement in the meaning of the words that passed his lips.

"There's been an accident."

"An accident? What do you mean?" She sat up, clutching the sheet to her.

"It's Jacob."

"Oh, God! No!"

"He was shot while attempting to illegally cross the river tonight with some escaped slaves."

"No! No!" She was kneeling now, almost screaming.

"His body slipped beneath the ice. It's not been recovered yet."

She did not know how her pain wracked him. She saw only his stoicism. Anger grew within her.

"Did you know? Did you send them after him?"

"Does it matter?"

She struggled with disbelief. "Does it matter! You bastard! You care for nothing, no one other than yourself. How could I ever have loved you? My God, Jacob!"

Once more an agonizing sob tore through her. She could not stop crying, even as she found her clothes and hurriedly dressed.

He stood fixed in place at the window. Why should she expect otherwise? Oh, how she hated him!

"You're an animal! You have no claim to human decency!" She gasped out the words of hatred between her wrenching sobs. "Do you also murder women and children? No doubt it makes little difference to you!"

My God, Jacob! No, it couldn't be true. It should have been her. Rachel, what of Rachel? She had to go to Rachel.

She stumbled to the door. Then she turned and spat out her final words to his back. "If I'm ever alone with you again, by God, I'll kill you myself!"

He heard the door slam behind her, the angry movement of her skirts. His face had not changed throughout her outburst. He had dared not let it.

Now that she was gone, he slowly closed his eyes. Tears seared his cheeks. Jacob's tragic death had ended it far more surely than he ever could have himself.

24

The smile that slithered across Pock's face said it all. Brad could barely restrain himself from attacking the man. He did not have to ask who it was who had been after Jacob that night. The answer stood before him, the look of a kill in his gleaming eyes.

"Well, Capt'n, seems the good citizens of Detroit are havin' better luck catchin' law-breakers than the highfalutin army."

"Better luck? Is that what murder is referred to these days?"

"Don't see how you could call an attempt to execute the laws of the land murder. Resistin' a citizen's arrest could lead to all kinds of accidents." He dragged the toe of his filthy boot across the highly polished wood floor and snickered.

Pock looked back up at him, as cunning as any good predator. "Besides, you got no proof of what happened out there. Them niggers sure ain't gonna come back to testify."

His laughter stopped short when Brad came around the desk toward him. He held his ground, even when the huge captain moved within inches of him.

Brad looked down with disgust and hatred at the mottled face and rotting teeth. The smell of stale urine and bourbon assaulted his nostrils, turning his stomach. When he spoke, it was with barely controlled anger. "Any more accidents, and I personally will see that you meet with an untimely accident of your own. Is that perfectly clear?"

"Is that a threat, Capt'n? 'Cause if it is, I'd watch your ass from now on, and the pretty little ass of that nigger-lover who's got you thinkin' with your cock 'stead of your head."

Brad struck the man then. He was standing so close that he could not take a full swing, but the blow still sent the smaller man careening across the room. Pock came to an abrupt stop when his back slammed into the wall next to the door. He rubbed his jaw, then looked up. There was no mistaking the hatred in his eyes.

"You better pray we don't meet some dark night while I'm doin' my duty as a law-abidin' citizen, 'cause you won't live to worry about things no more, Capt'n, and no one'd be the wiser." With that, he turned and left.

Brad kneaded his hand thoughtfully. What was happening? He had lost all sense of objectivity. He had intended not to care, just to do his duty, but he had become entangled. She had done this to him, with her fiery self-righteousness and moral inflexibility, with her golden hair and her silken skin.

* * *

It was late by the time Brad returned to his room at the hotel. Seymour Finney seemed thoughtful behind the counter as he crossed the lobby. There was no greeting. By the time he reached his room, he could feel the strain of the last night and day.

The room was as he had left it, as they had left it. The bedlinens lay in disarray. He stood with his back to the door, leaning his head against it. Slowly, he closed his eyes. He could still smell her—jasmine, sweat, and tears. There had been so many tears.

He stood there for a long time, reluctant to go on, to move ahead toward the inevitable. The vibration of the hesitant knock against his back disturbed his solitude. It was a moment before he could step away and turn to open the door.

Joey Whiton stood before him. His face was contorted with tears and bruises. The boy made one swipe of his face with a dirty coat sleeve, as if to repair the damage, but the agony in his face was beyond repair.

Brad could hardly speak. "My God, Joey, what happened?"

The boy opened his mouth, but no words came. Instead he took the two short steps toward Brad and clung to him, his small body wracked by sobs.

Brad moved back into the room and shut the door. He knelt then, and took the slender boy into his arms. They remained that way until the boy's body had stopped convulsing.

Brad pulled back and gently smoothed away the matted hair from the swelling along the side of Joey's face. He removed his handkerchief and attempted to remove some of the tears and grime, checking for other damage as he went. The boy winced under the light pressure.

He did not have to ask who had beaten the boy. He knew. But what else had happened to make the child so distraught?

"Are you all right?" he finally asked.

The boy nodded, although his expression seemed to belie the nod.

"Will you tell me what has happened?"

The boy's eyes filled once more with tears, and Brad reached out to hold him again. Against the blue serge of his jacket, he heard the first muffled words of explanation.

"It's my fault!"

There was such genuine anguish in his voice that Brad had to fight to keep his own voice calm.

"What is your fault?"

"Jacob." He started to cry again. Brad held him tightly, trying to drive away the terrors that haunted the boy.

"I know who killed Jacob, Joey. It was not your fault."

"But I told!"

"What did you tell?"

"About Jacob and the move."

"Who did you tell?" He moved the boy away so he could see his face.

"I told my father. He beats me until I tell. But no one's ever been hurt before. Now Jacob's dead because I told."

Brad clasped the boy to him. He didn't think it was possible to hate Pock any more than he already did. But the shaking child in his arms threw him into a rage—an all-encompassing, uncontrollable rage—

because there was little or nothing he could do. Pock had known it. He knew it. His hands were officially tied.

Brad reflected on the irony of Joey's words. How could this child be at fault? He was as much a victim as Jacob.

"It is not your fault, Joey. It is *my* fault for not being there to stop him from killing. That's why I am here. It was my fault, do you understand?" He almost shook the already battered boy in his intensity.

The boy nodded.

"I promise you this, Joey, I will never let it happen again. Do you understand? Never again!"

The vehemence of Brad's words seemed to bring some relief to the tormented child. He lay his head once more against Brad's shoulder, as if reluctant to leave its shelter.

Brad, torn apart by the boy's agony, brought a hand up to hold the boy to him. He felt the child wince slightly as he did so. He thought of the torments of his own childhood and cried inside with the boy.

He looked around the shambles of the room and thought only of the shambles of his life. He had successfully insulated himself from pain, indeed from all feeling whatsoever, until she had come into his life.

She had brought love into his life, and with that love, pain. She had said he was wrong to uphold the law when it led to injustice. He thought of Pock, and of the small boy cradled against his shoulder. Where was the justice in this?

Perhaps she was right. There was law, and then there was justice. Had he, by siding with the law, pitted himself against justice?

* * *

The keening and wailing of the congregation echoed in Rebecca's heart. Jacob's body had been found a week after the fatal shooting, when two hunters stumbled onto it a mile downriver, wedged near the shore where the ice had melted. He had been barely recognizable.

Rebecca had offered to identify the body for the distraught Rachel. She knew she would never forget that sight, the horrible image of the half-frozen, decaying body was burned onto her soul as a symbol of her guilt. Jacob should still be alive.

She should have been the one out on the ice. Somehow, she could have avoided the soldiers who had killed him. She had done it before, and she would have done it this time. But instead, all she had were terrifying memories of the battered remains of this warm and loving friend. It was a tragic way to remember all Jacob's life had represented.

Rebecca turned to Rachel beside her. A week of not knowing had taken its toll on her friend. Rachel's agony was now reduced to a stoic mask of pain. Acceptance had come with great difficulty, but it had come at last. She had said little to Rebecca since that night. She accepted her comfort, but said little.

Now she sat quietly, amid the uproar that marked the funeral. The incident had polarized the city. The army's spokesman, Captain Taylor, had denied any army involvement, but no one else took responsibility, and the events of the evening were enveloped in gossip.

Some whispered that the Angel of Passage had been out on the river as well, chased by a group of vigilantes intent on the large reward posted for his capture.

Others accused the army of lying about its role.

A few joked about it, saying it was a shame that all the niggers hadn't washed ashore like frozen carp.

Rebecca was too tired to think. In her mind, the truth was more than evident. The rhythm and cadence of the black minister captured her weary soul.

"Let us pray, my brothers and sisters, for our dear brother Jacob who has passed to a greater life, for a greater good than our limited minds can ever imagine."

"Amen, brother."

"He did not die in the comfort of his home. Nor in the companionship of his friends. Nooo, my good people, he died in the cold."

"In the cold!"

"In the company of brothers and sisters of color who had sought his help."

"With his brothers and sisters, Amen!"

"They found in him a kindred spirit. A man of faith, whose faith took him to the ultimate test, my friends. And did he fail that test? No! He did not fail! He passed it to the greater glory of the Almighty! Praise the Lord!"

"Praise the Lord!"

"Praise the Lord, Amen! There are evil men in the world . . . eeevil men."

"Amen, brother!"

"Who would send God's innocent people into torments nearly as great as the fires of Hell!"

"Amen!"

"Evil men who know nothing of God. Who know

nothing of God's love for his people, black *and* white."

"Praise be to God!"

"What is it, my brothers and sisters, that hardens their hearts, that turns them away from God's goodness? There are those of you who cry we should hate them. But I say to you, my brothers and sisters in Christ Jesus the Lord, that God commands us to forgive them their trespasses—"

"No!"

"Yes! Do good to those who harm us. For it is only in forgiveness that we rise above the evil. That we will find happiness with our brother Jacob in the tender embrace of a just God! Vengeance is mine sayeth the Lord!"

"Amen! Alleluia!"

Suddenly, there was music. It started with the minister's deep baritone, achingly rhythmic, haunting in its slow cadence.

"Swing low, sweet chariot, comin' for to carry me home. Swing low, sweet chariot. . . ."

Rebecca's lower lip trembled as the tears in her eyes traced a cold path down her cheeks. She bit her lip until the bitter taste of blood penetrated her mouth, and still she would not release it, as if the pain might make it all go away and awaken her from the nightmare.

Forgive your enemies. Vengeance belonged to the Lord. It was impossible. Her heart was breaking, torn apart with grief. There was no room in her heart for forgiveness, but neither was there enough life left in it for vengeance.

She had died a little bit on the night Jacob had died. The love in her heart, the hope she had so carefully nurtured, was all gone. What remained was barely enough to keep her moving to help those left behind by Jacob—Rachel and the children, and the slaves who were yet to come, seeking help and transport. She would assure them a place in what was left of her heart, but there was no room for anything else.

"Are you all right?" She felt the gentle touch of her father's hand on hers. She turned to him and nodded. He had insisted on accompanying her. They were two of only a handful of whites in the congregation. If George Cunningham's appearance at the funeral might be the topic of discussion among his peers, it seemed not to matter one whit to him. Rebecca had always admired her father, and at this moment she envied the certainty with which he lived his life. Her life had once been marked by that certainty, but no longer.

"Let us go forth, my brothers and sisters in joy! Let us remember our brother Jacob in our work to free all God's children of color. So that someday we may all meet in heaven to praise the Lord with an unending chorus! Alleluia!"

"Alleluia! Amen, brother!"

25

Brad stood for a long time outside the door to the house. It was something he was compelled to do, and yet he understood the futility of it. When he finally knocked, the jarring sound reverberated in the cold morning air.

To the startled face that greeted him, he made just one request: "May I come in?"

The door opened wider, and the warmth of the fire seeped into his heavy jacket. He took a single step inside, bending to avoid hitting his head.

"Who is it, Mary?" The voice came from the small sleeping room.

"Momma . . ."

"Mary? Was there someone at the door?" Rachel tucked Ezra into his cot at the foot of the bed, then checked the baby, who was asleep peacefully in her crib nearby. She glanced at the big double bed Jacob had hand fashioned out of pine before their wedding, so many years ago now. She couldn't stand to sleep alone in it any longer. Mary's presence in the big double bed had been welcome.

Now her daughter's voice sounded urgent. "Momma!"

There had been many visitors to the small house since Jacob's death. Friends had come with small gifts of food, offering prayers and condolences.

Now there was a visitor of a different sort. Rachel's face registered shock and disbelief at the large blue-uniformed figure that dominated the small room.

"I'm sorry for the intrusion." Brad found himself almost stammering. It felt more like a violation of this woman's grief than simply an intrusion into her home. He realized from just a brief look at Rachel's face that his entrance had been a fluke; if the mother had answered the door, instead of the daughter, he would still be standing out in the cold.

After her initial surprise, Rachel's face closed. No emotion at all was visible on her lined visage.

Brad was stunned by the change in her. She seemed to have aged ten years in the last few weeks. He recalled Christmas Eve, and her pain became for him a palpable thing.

"Captain Taylor."

"I wanted to explain."

"There is nothing to explain, Captain."

"But there is."

"No doubt, you were simply doing your duty." Her voice reeked of sarcasm.

"No."

"Ah, I see, now you go beyond your duty to kill good men."

"No . . . I mean, as I've said publicly, it was not my men out there that night. I gave no orders to pursue your husband and the others. Do you think, if I had been in charge, we would have shot an unarmed man?"

"Only God knows the answer to that, Captain."

"I don't make it a habit of using undue force, especially—"

"Especially when, Captain? When the criminal's worst crime is seeking freedom from injustice?"

"Especially when the crime is of a less serious nature."

"Should we be grateful for your new outlook, Captain Taylor? I thought our acts were so vile that you were sent specifically to stop these atrocities. Do you see now that the politics practiced in Washington are very different when you are forced to practice them in the reality of our city, or any place where human beings seek relief from a life where they are bartered like corn or potatoes?"

Brad said nothing.

She became increasingly agitated. "You have the gall to come to my home and say you made a slight mistake, Captain Taylor? My husband is dead! They were barely able to identify the body. My children are fatherless. And you come to me and ask for what? Forgiveness?

"I have always prided myself on being a religious person. But God has severely tested me in this. Jacob was my life, Captain. He gave me courage and sustenance. Do you have any idea what it is to love so completely that you are empty without the other?"

Suddenly, Rachel's rage seemed to waver. She saw something in Brad's face that gave her pause. Tears formed in her eyes.

"Perhaps you are just beginning to realize how

painful love can be. Jacob was my strength, and without him I falter. I will forgive you your self-righteousness, forgive you your insensitivity. I will even, with God's help, forgive you for his death. You see, Captain, it is hatred that destroys all that is good in life. It turns hope into despair, and without hope there is no good reason for life. Not to forgive you would be to make a mockery of Jacob's life, of all he worked for and all he died for. I loved him too much to do that."

She stopped a moment to compose herself.

"You can leave now. You have gotten what you wanted from me. I warn you, Captain, I have nothing left to give." Rachel had exhausted herself. She stood worn and battered.

Somehow, Brad realized, he had been party to this cruelty, as if he actually had pulled the trigger that fateful night on the ice.

Before he could leave, the patter of small bare feet caused him to turn. Ezra ran past his mother, his long nightshirt almost entangling his feet in his hurry. He stopped before the captain, ignorant of the bitter exchange that had just occurred. He looked up at Brad, holding in his hand a golden stone, twin to the one he had presented to Rebecca at Christmas.

A log settled in the fireplace. Its crackling seemed to be the only sound in the small room. Even the sounds of breathing had been momentarily suspended.

Brad forced a tormented smile. He took the small stone from the boy and carefully placed it in his left hand. His right hand settled on the dark curls of the child's head and almost caressingly moved down to his cheek, then behind the small ear. He removed his hand from the boy then, slowly, palm up.

The small gold stone lay nestled in his palm, glistening in the firelight. The boy's ebony face lit up with excitement. The gold-colored stone seemed to stand as small testimony to what few things were still right in the world.

"It is still magic, Ezra." His voice choked. He placed the precious stone in the small hand and hurriedly left the house.

The cold morning air stung Brad's face as he rode at a canter out of the city. But even in the biting wind there was not enough pain to bring him out of his dulled mental state. Nothing had been the same, not since the night Jacob had died.

He kicked his horse into a gallop and breathed the cold wind in deeply, greeting the pain as an old friend. He fled on the panting horse's back into white oblivion.

He should never have returned to Detroit. In doing so, he had lost his way. Somehow, fate should not have allowed it. He had put the pain behind him, and now it was back, transformed, but still recognizable.

Again, it found focus in love for a woman. This time it was not his mother, but his what? What could Rebecca be to him? What could she ever be? There was no future for them.

His love for this stubborn, determined woman had grown steadily, uncontrollably, but so had his capacity for pain. She hated him. For the first time, he admitted that she might be right. He was a moral coward, an object of derision. He had protected himself too well for too many years, insulating himself from all emotion.

He reigned in his horse and made a vow. Then he turned back toward the city.

The persistent knock reverberated through the foyer of the Cunningham home.

George Cunningham stuck his head out of his office. "Who is it, Maddie?" The figure at the door was still hidden from his view, but Maddie's agitation caused him some concern. He moved out into the hall, toward the entryway.

"Maddie? Is there some problem?"

"No, sir. I was just tellin' the capt'n here that Miz Cunningham left strict orders she was not to be disturbed, 'specially by him."

He took one look at the captain's face and dismissed the maid.

"Come in, Captain." He led the way to the back of the house, to his office. A huge fire burned in the grate, driving any chill away. "Take off your coat and warm yourself. You look like you've been out for some time."

George Cunningham sensed a change in the young officer. For the first time since they had met, almost a year ago, the self-assured, arrogant, handsome man who stood before him seemed to require compassion. He moved to the liquor cabinet and pulled out a bottle of his finest brandy. He poured two snifters and offered one to Brad, who stood immobile, staring out the windows toward the frozen river.

"Captain?"

"Thank you, sir."

"Why don't you join me by the fire."

Brad removed his heavy overcoat. A long moment passed before he joined the older man, taking a seat in one of two matching high-backed leather chairs that flanked the hearth. Still, he made no effort to speak.

George Cunningham sipped his brandy and studied the man who sat silently across from him. Why was nothing on earth without its price? Rebecca had once asked him if you could ever pay too high a price for something you wanted. It was for each to decide for themselves, he had responded. Now, as he watched the agony of the younger man, he knew it would not be an easy decision for Brad Taylor.

"You had nothing to do with Jacob's death, did you?"

Brad shook his head. He seemed lost in thought, gazing at the amber contents of his glass as it played against the firelight.

"Not by law. I knew nothing of it until it was over. Whatever your daughter may believe, I gave no orders. The group chasing Jacob that night were vigilantes. They had no authority from me to pursue those slaves." He paused, then continued more hesitantly, "But does that mean I am not responsible? Your daughter seems to think otherwise."

"And you, Captain, what do you think?"

"What do I think?" He laughed, seemingly at himself. "I think, perhaps, I should give up thinking."

"The failure to think, the failure to act is as much a decision as any."

"So you would not allow me even that escape?" Brad's eyes never left the brandy snifter.

"There is no escape from responsibility."

"You make it sound so simple." There was resentment in his voice. "Responsibility, is that the key? Responsibility to whom, to what? I have always lived my life by a code that served me well. I was responsible to myself, and to my role as a United States Army officer. It was very clear."

"And now, Captain, what has changed?"

Brad finally looked up. "What hasn't?"

He bolted from the chair and strode once more to the leaded window that overlooked the stables and the river. His back was rigid. He turned and turned the glass in his hands, unconscious of the repetitive task.

"And my daughter?"

"You need not worry about Rebecca." His voice softened. "I would never hurt her."

George Cunningham thought of his daughter and of the black-cowled spectre who ran slaves. "How can you be so sure, Captain?"

"I am not without honor."

"Sometimes it is not a matter of honor. Sometimes the choice is not ours to make. Sometimes fate makes our choices for us."

Brad laughed, again at himself, it seemed.

"Sometimes decisions we have made long before the moment control us. We have lost our freedom in a painstakingly slow process."

"I can't believe that."

"Can't, or won't believe it?"

"Both."

"It is not just you who have changed, you know. Rebecca has changed as well."

Brad looked up at this last comment.

"My daughter is in pain as well. You have torn her

apart. Leave her be. You are asking too much when you ask her to love you. She will not be able to do that without giving up so much of herself that she will be left an empty shell."

"I haven't asked her to love me."

There was a long pause.

"If you love her, Captain, leave her alone. This love cannot survive, not now, not the way things are. There will be war. You and I know that. She will be alone, with nothing to comfort her. Let her at least have her dreams, Captain. It will have to be enough."

"Dreams . . ." Brad leaned his head toward the windowpane until his forehead rested against it. "I once dreamed of becoming an army officer. Now I am living the dream, and it has become a nightmare, with no hope of ever waking up."

After a long pause, he turned suddenly back to the older man. "You need not tell her I came. It is just as well. When she left, I saw only the hatred in her eyes. I could bear not having her love, but I could not bear her hate." He picked up his overcoat and headed for the door.

"Thank you, Captain."

"No, thank you, sir, for sharing Rebecca with me. She is truly a remarkable woman. I will never forget her."

George Cunningham's thoughts turned once more to the Angel of Passage. His fervent prayer floated silently heavenward: I hope you will never know how truly remarkable, Captain.

Rebecca lifted the pen from the paper at the sound of someone's exit below. The muffled voices earlier had not attracted much of her attention. Now she stood up and went to the window. The panes were frosted with the cold. She used her warm hand to clear a small space and then looked out.

Her frosty view made the figure fuzzy, dreamlike. The broad blue shoulders, the dark hair curling over the collar, it had all too recently been warm flesh beneath her hands and silken strands between her fingers. She watched the delicate white crystals frost the glass anew obscuring the figure long before it moved out of sight. It was as if it had all been part of a dream, and he had never existed. Perhaps she did not exist. But that could not be true; the pain was too real.

She turned from the window and returned to the desk. She dipped her pen in ink and continued to write. All too soon, the letters were obscured. Her warm teardrops mingled with the ink and sent it fleeing across the page. Before long, there was nothing recognizable left in the letter, just as there was nothing recognizable left in her life.

26

"Come here, silly girl."

Charity giggled as she toddled her way across the green grass of Grand Circus Park to Rebecca's beckoning arms. Rebecca enfolded the laughing child and lay back, suspending her at arm's length. Charity squealed in delight. The weight of the child soon tired her arms, and she set her back on her feet and watched her stumble toward her mother and brother before she turned her attentions elsewhere.

She stared up at the blue sky. Huge white clouds tumbled across it, like kernels of popped corn flying from a fire. Suddenly, she was lost in memories of last spring, of that first picnic with Brad and Joey, of other fantasy clouds, and other times. She closed her eyes and tried to shift her thoughts back to the present. She willed the warm late-March sun to seep into her tired body, into all the chilled places of her soul.

She could smell the earth, the sweetness of its promise. Its feel beneath her fingertips was reassuring.

Her fear, if she voiced it, was that the winter was far from over. Six Southern states had seceded in the last months. The kindling was all ready. It needed but a match to start a war. Rumors were running rampant. She had tried to ignore them.

She spent much time with Rachel and the children. The tragedy had not driven the two friends apart, as she had feared. In the end, it had strengthened their friendship. They had both lost someone they loved on that terrible night.

"Ezra, come back here. Do not bother Rebecca."

"Oh, no, it's all right, Rachel. He's never a bother." Rebecca sat up as the rambunctious five-year-old came careening toward her. "Slow down, Ezra, you'll fall."

"No, I won't." He halted in front of her.

"What have you got there?"

Ezra was hiding something in his hand.

"It's a secret."

"You won't even share it with a friend?"

The child looked slightly guilty. "Well, maybe, 'cause you're a friend." He held out the object in his hand for her inspection.

"Why, it's wonderful, Ezra. Do you know it is a very special stone? See here . . ."

The child moved in to hang over Rebecca's arm and study the little rock.

"It is a fossil. What does this look like?" Her finger traced a pattern on the rock.

"It's like a leaf."

"Yes, long ago a leaf fell off a tree here into the mud. Years and years later the mud became rock, and the leaf is still there."

"Is it magic, then?"

"Well, I suppose you could say it's magic."

"No, magic like the rock I gave you at Christmas. Like the one the soldier said was magic. You remember, Miss Rebecca, the one he made come out my ear."

Rebecca stared numbly at the boy's eager face. She remembered. The memories she had tried to blot out came flooding back. "Perhaps it is a magic rock then, Ezra."

"Show me. Make it work." He looked so expectant that it made her heart ache.

"I'm afraid I don't know how, Ezra."

"But you said it was magic."

"Yes, I said perhaps it was magic. But sometimes magic rocks need special people to make them work."

"The soldier's special, isn't he?"

The small boy studied her face, waiting for her reply.

"Yes, he is special." Her voice cracked.

"Why are you crying?"

Rebecca wiped her eyes. "I'm not crying. The wind blew something in my eye."

"Momma used to cry a lot after Papa went to be with God. She doesn't cry so much now."

"That's because you take such good care of her. Your papa would be proud."

The boy smiled at the compliment. Then he saw something in the distance, and his eyes widened with excitement. Before Rebecca could turn to see what had caught his attention, he was off.

"Ezra, where are you going? Come back here."

Some evergreens hid him for a moment. When he reappeared, Rebecca gasped. Rachel turned toward Ezra at the sound, and her face drained of color.

Ezra happily dragged his find along by the hand. Rebecca started to get up, but in her agitated state she was confounded by her skirts and petticoats. She had barely gained a standing position when Ezra approached with his reluctant companion.

"I found the soldier, Miss Rebecca. He can show you about the magic stone." He turned toward the somber Brad. "Can't you?"

Brad's eyes never left Rebecca. "What stone is this?"

"Show him, Miss Rebecca. Show him the stone."

The boy grasped Rebecca's hand and held it out for Brad's inspection. "Open your hand so he can see the stone with the leaf. He'll know if it's magic or not."

Slowly Rebecca opened her hand. The dirty rock lay against her white palm, even whiter now because of her increasing pallor.

Brad's fingertips brushed against her palm as he turned the little stone over to inspect it. He looked over to Ezra. "It does look special, but I would have to look closer to see if it's truly magic."

"Let him look closer, Miss Rebecca."

Brad placed his hand under hers, cradling her slender white fingers in his palm. It took all his control to keep his touch light. He moved her hand up toward him, fighting the urge to kiss her wrist and follow the delicate line of her arm upward.

"Is it? Is it?"

"Yes, I believe it is." He picked the stone up in his left hand, displaying it clearly for the child's wondering eyes. His right hand gently encompassed Rebecca's, his thumb caressing the back ever so slowly as he turned it. Reluctantly, he let go.

He turned his hand so the small boy could see both sides. Then he placed it on Rebecca's cheek, cradling its silken smoothness for just a moment. She closed her eyes at his touch, and he nearly trembled as her eyelashes feathered his thumb. Then, afraid of losing control, he moved his hand with a flourish behind her ear. The small stone appeared.

Ezra's eager clapping was the only sound to disturb the tense silence.

"See, I told you! I told you! It is a magic rock, just like the others." The boy turned to Brad. "Tell her. Tell her it's magic."

Brad's eyes remained fixed on Rebecca's face. He was memorizing the features, feasting on the texture of it, reveling in her golden hair and eyes. "Yes, it is magic."

"Ezra, what are you doing?" Rachel's voice floated across the grassy knoll.

"It's the soldier, Momma. He's showing Miss Rebecca how my magic stone works."

"Come here, boy." His mother's unexpected sternness sent him scurrying in her direction.

"But, Momma—"

Rebecca should hate him. She had carefully nurtured her outrage. But now, standing here with him so close, she knew it had been simply a vain attempt to protect herself from other, more overpowering feelings.

There was pain in his eyes. For the first time since she had known him, he made no attempt to hide it. It tore at her, but she could not speak. She would be lost if she spoke. He seemed to be struggling as well—considering and then discarding words. When he finally spoke, it was heartrendingly simple.

"I'm sorry."

His look told her that the brief statement required no response.

He took her hand and raised it slowly to his lips. He did not kiss the back, but rather turned it gently in his and then pressed a kiss to her palm, so longingly tender that she thought she would die. When he turned and left, she did die a little.

"Rebecca? Are you all right?" Rachel hurried toward her friend.

Rebecca felt suddenly ill. She must have wavered as the blue-jacketed figure walked away, for Rachel took her arm in support.

"Sit down. You look like you're about to faint."

Rebecca sank to the ground, her head swimming.

"I feel slightly dizzy, that's all. It will pass."

"Do you need something? I can send Ezra home for a cool cloth."

"No, no, I'll be fine. I just need a moment. I just hadn't expected . . ."

Rachel studied her closely. "What did he say?"

Rebecca looked up, her eyes awash in tears. "He said he was sorry."

Rachel paused thoughtfully before she spoke. "Perhaps he is."

"How can you say that? He killed your husband!"

"It was not under his orders that those men pursued Jacob. Captain Taylor did not kill him. Jacob died because it was ordained by a higher power than the captain's."

"If only I had been on the river that night. If only I hadn't—"

"And you would be dead now. It would be no better, don't you see?"

Rebecca turned on her friend. "It would be better if I were dead and Jacob still alive."

"Better for whom, Rebecca? Better for Jacob, or better for you?"

Rachel had hit upon her pain. Now Rebecca was hysterical. "I wish I were dead! Do you know how many times since that night I've wished I were dead?"

"Don't speak that way. It's blasphemy!"

Rebecca had lost all control. Her eyes, nose, and voice overflowed with bitter tears. Her body moved spasmodically, wracked by sobs.

Rachel knelt before her and took her wet face in her hands. "You will survive the pain, Rebecca, just as I will. With God's help, we will all survive. And in surviving we will find strength. You must not talk of dying. Soon, I'm afraid, there will be too much dying."

Rebecca's crying subsided slowly. Rachel sat down beside her now.

"He came to me after Jacob's death. I did not tell you then, but I will tell you now. He tried to explain, but I would not listen. I was filled with too much pain. After he left, I was touched by his courage and concern. It could not have been easy for him, and he did not need to do it. No doubt, more than one eyebrow was raised at the sight of him at my doorway. I believe he came because he did care—because he saw the injustice of it.

"You have not loved poorly, Rebecca, just unwisely. I warned you long ago that our passions do not respect our minds. In another place, at another time, you might have found happiness together. But this is now. Too much has passed between you and too much has yet to come. Few relationships could withstand the strain of it. It is no doubt for the best. Something very terrible is coming, I feel it. It's as if Jacob is whispering in my ear, forewarning me."

Rebecca finally wiped her face, gaining strength from Rachel's words. "I miss Jacob so much. When I was reckless he was always sane and reliable. I have to get the *Deliverance* ready soon. I don't know how I'll do it without him."

Rachel smiled. "You will manage as you always have. I have great confidence in you."

27

Rebecca tugged at the heavy sail bags until they were all safely stowed aft. At some point, the black sails would have to be removed and checked for damage, but she could not do that now. She would need help, someone she could trust. Her thoughts fled to Jacob, bringing tears to her eyes. She would have to think of someone. The work must be continued.

It was the first day of April, 1861. The sun was warm, but the brisk southwest wind made her shiver slightly. She wore a lightweight muslin dress with its sleeves rolled back to allow free movement and to keep them from getting wet.

She studied her hands. They were raw and cracked. The lye soap solution she was working with stung them, penetrating each tiny opening in the skin. She had spent most of the morning scrubbing down the *Deliverance,* having refused her father's offer that Samuel, their driver, help with the arduous task.

It was something that Jacob had always done, and she was therefore compelled to do it herself this time. It was her penance. She was not Catholic, but suddenly the idea of penance performed to atone for sin made a good deal of sense to her. The physical pain of her red and roughened hands seemed little enough expiation. It was almost a relief from the emotional pain that had numbed her these past weeks. The work served as a cruel distraction.

The simple gown she wore was one of her oldest. Over it she had fastened a well-used apron of Bertie's. She had pulled back her golden hair and fastened it tightly. Now, her face marred by dirt, she worked on the last of the tasks, polishing the brass fittings of the black sloop. She did not hear the footsteps.

"Miss Cunningham!"

Rebecca started at the unexpected intrusion. She looked up to see Joey Whiton.

"Joey! What a nice surprise. What brings you all the way out here?"

"Mr. Finney sent me, ma'am—I mean, Miss—with a message. He even let me ride Big Blue." The boy nodded to the large gelding tethered near the Cunningham barn.

"It must be a very special message, indeed."

The boy acknowledged this. She could tell he was pleased with the responsibility.

Rebecca had straightened from her task and now stepped off the boat, extending her hand for the missive, but none was forthcoming.

"He didn't put nothin' in writin', Miss. He said I was to remember it exactly as he told it to me." He paused for a moment, recalling the precise words.

"The conductors will be meetin' at the usual place tonight at ten." He smiled then, pleased with himself.

"Why, thank you, Joey."

"You're welcome."

He seemed reluctant to leave.

"Are you hungry?" she asked him.

The boy perked up, though he seemed hesitant to admit his hunger.

"Bertie's made me a picnic lunch, and there is far too much food for me. Why don't you help by joining me for lunch?"

Rebecca almost laughed at his eager face. The offer was irresistible to the child.

"Can I help you with something first, Miss Cunningham? Mr. Finney said I don't have to be back 'til one."

"That's a kind offer, but I believe most of the work is done. The biggest service you can perform for me is to help make sure none of Bertie's roast chicken and hot biscuits are left in the basket." She retrieved a picnic basket from under the bench at the end of the dock. "Come on. We'll find a warm place protected from the wind."

They settled for a grassy knoll on the far side of a shed used to store unused equipment. Rebecca laid out the small cloth Bertie had included and emptied the contents of the large basket, filling the air with the most delectable smells.

As they ate Rebecca studied the boy. He seemed to be free of any bruises today. She tried not to think of Christmas Eve, and of Joey's father. It made her too angry. What kind of man would beat his own son? She was not naive, and yet it seemed almost incomprehensible. Joey was as much a slave as the Negroes she sought to help. And, as with them, there was no legal recourse—nothing to protect this child from his parent.

Was there nothing she could do for Joey? Perhaps they could be of mutual help. She could have Seymour Finney tell the boy's father that occasionally he might have to work late, with pay, of course, and would be allowed to sleep in the barn.

He was young and small, but he was also bright and surefooted. An evening helping her would mean one less night at home, one less night with his father and the danger that brought.

He already knew she was an abolitionist sympathizer. He need never know she was actually the Angel of Passage. She simply needed help getting away from the dock and later upon returning. She could easily wait to assume her disguise until after the boat left the Cunningham dock.

Of course, she would never have the boy accompany her. It would be far too dangerous. But he was obviously sympathetic to the cause, or Seymour, always cautious, would never have sent him with a verbal message that was clearly dangerous if it fell into the wrong hands.

As she lay back, her stomach filled with Bertie's wonderful cooking, she thought she would approach Seymour with her plan. She trusted his judgment.

The sun was wonderful. It had grown warmer, and the wind had slackened. Although the trees only hinted at leaves, it definitely felt like spring. Suddenly, the day held promise.

"Joey, do you know what an abolitionist is?"

"Yes, Miss. It's somebody who wants to free the slaves."

"Do you think they should be free?"

Joey pondered before he spoke. "If you're a slave, they can beat you anytime they want, make you do anything they want, even if you don't want to. I don't think there should be slaves—I don't think anybody should be a slave and have to do what somebody else wants, 'specially if it's bad."

Rebecca's heart was torn by this somber reply. No doubt, personal experience had formed his beliefs. This child was old beyond his years, aged by brutality and neglect. There was no justice in it.

"No, Joey, no one human being should be at the mercy of another, bought and sold, treated as chattel. It makes no sense, no sense at all."

"I think it would be unwise."

"Why do you say that, Seymour?"

"He is only a child."

"But he works hard for you. Has his work ever been less than satisfactory?"

"No, but my work does not endanger life. He works primarily in the stables, with the horses. There is also something I should warn you about. The boy's father is a shady figure, and he beats the boy. Rumors abound as to his mean temperament. You could jeopardize the boy, should his father find out."

"If you do as I suggest, he will not find out. In the end, it will probably save the child from more than one senseless beating."

She did not add that she had had personal experience with the pock-faced man's cruelty. She cared little about Joey's father. What harm could the man do her?

Seymour Finney paced his small office at the hotel.

"I still don't like it, Rebecca. There is something that troubles me, but I can't put words to it."

"That is because you are troubling yourself over nothing."

"Perhaps." He shook his head. "I will leave the decision to the others." He pulled out his pocket-watch. "We'd best be going if we are to reach DeBaptiste's on time."

George DeBaptiste spoke to those gathered in his home.

"There must be almost twenty. We've hidden them in safe houses throughout the city, but they will have to be moved soon. We think it best they be moved to Amherstburg. Our friends there are capable of handling such a large shipment. We have already sent word to prepare for the packages, and they have asked for some time. I told them we would be moving at the next new moon. That would be April eleventh. Are we all agreed?"

There was a murmur of approval from the small group. "We will have to move them in several trips. It will increase the danger, but it cannot be helped."

Rebecca spoke up, "I could move them all at once. I've made the trip and am familiar with it."

George DeBaptiste turned slightly to face her. "Can the *Deliverance* be ready by then?"

She nodded.

The head of the movement seemed to weigh her offer carefully. When he spoke, her heart sank.

"I don't believe it would be wise this time, Rebecca. I am concerned with your well-being. Jacob's loss was a tragedy for all of us, but I fear it has taken a serious toll on you."

"All the more reason I should go. I need to feel useful again. I cannot bear to stand idly by any longer. You know my loyalty and my skill. How can you deny me this?"

There was a whispered undercurrent in the room. Rebecca held her ground. It had to be her. It would be her true redemption for that other terrible night. She desperately sought another argument, anything that might sway the soft-spoken Negro in her direction. "I believe the Angel of Passage needs to make his presence known again. The community needs a reminder. They fear war, yet there are worse evils than a just war. The black spectre will once again provide a means of escape for those poor slaves, and a symbol of the grim future that awaits us all if injustices are not corrected."

"Have you found anyone to aid you?" DeBaptiste asked. "Surely you cannot intend to work alone?"

All eyes turned her way. She steadied herself. She needed to be as unemotional and as logical as she could to win their agreement.

"You forget, George, that I have worked alone before. But in answer to your question, yes. I have found someone I believe could provide enough assistance to allow me to safely move the packages."

She saw Seymour Finney watching her from the corner of the small room. "There is a boy. He works for Seymour. He could help me rig the boat and be there when I return. It is all I would need. The rest I can accomplish myself."

George DeBaptiste turned away from Rebecca. "And what do you think of this scheme, Seymour?"

Rebecca held her breath, willing Seymour to give her the benefit of the doubt.

"I believe the boy would be trustworthy. He is dependable—of that I have no doubt. It is up to Rebecca to judge what risk his participation would bring to her and the others."

Seymour had chosen to be noncommittal. Rebecca hoped his lack of objection would be enough to convince the others.

"Rebecca, you have served us well. Perhaps it is time for the Angel of Passage to make an appearance. It is rumored that Captain Taylor has requested reassignment. He seems much less rabid in his pursuit. The Angel of Passage might well rally the people of the city around us, and more expediently send the captain back to Washington."

DeBaptiste had agreed. She should be elated, but she was not. What had he said, reassignment? That she might expedite his departure? Why did the irony of it torture her? It was all over.

"You may use the boy. But be careful, Rebecca. Just because the captain has had a change of heart does not mean he will not uphold the law when forced into it. There are others in the community with no scruples who would find great pleasure in forcing the captain to arrest you."

Brad, arrest her? What perverse plan had driven them to this point? Surely God was laughing at her folly. She had allowed herself to fall in love with the enemy, and this might be her retribution. Imprisoned by the man she loved. She could not let it happen. It could never come to that point, it would break her completely.

"You can depend on me. I will not fail in this."

She turned and headed for the door. When she was abreast of Seymour Finney, he spoke for her ears only. "I hope to God you know what you are about, Rebecca."

So did she.

The scruffy little man straightened up as the door opened. From his hiding place across the street, he could see clearly the faces of those departing. He smiled as the woman crossed the threshold. So, the captain's bitch was at it again. Perhaps there was a way to get revenge on the captain that he had not thought of before. Pock's face brightened with a certain malevolent delight. He would have to have another little talk with his son. Perhaps he could kill two birds with one stone, so to speak.

28

Rebecca nodded to Joey on shore, and the boy released the lines. The sloop moved silently out into the darkness. She studied the sky. There was no moon, but neither were any stars visible. The clouds had started to roll in that afternoon, dark and ominous, but there had been no rain, at least not yet. The first leg of her trip should go smoothly. She would have to travel over a mile up-river to pick up her cargo, but the wind would be at her back.

Over the past several days, the slaves had been moved in small groups into the countryside, to the farm of a "conductor." The small house with its secret room and ample cellar had quick access to the river, and it was far enough removed that no one would be watching it. A small landing would permit safe boarding for the fugitives who would be in her care.

Rebecca shivered. There was an eerie stillness as the black craft moved out into the river. Then the boat's infamous sails caught the strong southwest wind, and the wheel in her hand protested. She expertly guided the sloop toward its destination. The river was choppy, but not dangerously so. It provided a steady rhythm as the boat plodded forward.

She turned and watched as the single lamp Joey held on shore became a small speck, no larger than a firefly. The boy had proved his worth over the last few days. Together they had managed to lay out the sails and check them for rips and tears. Joey had cleaned the cabin and stowed away the blankets and food that might prove a necessity if things did not go smoothly. Just before she left, he had helped her affix the name *Tremont II* to the stern. She had no doubt he would be there upon her return, whatever the hour. Seymour Finney's concerns would prove unwarranted.

She searched the shoreline ahead for the fire that would signal her destination. In the darkness, she would have to rely on it to prevent her from grounding the sloop on Hog Island. With no sign of the fire yet, she reached down and opened a compartment beside the wheel. Withdrawing a length of rope, she secured the wheel so that it had only an inch of play. Then she released the mainsail slightly, slowing and stabilizing the sailboat's progress.

Quickly, she stripped off the thin muslin dress she wore. Over her simple chemise and pantalets she pulled on a man's shirt and woolen pants she had retrieved. Then she picked up the last of the items and paused for a moment. The wool was heavy and coarse. She fingered it thoughtfully, then lifted it high to shake out its folds.

Her face showed a new resolve as she skillfully twirled the cape around herself until the black fabric hid her completely. She reached back and pulled up the heavy cowl until her face was obscured. She moved then to release the wheel and pull in the main sail. The sloop responded to her touch and flew into the night.

A slow, enigmatic smile crossed her hidden face. Once again, the Angel of Passage was on the water.

Joey sat alone in the darkness, awaiting Rebecca's return. As time passed, he found it harder and harder to keep his eyes open. He lay back, vowing only to rest, not to sleep.

"So there y'are, boy."

The low raspy voice awoke Joey with a start. Its familiarity filled him with terror.

"Now what would you be doin' sittin' in a rich man's backyard this hour of night? Holdin' a vigil for some black demon? Not a healthy job for a God-fearin' boy, I would think."

Joey jumped to his feet. "I was just doin' a favor for Miss Cunningham. That's all, Pa."

"Now what kind of favor would have a young boy, who needs his sleep, out on a night when it's bound to storm?"

"I'll be all right, Pa. No need to worry."

"Ah, but you're my son, boy. A father's meant to worry."

Joey didn't see it coming. The blow sent him reeling sideways to the ground. He whimpered once and slowly regained his footing.

"What was that for, Pa?"

"Don't sass me, boy, or you'll get another. Where is she?"

"She's not here." Joey stammered.

Pock grabbed the boy by the arm. His painful grip caused Joey to wince. He dragged his son toward the dock. "She's out on her damned boat, isn't she? Isn't that just the thing a lady would do at this hour of the night?"

Once more he struck the boy on the head. Only his iron grip on Joey's upper arm kept the boy from being propelled off the dock into the water.

"Go ahead, protect her. I know you. You can't lie to me, boy. I can see it in your eyes." He grabbed the youngster's face with his free hand. His dirty fingers held the tender bruised flesh of Joey's cheeks. "I know she's out there helpin' her goddamn nigger friends! I thought there was somethin' mighty peculiar about old Finney askin' if you could work late, so I went sniffin' around. I got a good nose for trouble. Imagine my surprise, boy, when I tracked you to the highfalutin Cunninghams' place. Why, I asked myself, would a woman like her need my boy in the middle of the night? I thought it was my duty as your pa to protect you from gettin' yourself into trouble with the law."

"No! It's not like that, Pa."

"Well, maybe you should be tellin' your pa exactly what it *is* like." His filthy fingernails dug into the pale white skin until small crescents of red began to appear.

Joey gasped in pain. "I'll not tell you, Pa. I won't let you hurt her."

"What's this? You got a problem all of a sudden with tellin' your pa what's goin' on? You never have before, boy. 'Course, sometimes it's taken a bit of persuasion." He suddenly released Joey's face and jerked the boy's arm behind him until the child sobbed. "Maybe what we need here is a little persuasion." Pock half pulled, half dragged his son off the Cunningham dock. Once on shore, he hurled him to the ground. As Joey struggled to regain the wind knocked out of his lungs, Pock searched the ground nearby. He picked up a slender willow branch.

"Now we'll see what a little persuasion can do." His first blow snapped against the boy's chest. The slender end of the switch caught Joey's face. A crimson line formed where the wood had torn through the flesh. Joey turned then onto his stomach, cowering at the first blow from the terrible beating that would come. The second strike covered his back, raising a welt. The third blow never came.

George Cunningham sat in his study, looking out toward the river. His offer to help Rebecca had been soundly rejected. Her plea had made sense: his presence in the house would provide an alibi for her, should anyone come inquiring after her whereabouts.

He had barely made out her departure in the moonless night. Now he sat and worried. Gone were the days when he could go to bed and fall asleep easily. Now his daughter's absences put a deep fear into his soul. He would not sleep until she returned, and that might not be before the wee hours of the morning.

Anticipating a long wait, he had opened the windows slightly to let in some night air. When the *Deliverance* had pulled away, he had heard the faint jangle of its rigging. Since then, the night had been quiet. Now a faint sound, a voice, seemed to wend its way up from the water. He concentrated on the tone and timbre of the sound. It was a man, an angry man.

He rose quickly from his chair. Proceeding through the house to the kitchen, he lit the oil lamp kept by the door, and went out into the darkness. When he reached the stables, he realized there were two voices, both down near the water. The second voice was so light and soft it had been lost to him before. At first he thought it a woman's voice, as he drew closer he realized it was a child's. In the distance, he could see a blur of white amid the blackness. He could hear whimpering, low and muffled.

"Who's there? Is someone there?" Footsteps retreated across the ground. He hurried forward, his lamp held high against the darkness.

"My God!" George Cunningham rushed to Joey's prostrate figure. Kneeling beside the boy, he gently turned him over. The lamplight fell across the pale face, now swollen with bruises. A single slash of red ran from his eye down to his jaw. The older man drew out a handkerchief, desperate to help somehow.

"Joey! What happened? Who hurt you like this? Where is Rebecca?" He looked frantically toward the dock. Somewhat reassured by the absence of the *Deliverance,* he turned his attention back to the boy.

"Can you sit up?" At the boy's nod, he placed his hand behind the child's shoulders and helped him to a sitting position. Joey winced as he moved. Rebecca's father slid Joey's suspenders off his shoulders and lifted the boy's flannel shirt. The single red weal marked the boy's courage. The older man found it difficult to believe the youngster had not screamed out at the infliction of such a wound.

"Joey?" He waited a moment until the boy looked up at him. "Will you talk to me?"

The boy nodded.

"Why are you here, son?"

"I was helpin' Miss Cunningham."

"Damn!" The older man's curse reverberated in the night. "Where is Rebecca?"

"She's gone, sir." Joey's voice was barely above a whisper.

"Is she safe?"

"Yes, sir."

"Who did this to you?"

"My pa."

"Why? Why did he beat you?"

"He wanted to know about Miss Cunningham. What she was about."

"What did you tell him?"

The youngster's face contorted in pain. "I didn't tell him nothin', sir. But it made no difference. He knows."

"Knows what?" Cunningham was near panic. Surely a man who would beat his own son for information was a violent force to be reckoned with.

"He knows that Miss Cunningham is on the water with the boat."

"Does he know where she's going?"

"I don't know, sir."

"Does he have other sources?" He almost shook the boy in his urgency. "Could he find out?"

Fear showed on the boy's face. "Yes, sir."

"Can you stand?"

Again the boy nodded.

The man offered his support, and together they headed for the house. As they passed the stables Cunningham yelled.

"Samuel! Samuel! God damn! Samuel!" A sleep-weary face appeared at the small window. "Samuel, saddle Rebecca's horse and my own and bring them up to the kitchen. Now!" A puzzled look crossed the stablehand's face before he quickly disappeared to do as bidden.

George Cunningham half-carried Joey into the dark kitchen. He set the lamp on the long oak table and sat Joey there as well. He used the hand pump to fill a basin, grabbed one of Bertie's clean towels, and returned to the table. He wrung out the towel and offered it to the boy. The child took it from him and held its coolness to his face.

"I need to ask you something, Joey. Will you tell me all you know?"

"Yessir."

"Could your father have known about Jacob, the night he died?"

The child's eyes filled with tears. He bit his lip in an effort to control them. His chest heaved. When he spoke, his voice was tremulous, on the verge of losing all control.

"He knew."

"Was he out on the water that night, too?"

"Yes."

"Did he kill Jacob?" George Cunningham did not need an answer to his last question. The boy's tormented face was answer enough.

"If we are to assure Rebecca's safety, you will need to help me. Will you help?"

The boy brightened. "Yessir."

"Good! I am going to try and warn Rebecca about your father. Perhaps I can reach her before she has boarded her passengers. If I am too late, we have only one choice. You must ride to Captain Taylor." At the captain's name, the boy's face showed hope.

"Tell him what you know. He must be persuaded to try to intercept your father before he has a chance to get on the water. After that, I fear there is nothing we can do. Samuel will be bringing Rebecca's horse shortly. You are to use it to ride to the captain. Do you understand?"

"Yessir, I understand. I won't stop for nothin'." The boy's response was so earnest and passionate that it pained George Cunningham even more to think that they might already be too late.

The sound of Samuel approaching with the horses ended their conversation. Joey handed back the bloodied towel. "Thank you, sir. I won't let Miss Cunningham down."

"She knows that, son." He followed the boy out into the yard and gave him a hand in mounting. "Be careful."

"Yessir."

George Cunningham stood for a moment, watching as the child and horse were quickly swallowed up by the darkness. Then he turned and mounted his own large gelding. He turned to the puzzled Samuel. "Samuel, you know Miss Cunningham's dressmaker, Rachel?"

"Yes, Mr. Cunningham."

"I want you to go to her and tell her, 'The packages that were in transit may have run into a problem. They may end up being delivered late and damaged.' Do you understand?"

"You want me to go *now,* sir?" The man looked completely confused.

"Yes, now. Wake her if you have to. Do not stop anywhere. You are to leave as soon as I'm gone. Is that clear?"

"Yes, sir."

"Repeat the message."

"I am to tell her that 'the packages that were in transit may have run into a problem. They may end up being delivered . . .'"

"'. . . delivered late and damaged.' It is important that you remember the message exactly."

"'They may end up being delivered late and damaged.' I've got it now."

"Good. When you are done, return here. If I have not returned by daybreak, you are to go to the home of William Webb on East Congress."

The stablehand's eyes grew at the mention of this name.

"You are to deliver the same message." George Cunningham knew there was some risk in this, but Samuel was a longstanding employee of the Cunninghams. He trusted the man's loyalty. He would take the risk.

When Samuel nodded, George Cunningham kicked his horse into an uncustomary gallop. He headed out on Jefferson and prayed that he could find the little farm before his daughter had left it far behind.

29

Rebecca searched the black shoreline. She was beginning to worry. Suddenly, she saw what she was looking for, a tiny flicker of light in the distance. She pulled the boat around, setting a course slightly upwind of the small beacon. The light grew steadily as the brisk southwest wind pushed her forward. Still, it seemed as if she would never reach her destination. She tried to ignore the strange foreboding that hung around her like a deathly pall. She trimmed the sail to speed her progress. She would not think tonight, she would simply do. It was the only way she would survive.

As the black craft with its inky sails approached the shore, she could make out the outlines of the figures that anxiously awaited her arrival. From her vantage point, they lacked both face and figure, an appropriate accompaniment to her ghostly presence as the Angel of Passage.

She turned her thoughts to Theodore and Emiline

Crockett, the Quakers whose devotion to their faith was matched only by their devotion to the abolitionist movement. With every hour they kept their guests, they risked discovery, yet nothing could deter them from helping.

It was Theodore who greeted Rebecca as she threw him the lines that would temporarily secure the sloop to the dock.

"Thou art timely as usual, Rebecca."

She smiled and pushed back the cowl of the cape. "I pride myself in it, Theodore. Is everything well here?"

"Yes, Emiline has given them a goodly amount to eat and they have been clothed for the trip."

Rebecca nodded.

"Is all well with thee?"

"Yes, of course." Rebecca's response was a little too quick, and Theodore looked to question her. She smiled once more. "It has been a difficult spring, that's all, what with Jacob's death . . ."

"'Twas tragic, dear Jacob. But thou must not dwell on the dead, child. They are with their Maker. 'Tis the living we must concern ourselves with this night."

He was right, she told herself. It was on the living, who held hope for the future, that she would concentrate. "Are they ready to board?"

"Yes, I will tell them thou art here. Come, thou must greet Emiline. She would be heartbroken if thou didst not take a moment."

Rebecca followed him toward the bonfire. One of the shadows moved toward her.

"Rebecca!" Emiline Crockett's face, flushed with the heat of the fire, materialized before her.

"Emiline! How good to see you."

The short, heavy-set woman reached up to embrace Rebecca's tall figure and then took a step back. Studying Rebecca carefully, she must have seen something awry, for her voice when she spoke was solicitous. "Thou art well?"

Rebecca smiled once more and added a nod for increased emphasis. "Yes, I am well."

The warm, round face of the woman still showed some doubt, but she was too polite to question any further.

"We will have to visit another time. Now I must go help Theodore. Thou must be on thy way, I know." She bustled off into the night.

Rebecca turned back to the fire. Several of the Negroes had already started to douse the bonfire. The intensity of one man in particular caught her interest. She gasped slightly as he turned away. His bare back, lit by what remained of the fire, looked ghastly. A network of ragged red welts crossed and recrossed the black skin until it resembled raw red meat.

It was such a horrible sight that Rebecca wondered how the man had survived. But he had survived, just as she would. There were too many things still left to do. She would not let herself wallow in self-pity.

This was her life once again. She would not let herself forget that.

George Cunningham cursed his aging body. He was forced to rein in his galloping horse. He could not warn his daughter if he was unseated before he reached her. Worry furrowed his brow as the worst possible thoughts took possession of him.

He had spoken the truth when he had said that he was too old to survive another loss. It was incomprehensible to imagine life without Rebecca. That she might be imprisoned or, worse yet, killed, had caused him greater fear than anything he had ever experienced.

He could not be too late, for if he were, her life might well rest with the one man who had sworn to capture her. What were her chances then, he wondered fearfully. Had he done the right thing in sending Joey off to the captain? Was love enough to make this bitter and stern man break the very oaths that bound him to his duty?

It was difficult to imagine Bradford Taylor not upholding the law. George Cunningham wondered if he had made a terrible mistake. Had he tragically sealed his daughter's fate more surely than even the violent man who pursued her? Struck anew with terror, he once more spurred his horse into a gallop.

The Crocketts' home appeared quiet. That did not necessarily mean he had missed her. They would intentionally keep activity to a minimum to allay any suspicion. He pulled up his horse and proceeded cautiously toward the white farmhouse. As he dismounted, he fervently prayed that she was still there. His knock echoed in the night's silence.

"George!" Theodore Crockett's face immediately showed concern. "What has happened?"

"Is Rebecca still here?"

A flash of lightning burned itself across the sky, lighting the two men's faces. The answer was there for George Cunningham to see. The crack of thunder that followed shook the souls of both men. The worst had happened.

* * *

The thunder rolled across the black skies to the city, masking the sound of the door being pushed open at the small bar on Atwater. The disparate group did not hear the entrance of their compatriot. Within moments, though, an awareness of his presence spread an uneasy quietness over the previously boisterous crowd. Even those who did not know him well felt something amiss.

Pock looked particulary driven, almost feverish in his perverted quest tonight. Even though they shared his views, most of those who still remained at the all-night establishment seemed to recoil at the sight of the heavily armed, possessed soul who stood defiantly like Satan's own issue. They waited for him to speak.

"Where's Ben?" It was more of a demand than a question.

"Out back. He went to piss."

Pock swaggered up to the bar and placed his shotgun down for all to see. "Give me a whiskey."

The sought-after Ben came in the back door, just as the bartender offered Pock the drink. He was still buttoning his stained trousers around his fat belly, which hung in folds over the waistband of his pants.

"Damn, but that lightning sure scared the shit out o' me."

There was a snicker or two from the group.

"Sure as I was born, it's gonna pour down like the flood tonight. Only a fool'd be stupid enough . . ." He stopped short as he caught sight of the familiar figure at the bar.

Pock nodded his head in the direction of an unoccupied table slightly removed from the others. Ben moved toward the dark corner. When they were both seated, Pock spoke, his voice loud over the dull murmur of the disorderly crowd.

"A drink for my friend!"

Once the bartender had departed, Pock spoke in an undertone. "What d' ya hear from yer friend over yonder?" He indicated the river and beyond.

Ben shifted uncomfortably in his chair. "Not been hearin' much lately. Things seem to be slowin' down a bit."

Pock removed a silver coin from his pocket and placed it on the table.

"Like I said, them niggers must be layin' low."

Pock raised the shotgun in his left hand and lay it on the small table beside the coin. "There must be a thing or two that might be of interest to a law-abidin' soul like me. I think you should try a little harder. What d'you think?"

Pock's feral look caused Ben to swallow hard. The informant took a large swallow of the potent alcohol before he replied, "Maybe I did hear a thing or two. Seems there's been a bit of activity downriver. Amherstburg. A friend says them two niggers named Finney been buyin' up a lot o' stores for just two skinny 'coons. Don't suppose they'd be 'spectin' company now, would ya?"

Pock smiled. The effect was anything but pleasant.

Ben, meanwhile, looked greatly relieved that he had been able to provide the information the little son of a bitch wanted. He took another swig from his glass and breathed a little easier.

"Have you still got yer boat docked at old Cormick's pier?" Pock asked him.

Ben nodded.

Pock rose abruptly and addressed the room.

"Anybody here lookin' to catch themselves a little black ass tonight?" When there was no answer, his voice became challenging. "What's the matter, lost your belly for it? Or are ya afraid of gettin' yerselves a little wet?" Still there was no answer. "Suit yerselves, but I aim to make myself a little hard cash tonight, maybe even'll be famous. You lily-livers can sit here, all the same to me." With that he turned, signaled Ben to follow, and left.

Brad awoke with a start. The insistent pounding at his door had been incorporated into his nightmare. He had been dreaming of his childhood, of his father. He had not done that in many years. His body was damp and clammy, soaked with sweat. Temporarily disoriented, he struggled to regain his bearings. He could not determine the hour. The rain had started. Lightning lit the room before a loud crack of thunder buried what sounded like a voice at the door. He pulled on his trousers and moved silently toward the intrusion.

He could hear the voice now. It was Joey Whiton's. What had sent the child to his door in the middle of the night? He felt a new fear as he opened the door.

"Captain! Captain!" A look of relief passed briefly over Joey's face.

This was all the boy could get out before the tears came. The child was rain-soaked. His red hair clung to his head, leaving trails of white scalp. His clothing adhered to his thin body as if glued there. His face was tormented, streaked with grime, rain, and now tears.

Brad knelt to get a better look at the youngster. There were bruises, always bruises. This time Joey's face was freshly swollen. A livid, blood-marked welt trailed down one side of his face. The boy sobbed. His small body convulsed as Brad gathered him in his arms.

Brad held the shaking child, fighting the urge to demand answers to all the frightening possibilities that ran unchecked through his mind.

"Shhhh. You're all right now. You're safe."

The boy clung to him. The cold rain that soaked Joey mixed with Brad's warm sweat. Slowly, the boy stopped shaking. It took several moments before the boy steadied himself, and still several more before he pulled away from the comfort of Brad's arms.

"You've got to help, Captain. You promised!" The tortured request filled Brad with dread.

"What's wrong?"

"It's Miss Cunningham. She's out on her boat helpin' to move some slaves."

Brad grasped the boy's shoulder, desperate for more information.

"When did she leave?"

"I don't know. I fell asleep."

Brad thought of Rebecca and of the Angel of Passage. Perhaps she was with him. Perhaps . . . the improbable thought that suddenly crossed his mind then sent a chill through him.

"Surely she knows what she's doing," he tried to reassure both himself and the boy.

"But you don't understand, Captain. *Pa knows!* I didn't tell him. I swear, Captain!" The boy was passionately adamant. "I would'a let him beat me 'til I was dead this time, but I wouldn'ta told! You believe me, don't you?"

"Yes, I believe you, Joey." And he did. "What *exactly* does your father know?"

"He saw her boat wasn't there. He sorta figured it out. Mr. Finney told him I was workin' late, and he musta come lookin' for me. But I didn't tell him nothin'! He don't know where she's goin', 'least not yet."

"What do you mean, not yet?" The words sent cold terror through Brad.

"Pa's got all kinds of ways of findin' out what he wants to know."

Brad didn't doubt it for a second.

"He ran off soon's he heard Mr. Cunningham comin'. When Pa finds out where she's headed, he's gonna be after her fer sure. Mr. Cunningham told me to come here and tell you."

"George Cunningham sent you to me?"

"Yessir. He's trying to warn her himself. But I think he's gonna be too late."

Too late. Brad had always been too late to stop the pain, too late or too weak. He was no longer weak, and he prayed he was not too late. He rose suddenly and grabbed his jacket off the back of the chair.

"Joey, will you do me a favor?"

"Sure, Captain, anything."

"Go to the stable and saddle my horse. I'll be right down."

"Yessir." Joey hurried out of the room to do as he was bidden.

Brad struggled with the unwieldy buttons on his jacket. Every article of clothing seemed to fight him. He cursed under his breath, but it was not anger that drove him. It was fear.

Joey held the big horse, which he had saddled and bridled. When Brad entered by the barn door a sudden gust of wind swept a torrent of rain in after him. The storm had not let up. If anything, it had worsened. The barn doors clattered loudly, as if protesting the affront. He mounted the horse and looked down at Joey.

The boy still held the bridle, unwilling to let the horse and its rider go.

"Captain . . ."

Brad studied the small somber face. It was calm now, determined.

"You gotta take me with you." The boy paused and then added with conviction, "I've paid for the right."

Brad saw his own face in the boy's. The boy had paid for far more than what he requested.

He bent down and extended his arm. As Joey grabbed hold, he swung the boy up behind him. Yes, Joey, he thought bitterly, you have more than earned the right.

30

Rebecca pulled in the sheeting. The rain was blinding. She felt the same fear she had felt that day in the storm on Lake St. Clair. This time, there were many more lives at stake. She considered turning back to the Crocketts', but in the end she decided it would be just as dangerous.

She struggled with the wheel as the boat heeled over still further. She was riding a tight tack, beating into the southwesterly wind. She strained to see the Canadian shore. She knew it was fast approaching, and yet it was so black that she feared she would miss it and run aground. Suddenly, it loomed before her. She frantically turned the wheel, and the boat's prow struggled with the gale-force wind until it threw itself over on the new tack.

They were headed back toward the city of Detroit, almost to the foot of Woodward Avenue. The sloop had lost ground in the driving winds. It seemed that fate had taken a hand in their journey. They would be forced to approach the shores of disaster before they could tack again and head once more downriver.

Because they were sailing so close to the wind, their course was slow and torturous. If something went wrong, Rebecca prayed it would not be on the U.S. shore, where there would be little hope. On the banks of the city of Detroit, their fate would be certain, sealed by a man she had once loved. How long ago it seemed when she had first seen him there, a powerful man raging at the audacity of those who defied him. So very, very long ago.

The two men moved through the darkened alleyways, one small and lean, the other corpulent to the point of obesity. Their speed was hindered by the waddling gait of the second one, whose fat seemed to reverberate with every step he took.

"Move your fat ass, Ben. We'll never catch 'em."

Ben wheezed his reply. "It won't do you one bit of good if I die tryin' to get there."

"Maybe if you moved your ass more you wouldn't—Goddamn!"

"What is it?"

"It's them."

"Who?"

The two men had reached the river. Before them, materializing out of the darkness and rain, was the black sloop of the Angel of Passage. There was no doubt in their minds of the boat's identity, for the creature himself stood at the wheel.

The two men stood mesmerized by the eerie sight. For all the noise and fury of the storm, the effect was that of a vision without sound or speed.

Pock's response was one of immediate visceral excitement. His mouth nearly salivated with desire. For his portly friend, the reaction was equally immediate, but it was pure fear.

"Hell! Come on. We're gonna lose 'em if they don't ground themselves first."

Ben stared at Pock. He seemed to be assessing which was the greater threat to him, his friend or the Angel of Passage. It did not take him long to make up his mind.

Ben was close on Pock's tail as Pock ran through the rain to the wharf. A small, well-weathered scow sat tethered to the leeward side, cowering from the rough water and fierce winds. Ben struggled to get his great weight into the small, flat-bottomed boat. He lowered the two bilge boards and nodded to Pock.

Pock released the lines and agilely jumped aboard. He raised the single sail, and the boat jerked out into the river. The noise of the rain and the wind obliterated the shouts that tried to stop them.

Joey's voice was a hoarse croak by the time he reached the wharf. He had seen them first. Before Brad could stop him, the boy had leapt down from behind him and ran for the two familiar figures on the long wooden pier. Joey's beleaguered cry was lost in the wind.

"Pa . . . Pa . . . stop! Pa . . . please!"

As the scow was propelled out still farther, Joey's body sagged with helplessness.

Brad dismounted and quickly tethered his horse. He moved up behind Joey, his eyes straining to see into the sheet of rain that still pummeled them. He could see Pock and his companion. They seemed excited. They were pointing. He looked still farther out, doubtful he could see anything more.

Suddenly, the sky was ablaze with light. The ragged brilliance threatened to tear the blackness in two. There, before him, a tableau in silhouette, was the notorious black-sailed boat and the mysterious Angel of Passage. The perverted little pock-faced man he had dealt with all these months was in pursuit.

Now, Brad would have to choose. The irony of it did not escape him.

"Joey!" He had to shout, even though the boy was a mere foot away. The reverberation of the thunder that followed the eerie light seemed to move the earth with its intensity. "We've got to find a boat."

He searched the dock. Finding nothing suitable, he moved on to the adjoining dock, where he found what he was looking for, a small inland scow. Unlike the one Pock had commandeered, it was sloop-rigged. Its flat bottom would assure speed, and its double sails would mean they could outdistance Pock, who already had a considerable head start.

As for the Angel of Passage, it appeared to Brad that he was struggling alone with the large sailboat. That could not help but slow him. There was something peculiar about the flash he had seen of the man, something hauntingly familiar in his movements. For a heartbeat, a mind-numbing possibility once again took possession of him.

Rebecca berated herself. She should have turned back. Her arms ached, and she was exhausted. It was still miles downriver to Amherstburg, and the rain was unrelenting. She started to weigh her options. In her mind, she went over the shoreline, taking note of any location that would offer them a sympathetic reception. There were several small children in the group who would need shelter soon after they were ashore. They could not walk the miles to Amherstburg.

Suddenly the hatch flew open and a man appeared. He was big, black, and unbowed by the storm. It was the same man whose back had given Rebecca new resolve earlier.

"Thought you might be needin' some help!" His deep voice carried over the wind like the voice of God. "Name's Jacob." Spent some time on boats. Knows just 'bout everythin' there is to know."

Tears of relief welled up in Rebecca's eyes. She couldn't believe it. Jacob! Had he said his name was Jacob? A great smile crossed her face. She sent her thanks to another man in another place, a friend who had sent her a replacement in her hour of need.

"Well, Jacob, we have our work cut out for us!" she yelled.

"Yes, ma'am!"

"I need you forward as watch. When you see the shore, signal me, then you'll have to help me trim the sails after we tack."

"Yes'm."

She watched as her new crewmate made his way forward to the bow with the ease of many years' experience. He stood there, alert to his surroundings. A thought crossed her mind. What an appropriate figurehead he made: strong, free, and black!

Brad was grateful for Joey's agility. The boy moved all over the boat with a familiarity that gave Brad some comfort. He thought only of the insanity of what he was doing. Still, he could not turn back. Something was driving him, something more powerful than the hate that had been his constant companion for so many years.

He pulled his sodden hat still lower over his eyes in a vain attempt to shield them from the rain. Damn! He couldn't see a thing in this storm. Frustration added to the fear that held his heart.

They had initially made good time, beating into the storm, but now the wind seemed to have shifted. When all seemed hopeless, another bolt of lightning seemed to offer hope. Joey yelled. There, some five hundred feet ahead of them, was the black boat. To the right, on a collision course, was Pock's vessel.

Brad's agonized scream was swallowed up in the wind. "Rebecca!"

Rebecca sensed it rather than heard it, her name shouted in warning. She searched the darkness. Then she saw it, dead ahead!

"Jacob!" Her scream put him on the alert. He released the jib to slow them as Rebecca scrambled to tack the boat. For a moment, the big sail luffed erratically. She feared they would end up in irons, facing into the wind and unable to move in either direction. She signaled Jacob, and he shifted his weight as she worked the wheel and prayed.

The black boat hesitated before the mainsail finally caught the wind. Jacob pulled in the jib, and the boat slowly took its new course toward the Canadian shore. They had avoided a collision, but Rebecca had seen the face of the man who pursued them, and she knew Pock would not be dissuaded.

She signaled Jacob aft.

"That was no accident. We are being pursued!" Her voice was hoarse from shouting. "I can't chance a collision or being caught in U.S. waters. We will have to ground the boat on the Canadian shore. As far as I can tell, we are still more than five miles north of Amherstburg. After we've landed, you'll have to guide the others south along the river. You know who to ask for?"

"Yes'm. Ben and Hannah Finney."

She nodded.

"Don't worry 'bout us, ma'am. We been watchin' out fer ourselves a long time. We ain't 'bout to come this close and not make it."

"You understand they are after me. I'll help you with the women and children, then I'll head upriver. They will follow me."

"Yes'm, I understand. Thanks."

Rebecca smiled. "You're welcome."

Her response was punctuated by a shotgun blast that rent the mainsail immediately over their heads. They both ducked instinctively.

"Hurry now. Tell them below what is to happen. Tell them to brace themselves, for when we hit it will be hard."

Jacob gave her a small salute before he disappeared below. When he returned, Rebecca shouted final directions over the noise of the storm.

"I don't know how close we'll be able to get to shore. The depth of the river bottom varies greatly, and I'm not sure exactly where we are." She studied the darkness for some clue.

Lightning once more lit the sky, immediately followed by another shotgun blast, which just missed them to starboard. As if in echo, thunder rolled across the water.

The lightning had given Rebecca a better idea of their location, but it had also made them easy targets. She prayed for darkness until after she grounded the *Deliverance* and her passengers were safely ashore.

"You will have to call out the distance as we approach. When I signal, lower the jib. And watch yourself. I'm not sure what damage the impact may cause."

Jacob nodded and once more moved to the bow. Then they waited, searching the darkness for any sign of land. Rebecca turned to check on their pursuers. The boat was not gaining on them. If anything, it had lost some ground. Evidently, whoever was sailing it was not experienced.

She was about to turn back when something else caught her eye. Her heart sank. It was a second boat! It was still well downwind of them, and on the same exact tack. And it *was* gaining! Both boats would probably reach them at the same time. How many would she have to deal with? By law, they had no rights to arrest her in Canada. But somehow she sensed that her pursuers would not concern themselves with the niceties of the law.

Jacob's powerful voice sounded the distance. He had seen the shore.

"Five hundred!"

They sailed on.

"Four hundred!"

The wind propelled them faster than Rebecca wanted, but she would not slow the boat. She feared the force of the impact, but even more she feared the men that followed them.

"Three hundred!"

She tried to brace herself by wedging her feet against the wheel support and putting what little strength she had left into her arms to help break her impact against the wheel.

"Two hundred!"

Dear God, she prayed silently, take these people to safety!

"One hundred!"

She saw Jacob brace himself and reach for the jib clew.

They hit harder than Rebecca ever thought possible. The *Deliverance* bucked in protest, and the great mast swayed. Suddenly, a horrifying cracking sound filled her ears.

"Jacob! Jump!"

The mast had broken on impact and was careening forward. Jacob barely missed being crushed between the heavy mast and the forward deck. He hit the water, only to reappear moments later toward the back of the boat. The water was up to his neck, but still it was good that he could stand at all. The impact of the boat had driven the keel through silt and muck, leaving them maybe twenty feet from shore.

"Get the little ones out first, ma'am. Hand 'em to me an' I'll sees they get to land."

Rebecca opened the hatch. There had been no sound from below throughout the ordeal. Rebecca wondered if she could have been as quiet. She could hear the muffled crying of the children now and the soothing voices of the women. Several of the men hurried to help the women and children.

"Tell the women to go to the front of the boat. They can use the broken mast to work themselves to land. Jacob will carry the children on his shoulders."

"We can all help with the children, ma'am." The slender, fair-skinned man took a child and went to the edge of the boat. He jumped into the water, turned, and encouraged a boy of eight to follow suit. When the child hit the water, the man raised him onto his shoulders and struggled toward shore. And so it went, men, women, and children—wet and tired, but alive, and with God's help safe and free.

Rebecca checked the approaching boats. She had been right. They would land within moments of one another. She had but minutes to get away. She helped the last of the women forward and then jumped into the river herself.

The water was frigid and well above her waist. The heavy cloak dragged her down, but she would not abandon it. She hoped it would draw the pursuers to her rather than to the escaped slaves.

"Godspeed, Jacob."

"Godspeed to you, ma'am."

It was all the good-bye there would be.

31

"Thank you, God!" Rebecca whispered. The storm was letting up. She waited until she could make out Pock's face before she headed north along the river. He could not miss her escape. He must take the bait. Too many lives depended on it! A bullet whizzed past her ear, and she smiled bitterly. He had seen her.

She moved faster then, pulling the hood close around her head. She had no weapon. She had never felt the need. Perhaps it had been a mistake.

The brambles snagged the wet cloak, and she ducked to avoid the low, overhanging branches. It was so dark she had to fight to keep her balance as tree stumps caught her legs and the heavy hem of the black garment. She was forced to slow her pace. The sodden cape seemed to betray her every step, catching on the underbrush and sending the barren branches shaking like some ancient rattle signaling her presence.

Still, she dared not part with it. There was little foliage to hide her, and without the protection of the cape, her golden hair would be a beacon to Pock. As she approached an opening, she paused.

There was no sound other than that of the trees trying to shed themselves of the unwanted water, but all the noise and fury of the past hours seemed to reverberate in her head. She tried to quiet her thoughts, to concentrate on the here and now. She listened again. There was no sound of footsteps, no clue as to where her pursuers were. Had they decided instead to follow the slaves? Had she lost them? Or, like her, were they waiting and listening?

Brad pulled up the center board. The flat-bottomed craft moved past the hulk of the black sailboat to shore. Joey scurried forward to lower the jib, while Brad released the boom. The high winds had calmed almost as suddenly as they had arisen. The air was clean and crisp. The only sound they could hear was a strange wheezing.

Joey jumped from the bow almost before it touched land. He hurried toward the noise.

"Here, Capt'n!"

"What is it?" Brad followed the boy.

It was the other boat, the one Pock used to chase Rebecca, but Pock was nowhere to be seen. On the ground, gasping for breath, was a man Brad did not recognize. The man was a mass of trembling flesh.

"Where is he?"

"Who?" The man's breathing seemed to have steadied somewhat.

"Pock!"

"He went after that demon, the one they call the Angel of Passage."

"Which way did they go?"

The man pointed a pudgy finger north along the river.

"Don't let me find you here when I return. Your sailing companion won't be needing you to get home. Do you understand?"

Ben shook his head, and Brad knew he would be obeyed. In the end, this man's loyalties were only to himself. This thought gave Brad a moment's pause; it described himself, not so very long ago.

He turned to Joey. "Stay with the boat until I return."

"No! I'm coming!"

Brad stared at the boy. His initial annoyance turned in to a grudging admiration. He turned and headed into the underbrush with Joey at his heels.

Rebecca was tiring. She was stumbling more with every step. If only she could stop and rest for a moment. She decided to take the risk, for a few minutes at least. Perhaps she had lost them after all.

She paused among some pine trees about fifty feet in from the water. She could smell smoke now. She must be near a farm of some sort. In the darkness, she had no idea how close it was or whether its occupants might be sympathetic to an unexpected night visitor.

It was not long before she decided stopping had been a mistake. She stood with her back pressed to the trunk of a tall pine, inhaling its sweetness. Beneath her feet, the ground was slippery with the tree's needles. She lay back her head and felt the slight prick of a single needle. It seemed to trigger her body, and she started shaking.

The cold and the rain, the fear and concern, all had taken their toll. She clasped her hands together under the wet cape to keep them from trembling. When that failed, she crossed her arms, hugging them tightly to her body. Even then, the unbidden movement seemed to snake through her body, leaving her quivering under the wet black wool.

She tried to focus her senses on other things. She closed her eyes for a moment's respite. She could smell the rough wool of the cape, mixed with the pungent odor of pine. That, and the mind-numbing cold, brought back memories of another aborted sail. How far she had come since then. It was impossible to go back.

She opened her eyes at the sound. She wasn't even sure it was a sound. She stopped breathing, to listen intently. Again, she heard it, the cracking of small twigs. It was no animal that disturbed the night.

Forcing herself away from the tree, she tried to determine the direction of the sound, but her ears seemed to betray her. It seemed to come from all directions. She crouched low and headed still farther north, avoiding open spaces as much as possible. She traveled another quarter of a mile or so before she stopped. Her breathing was fast and hard. She tried to quiet it. She could not hear. Where were they?

Now she heard them. They were still behind her.

She would have to move through a clearing. It looked like fallow farmland. To go around would take too long. She strained to look behind her, but she could not see. She moved across the previously tilled field. The several hundred feet to the protection of the trees on the far side seemed an eternity.

She was within twenty feet when she chanced to look back. A figure had just emerged from the woods behind her. Barely distinguishable from the background, the figure occupied her mind exclusively. She wondered if she could reach the trees before he fired.

She did not see the man who stepped from behind a tree not ten feet ahead of her, pistol in hand.

"Well, well, who might we have here?"

Rebecca stopped so suddenly that she almost fell over. She was staring into the barrel of a pistol whose owner was all too familiar.

Pock's eyes gleamed in sadistic pleasure. They appeared to glow in the dark, like some prowling night animal's. He *was* a prowling night animal, a scavenger who lived off others. Rebecca shook now with disgust and shrank further back into the blackness of her cowl.

"Seems like the first order of business is to relieve you of any weapons."

Rebecca opened her hands slowly and held the cape wide for Pock's perusal, hoping to stall for time.

"Seems mighty stupid to be out without some protection. But then, you must be pretty stupid to be helpin' niggers."

Rebecca kept her peace. He could not know her identity yet, or he would have said something.

"Don't care much for the thought of havin' to drag you all the way back for the reward. But one thing's fer certain. Be a lot easier once yer dead. Don't have to worry 'bout no fancy tricks then."

Still she said nothing.

"Why don't you just lower that there hood, so's I

can see your face? It gives me pleasure knowin' I'll be the first to know the identity of the famous Angel of Passage. Be a good story to tell the boys, how I single-handedly caught the ferocious outlaw who's been breakin' the law. Seein' how I'm just a law-abiding citizen doin' my duty. There can't be much harm in gettin' a little fame as well as a little cash for my hard work."

Rebecca stood impassively. She would not demean herself or the movement by giving in to this despicable man's demands.

"You don't seem to hear too good, do you? I said to lower the damn thing!"

When there was still no movement, he raised his pistol.

"Makes no nevermind to me, I'd just as soon find out after you're dead!"

Staring down the pistol barrel, Rebecca felt a strange sense of relief. It was over, then. Perhaps it was for the best.

The deafening sound of the gunshot reverberated through the silence. Rebecca waited for the pain in a kind of daze. But when it did not come, she stood swaying in confusion.

Pock still stood before her. His smirk had changed to an expression of surprise. Then she saw it, the widening red stain on his chest. She looked back to his face and saw some kind of recognition. He slumped to his knees and then fell face-forward onto the ground. For a moment she was stunned, then she turned slowly.

There he was, a huge shadow of a man, a memory from that first night so long ago when he had stood on shore. That had been the beginning. Now they were nearing the end. She knew him now, his strengths and his weaknesses. She felt suddenly safe. Still, there was a doubt. Was she safe, or was he simply another danger for her?

They stood silently for a long time, neither speaking and neither moving. The gentle wind whispered through the trees, blowing away the last traces of the heavy rain. In the distance, the river once more reassuringly lapped the banks.

He moved first. It was to re-holster his pistol. Then he moved toward her. She could not have moved if she had wanted to.

He stopped before her, so close she could smell the wet wool of his uniform and the faint odor of cologne. No, she could not move. This was the confrontation she had dreaded. Would it be the end, or just the beginning?

He raised his hands to the heavy folds of the cowl. Slowly, ever so slowly, he pushed back the wool, his hands grazing her cheeks softly until her hair tumbled out over her shoulders. He moved to cradle her face in his hands, gently forcing her to look at him.

"You are a fool, Rebecca."

The accusation hurt.

"My God, you are a fool!"

He kissed her then, so passionately that she thought she would die from it. She was being devoured, and she had no defenses left any longer. She had no will, no life apart from this man.

She responded, returning the passion, and their mouths bruised each other's, each attempting to take possession of the other's soul. He held her so tightly she could barely breathe, but breathing had become unimportant. Her hands caught at his black hair, holding him to her, unwilling to ever let him go again.

Suddenly there was commotion. Joey rushed into the clearing. A light appeared less than a hundred feet to their left. The residents of a small farmhouse had been awakened by the gunshot. A lantern shone in a window. Another seemed to be approaching.

Brad stepped back, removing Rebecca's arms from around his neck.

Joey ran up. He stared first at Rebecca, then at the prostrate figure of his father. He did not have to be told.

Brad addressed the boy. "Stay here with her. See that she gets home safely."

Joey nodded somberly.

Brad bent over Pock's body and lifted it onto his shoulders. As the shouts from the farmhouse neared, Brad disappeared into the woods—a ghostly intervention come and gone so quickly that Rebecca could scarcely believe he had been there.

Brad reached the water and threw Pock's body into the bottom of the scow. He hopped onto the small boat and moved out to the river. The gentle southwesterly wind caught the mainsail, and the boat steadied its course. When he reached the middle, he released the sail and let the boat bob in the darkness. He searched the back of the boat until he found the anchor and released it. Then he took the loose end and fastened it tightly around the middle of the body. He pushed the corpse into the black water.

With any luck, the body would never surface. If it

did, it would probably be unrecognizable. Brad wondered if anyone would be concerned about the disappearance of the little man called Pock. Somehow, he doubted it.

He sat back in the small boat and pulled in the sail. He was alone on the wide river, more alone than he had ever been in his life. He did not like the feeling. He had just killed a man and covered up the killing. He had helped the very person he had been sent to arrest. He had betrayed his commission as a United States Army officer.

Yet, for the first time in his life, he felt at peace, a strange kind of peace. It was as if he had finally come to terms with his past. The memories were still there, vivid and appalling, but they no longer haunted him. It was over. It was finally over. It was time to move on.

32

Rebecca awoke exhausted and disoriented. She looked around her and found some comfort in the familiarity of her room. Then she saw Joey, asleep on the floor at the foot of her bed. She remembered how he had refused to leave her last night, despite his exhaustion. He looked so young under the brightly patterned quilt. She smiled, but the smile was short-lived. Memories of the previous night came back in a fury. Her mind was a confused jumble of the vivid sounds and sights, of wind and rain, of her beloved boat careening, of gunshots and blood.

Through it all came a single overriding thought. Brad had not arrested her. He had protected her.

Joey stirred, and Rebecca sat up. She threw her feet over the side and grabbed her wrapper. Light streamed in the window. It was not morning. She judged it to be late afternoon. She rose and went to the window. It was April 12, 1861, and it was a beautiful day. She opened the window. The air was mild and full of promise. She smiled. Perhaps happiness was not beyond her grasp after all. There was hope, she told herself. There was hope.

"Miss Cunningham?"

"Yes, Joey." She turned.

"Are you all right?"

She smiled. "Yes, Joey, I believe I am."

"Good."

"You were very brave last night. I was glad that you were with me."

The boy blushed at the compliment.

"But your mother will be worried. I suggest you go to her."

"Yes, miss."

"And, Joey—" Rebecca walked over to where the boy stood.

"You don't have to worry about me sayin' anything, miss." There was an intensity in his eyes that brooked any contradiction.

Rebecca bent over and placed a soft kiss on his cheek. "I wasn't worried."

Joey reddened before he turned to leave.

"Joey, thank you."

"You're welcome, miss." A big smile lit his face.

Rebecca called for Maddie to prepare her bath. Every muscle in her body ached. She still felt chilled, despite the warm day. When Maddie was on her way out, she stopped her.

"The house is very quiet. Is Father at home?"

"No, miss. There was some hubbub down by the post office. Samuel brought word to your father, and he set out right away."

Rebecca was suddenly concerned. What had happened? Did it have anything to do with last night? She abandoned her plans for a leisurely bath. Instead, she quickly washed herself and her hair before dressing in a simple brown skirt and white blouse. She pulled her wet hair back into a bun and hurried downstairs.

She had just reached the foot of the staircase when her father entered. He looked shaken. There was an unnatural pallor to his face.

"Father!" It was a hoarse whisper filled with horror. "What has happened?"

She feared the worst, but when he spoke she knew her worst fears did not encompass the horror of the news.

"It's begun." His voice was lifeless, desolate.

"What, Father? What has begun?"

"The war. The war has begun."

"Oh, God, no!"

She rushed to her father's side. He was so pale. She took his arm and guided him along the hall to the library. Once he was seated, she hurried to get him a drink.

"What have you found out?" She handed him the brandy.

"Beauregard and Confederate troops demanded the surrender of Fort Sumter. Major Anderson refused. The Union troops have been under bombardment all day. They are not expected to hold the Fort. If Sumter falls, Lincoln will be forced to retake it. It is what we have feared. Civil war!"

Brad awoke with a start. Again there was the pounding at the door. He felt as if he had not slept at all. When he pulled on his pants and looked at his pocket watch, he realized he had slept soundly for hours. It was almost four in the afternoon.

"Captain Taylor!" Again the knocking. "Captain Taylor!"

Brad opened the door. A corporal from the garrison saluted.

"Captain, Major Harcourt sent me with a message. He wishes to see you immediately. And, Captain, this came for you as well." He handed Brad a telegram.

The young corporal was in high color and obviously disturbed.

"Is there anything else, Corporal?"

"Have you heard, sir?"

"Heard what?"

"It's war, sir! They've fired on Fort Sumter!" The young man found it hard to suppress his excitement.

War! "Thank you, Corporal. Tell Major Harcourt I'll be with him directly."

"Yes, sir!" There was a precision to the corporal's salute that Brad had never seen there before.

War! Brad turned back into the room. He opened the telegram. He was being recalled immediately to Washington. In the face of the cruel reality of war, he was forced to acknowledge the plans he had been harboring in his heart, hopes and dreams that were an impossibility now. Perhaps it was for the best. He had been foolish to think otherwise.

He dressed quickly and descended the stairs to the lobby. There was a strange quiet in the room. Normally it would have been alive with activity. Only Seymour Finney was there, standing at the door, watching the crowd that moved up Woodward toward the post office. As Brad approached, Finney stepped to one side. When Brad came abreast, the hotelkeeper spoke quietly.

"Captain, thank you."

Brad studied the man. Seymour Finney knew. How many others did as well? No doubt, they all knew. He should feel threatened. They held his career, his life, in their hands. Yet he felt safe. These people, who risked their lives for others, kept their confidences well.

He nodded an acknowledgment to Finney. These people had earned his admiration and respect.

"Father, I'm going into town. I can't stand it any longer. Perhaps there is some news. Perhaps the incident has ended peacefully."

George Cunningham smiled at his daughter. His smile was sympathetic. Somehow, he could not crush all her hopes. There seemed to be something urgent about her need to believe that it was not true.

"Go, Rebecca. Have Samuel get the carriage for you." He wanted to warn her, to cushion the blow, but he knew he could not protect her from the terrible reality of what was happening.

Rebecca fidgeted while Samuel harnessed the horses. It seemed to take an eternity. When he finished, she did not wait for his help but climbed in herself.

"Take me to the post office, Samuel."

"Yes, miss."

The streets were filled with people, agitated people, people who had come out of their homes and places of business to find companionship, to find reassurance.

She saw the flag before she saw anything else, the huge flag that flew over City Hall, the one that had looked as if it had been stained red the night of the ball for the Prince of Wales, so long ago. Perhaps it had been a premonition after all.

Samuel had to slow the carriage to a crawl. They were amidst a throng of people and carriages, all heading in the same direction.

"Samuel, stop the carriage. I'm going to walk. There are too many people. You can return the carriage to the house and tell my father that I'll walk home."

Seeing Samuel's concerned look, she tried to reassure him. "I'll be fine. I can always go to Rachel's."

He nodded.

She struggled to move through the crowd. She was working her way toward the somber facade of the three-story building, where the telegraph communications were being posted on a bulletin board. As Rebecca made her way forward, several men doffed their hats in recognition. After many difficult minutes, she reached the front. Someone stepped aside so she could read the notices. She pored over the bulletins, but they all said the same thing. It was war!

"Rebecca." The familiar, quiet voice caused Rebecca to turn.

"Oh, Rachel!"

Rachel's stricken face reflected her own. She moved away from the bulletins, toward her friend. "Oh my God, Rachel!"

Rachel took both of Rebecca's hands in her own. "Come, we must talk."

They moved off toward the back of the crowd. "I heard about last night. Are you all right?"

"Yes, yes." For the hundredth time since she had first heard the news of war, Rebecca's thoughts returned to last night, to the hope she had felt, which was now lost. What chance was there for them now? Still, she could not but hope. To do otherwise would be to die.

The slight tightening of Rachel's hand on her arm caused her to look up.

He stood a hundred feet away, on the far side of the milling crowd. How long had he been standing there? She did not know. But he was there, safe and well. She felt Rachel's presence float away. He was approaching her, and all the noise and activity around her disappeared. It was as if they were alone, isolated, if only for the moment, from the cruelty of the world.

When he reached her he did not say a word. She watched him study her. He seemed to take in every detail, every nuance of her eyes, her hair, her skin, the curve of her ear, and the line of her neck.

When he spoke, his voice was heavy with emotion.

"You were a fool, Rebecca. . . ." His voice was warm, loving, caressing. There was no accusation. He moved his hand to her cheek, barely touching it. "But I find I have grown very fond of fools of late. They have a way of looking at things that simplifies them, clarifies them." He smiled, but the smile was bittersweet. He moved his hand away.

"Rebecca . . ." He paused, struggling for the right words. "Long ago I gave up hope. I thought it impossible to find true courage and warmth, purity, and fidelity in this world. They were words without substance, without face or form. Then fate led me to you." His eyes devoured her. "You are all these things and more. You mean more to me than anyone or anything ever has in my life. I'm sorry for the hurt I've caused you." He started to reach out to touch her again but stopped himself. "I don't know where our lives will take us. . . ."

His voice trailed off.

It was a moment before he began again, with more control, but just as softly. "I've been recalled to Washington immediately. I'm to leave within the hour."

"No!" She wanted to scream, but it came out as a whisper. There was so much left unsettled. They had just begun.

She could see the pain in his face, but she could not know that it took all his strength and every bit of his willpower for him to do what he had determined was the best thing for the woman he loved. He could not damn her to years of uncertainty, years of waiting. He would free her to love again. Her pain would heal, as his must as well.

He continued, his voice intimate. "Perhaps fate will be kind to us, and our paths will cross again." Slowly he bent until she could smell his hair, his breath, his body. He brushed her lips with his. The faint, feathery touch seared her lips more than their most passionate moments had. She heard his whispered good-bye.

"Until then, my love . . ."

What had she heard? He was saying good-bye. But was it also a promise?

He turned then, and walked away. She watched him until she could no longer see him. She did not call out. She did not move. She stood, silenced and nailed to the ground by her pain.

She did not hear Rachel approach. She heard her quiet inquiry.

"Did you tell him?"

Rebecca shook her head. Somehow, it was not the reason she wanted him to return to her, if he *would* return after the nightmare that was surely coming.

"You are a fool, Rebecca." It was a gentle reprimand.

Rebecca smiled then, even as the tears streamed down her cheeks. Her hand went to the child growing in her womb. "Yes, Rachel, I am indeed a fool!"

33

Rachel mopped the agonized sweat off Rebecca's forehead.

"You are doing well. You must be strong."

Rebecca nodded. She gasped as the pain began again. "You have to help me. I want to get up."

Rachel turned to the doctor. When he nodded his approval, she put an arm around Rebecca and helped her once more to stand.

Rebecca moved to the window. "Can you open the window for me?" Once more Rachel hesitated, then she released her friend long enough to do as she was bidden.

Rebecca inhaled the warmth of the Indian summer. It had been a beautiful September, and now October was promising much of the same. Only the reports of the war marred the day. She looked out at her beloved river. Her thoughts fled, as they so often did, to the past.

She braced herself against the windowsill as once

more the vise-like grip took hold of her womb. She tried to distract herself from the pain. She inhaled deeply, in an attempt to blot out all the agony of the past few months. She thought of her father waiting and worrying downstairs. Tears welled up in her eyes and trailed down her cheeks.

"Rebecca?"

"I'm all right." She had to pause until the contraction had passed, and then the words tumbled out. "I can't help it, Rachel. I've caused Father so much pain. Only those who were truly kind have chosen to believe his story about my marrying a family friend killed in the war. I know he only means to protect me, but I worry about him. I can see his sadness at being shunned by so many of his old friends. It matters little to me to be shunned so, but Father gives only kindness and expects it in return. Oh, Rachel, he's been so good about all this."

Rachel put an arm around her friend. "Your father is a very understanding man. He acts only out of love."

Love, Rebecca thought. Would she love her child as well? This child who might never know the love of a father?

She sobbed then as her thoughts went to Brad.

"Are you all right?"

"Yes, yes. It was just that I was thinking of Brad, of how much I wish he were here. Is that wrong?" Pain shadowed her eyes once more as her voice choked in another sob.

"Hush . . . hush. You will drain yourself of all your strength worrying about what cannot be. Think about what is! You have a child struggling to be born. You must help. You must be strong! He would want that. He admired you, Rebecca. He admired your strength. You must not let him down. It is his child as well."

Rebecca nodded. Rachel was right. She could not afford to lose herself in despair. There was another life, another person who needed her.

"Let's walk, Rachel. If this baby is as stubborn as his father, we will need all the persuasion we can command just to force him to make an appearance."

She smiled then, and together the women walked back and forth across the room, stopping when the contractions came. Finally, when even walking became impossible, Rebecca allowed Rachel to put her to bed.

Rebecca tried to cooperate with her body. She willed him to be born, this son of hers. She was certain it would be a son, with black hair and black eyes and a look about him that would cause her heart to jump.

She heard the doctor now ordering Rachel around. It all seemed to be happening in the background to her own struggle. "Push now." She heard the order and attempted to obey. "Push again." Again she tried, until she thought the pain would rend her in two. "You must help, Rebecca, push!" She pushed, ignoring the pain until she suddenly felt a great release.

The doctor was talking now, but she was barely aware of what was happening. She could hear only the crying, the spasmodic, helpless wail of new life. "Let me see him. Please! Let me see him."

The doctor laid the struggling infant on her belly, and she looked down. A son! A son with dark hair and dark eyes, and a look about him . . . She gently moved the child to her breast, urging him to suckle, and when he did she lay her head back on the pillow and closed her eyes. She sobbed then. She had a son. A son so like his father that it made her heart break all over again.

Brad lay in the red soil, barely hidden in the shallow ditch. The icy rain had begun just after dawn. It had turned the red clay into a quagmire. He would be hard pressed to get the information General Burnside had wanted. It had been days since he had seen a Union soldier, even longer since he'd been in camp. But perhaps that was just as well. The last time he had seen the Army of the Potomac at their camp on the frozen banks of the Rappahannock, it had been little more than a cesspool, with hundreds dying from dysentery, typhoid, and pneumonia. Perhaps the dangers he faced as an intelligence officer were no worse than the dangers he would have faced in camp.

He had thought ironically during that last visit that a firing squad might not be the worst thing that could happen to him. He looked down at the Confederate uniform that clothed him. If he were caught, it would brand him a spy and assure a quick death. Perhaps it would prove to be a blessing in disguise.

He would have few regrets. No, he would have only one regret. He lay in the mud and tried to remember her the way she had been that last day—tragically beautiful, and full of pain. Once more he had hurt her. He had seen no other way. What future would there have been for them? He had made the right decision. Lying now in this red hellhole convinced him of that.

Perhaps there would be time later to rectify the

wrong he had done her. What would he do? He laughed at himself for still harboring dreams amid this nightmare. He still thought that after this horror there might be happiness. He was a fool.

What had he said to her? Something about fools, that they simplified things, clarified things. The past two years had done that for him. Things that had once been critically important to him seemed to matter no longer. People had taken a new order of importance in his life. If he survived this hell, things would be different. *If* he survived.

George Cunningham sat in a swing on the lawn of his home. It was a beautiful summer, the summer of 1863. The weather had been neither too hot nor too rainy. He let his mind wander for a moment. His thoughts were anything but hopeful. General Burnside had spent the winter camped at Falmouth, Virginia, on the Rappahannock River. The disastrous winter was being referred to as the Valley Forge of the war. He knew from reliable sources that Washington was bogged down by politics.

Most disturbing, however, was an unsettling turn of events in Michigan politics. There was growing opposition to the war. That, in and of itself, was not reprehensible. George Cunningham wished the war over as fervently as anyone.

But similar factions in nearby Indiana and Illinois had gained control of those legislatures and had officially called for an armistice. Linked inextricably to the armistice was the repeal of the Emancipation Proclamation, a loss of the very thing that so many of them had struggled for so long to attain! It seemed to make a mockery of the entire struggle, to make a mockery of all the lives already tragically lost.

A sound distracted him from his morbid thoughts.

"Come to your grandpa, young fella." George Cunningham held out his arms to the toddler. The boy barely managed to stumble over the uneven grass.

"What have you got there, my boy?"

The child clutched a small wooden object in his hand.

"Show me."

The unidentified offering was held out for inspection.

George Cunningham looked puzzled for a moment. He picked up the wooden object to study it more closely. It was a soldier. The paint was well worn. It was not new, yet he had never seen it before. He fingered it thoughtfully until some small scratchings on its back caught his attention. He rubbed his thumb thoughtfully over the ragged signature. *B. Taylor.*

"There you are, you rascal! You know Rachel and Mary have been looking for you for your bath."

George Cunningham looked up guiltily as his daughter approached.

She saw the soldier in her father's hand, and her face paled. She picked up the boy and handed him to Mary, who had followed her out. After Mary had taken the boy inside, she turned to face her father's unspoken question.

She did not speak at first. Rather, she came and sat beside him quietly on the wide swing and stared at the toy in his hand. Finally, she reached over and gently retrieved the little soldier. She lay her head on her father's shoulder then, and together they swung in silence. Rebecca rubbed her thumb over the cut name, as if she were conjuring a genie from a bottle.

"I can't sit idly by any longer, Father. I am going mad. They are looking for women to help at the soldiers' hospital. I've told Mrs. Couzens that I would help in any way I could. The baby is happy now, with Rachel and her children here."

They continued to swing in silence.

"I'm sorry, Father."

"Sorry? For what?"

"For living in the past so much. For being unwilling to face a future not to my liking. I've always been in control. I've always had things my way. It has been difficult for me to accept that this . . ."

His hand covered hers, closing it around the soldier. "He loved you, Rebecca. Don't ever doubt that. I have seen enough of love to know that you did not misplace your love. He was a man haunted by his past. He will have to come to peace with it before he can come to you. With the war that may be difficult, if not impossible." He did not voice his worst fear, which he was sure was also his daughter's—that Brad Taylor might already be dead. "It's just that love isn't always what we hope it will be."

"But it was for you and Mother."

"Yes, it was for your mother and me. But we lived in quieter times, less turbulent times. It would take an extraordinary love to survive what you two have been through. There is still room for hope, don't misunderstand me. I just don't want to see you hurt any more than you have been already. I will not be around forever. I would like to know you are happy before I die . . ."

"Father! You will live a long life yet!"

He smiled then and kissed the top of her head tenderly. He hoped she was right, about his life and her hopes.

34

The smell of putrefying gangrene clogged Rebecca's nostrils until she thought she would gag. When she first volunteered to help with the wounded, she had had no idea of the tremendous personal toll it would take. Today, almost two years after she started, she still could not eat before she came to the hospital. She was still afraid she would embarrass herself by vomiting.

"You're the prettiest thing I've seen in a long time, ma'am."

She looked down at the young soldier and wondered how he would take the news that his leg was to be sacrificed today. She wondered if he had a wife or girlfriend who would stand by him after the ordeal. She wondered if he still harbored hopes for a bright future. She hoped so, for somehow his hope might bolster her own.

"Well, soldier, you're in fine spirits today." She took the cloth she had in her hand, wrung it in cool water, and mopped his sweaty brow.

"Yes, ma'am. I'm practically home."

"Where's home?"

"Jackson, ma'am. Jackson, Michigan. Home of Abe Lincoln's party!"

She smiled at the last statement. He was so exuberant, she could not help herself.

"I think you are right. After today, the worst will be over and you'll be ready to head home."

"The worst was over the day I got shot, ma'am. I wasn't dead, and I knew then I wasn't headed to some Reb prison to rot. Saw a man once got himself out of the Reb prison at Richmond. Said he'd rather die with a clean shot than lie starvin', waitin' to die from the typhoid or some other scourge."

"Well, then, you should be counting your blessings."

"I am, ma'am. That I am. Got me a sweet little miss waitin' for me back home. Told her I'd be there in the wink of an eye and we'd be married even quicker."

"Sounds like congratulations are in store!"

"Yes, ma'am!"

Rebecca smiled again and said a silent prayer that the boy would survive the operation and make it home. She had seen too many who had not.

She was tired. She had been at the hospital since before dawn and, although it was only midday, she felt like she had already spent a lifetime here.

As she walked through the ward she studied the men who had survived, often at great cost. She could not help but think of all those who had not survived, and all those who still would not. Christmas had come and gone again. Finally, there was some hope for an end to the war. Lincoln had found the military leaders he had been searching for. Ulysses S. Grant had been pulled back from disgrace to give some shape to the Federal campaign, and he was finally seeing success. Sherman had taken Atlanta and was even now moving through Georgia to the sea.

The week before, she and Rachel had wept with joy as word had come that Congress had voted 119 to 56 to pass the Thirteenth Amendment, abolishing slavery. There was no going back, only forward.

She stood in a corner of the large ward and stared out the frosty window into the bleak February day. She could not completely block out the crying and moaning that punctuated the silence with pain.

She wondered if he was alive. For the first time, she tried to deal with something she had always been unwilling to even consider. The past two years had brought her face to face with death, with young men whose lives were extinguished before they ever got to love or live. For every soldier she saw die, she knew there were hundreds, thousands who had died on the battlefield, alone, far from family and friends. Perhaps he was dead. Perhaps he had died years ago, and she did not know.

She raised a finger and pressed it against the frosty pane, leaving a warm melted circle in the cold whiteness. She studied it like a sorcerer's crystal ball, willing it to show her the truth. Within moments, the shiny surface was engulfed in delicate white feathery lines, until it was barely distinguishable from the rest of the icy window. Still, she had seen what she had wanted to see. He was not dead. Suddenly, very eerily, she was certain of it.

* * *

Brad walked through the pestilence. As far as he could see, men lay in holes scratched out of the red earth, a single blanket their meager protection from the elements. Andersonville, Georgia, would surely become synonymous with hell. It was a place where a teaspoon of salt, three tablespoons of beans, and a half-pint of cornmeal were considered sustenance, where a single foul trickle with the ironic name of Sweet Water Branch served as both sewer and well to the thirty-three thousand men who called this hell-hole home. A man died every few minutes, like clockwork. A rat became a feast. No tent or structure marked the landscape; they were strictly forbidden by the commandant. Surely the man, called Wirz, was from the devil's own sperm.

"Capt'n."

Brad nodded at the skeletal figure that acknowledged his presence. The men who had not died looked as if they had defied death by will alone. There was nothing in their emaciated bodies to explain why they still lived.

Brad had been luckier than most. He had been caught only months ago, after an aborted effort to gain some urgent information for General Grant. Moments before his capture, he had managed to swap his stolen Reb uniform for one off a fallen Union soldier. He owed that dead man a debt of gratitude, for his blood-stained uniform had saved Brad from the firing squad.

He had been sent first to Richmond. As the war progressed and Sherman's march continued, he had been sent farther south to Andersonville. Here, dying seemed a welcome release. He had lost so much weight in the short months of his captivity that the dead man's uniform, once tight, now hung loosely over his body.

He tried to walk every day. It seemed to keep up his strength, if not his morale. He was careful never to venture too close to the stockade that marked the borders of their personal netherworld. To do so was to risk being shot. He had seen a man shot there. He had wondered if the man had wandered unawares into the deadly no-man's-land, or if the poor soul had merely seen a means of escape from miseries too terrible to withstand any longer.

As Brad reached the western perimeter of the camp, he could smell death. It rose from the mass grave that was constantly being lengthened for new occupants. They must not have filled it yet, he thought with a certain detachment. It was simply an item to be noted.

The sun was low in the sky. He studied it as it fled behind some trees, making its escape. Perhaps, like him, it had had its belly full of death for the day. He tried to conjure up the thoughts that had kept him alive these past months.

He could block out the sounds and the sights. It was the smells he found he could not rid himself of. He tried harder, willing himself to another place, another time. She was there—loving or angry, laughing or hurt—but she was there, as clear as if it had only been yesterday. He concentrated on the glint of the sun in her hair, the lustre of her pale skin, the dimple in the lobe of her ear, the line of her neck as it met her bare shoulders.

He could hear her voice challenging him. ". . . And

you, Captain, do you have any secrets?" Secrets. Their relationship had been full of secrets until the end. Then, when there were no more secrets, there was no time. He tried to concentrate again. He was getting distracted by useless thoughts. He remembered her hands as they tended to the gash across his back. Her hands . . .

"Capt'n."

He forced his eyes closed still tighter, trying to block out the sound.

"Capt'n, please . . ."

He knew the sound. It was a death rattle.

He turned, carefully wiping any sign of pain off his face.

"Yes, soldier."

"Will you do me a favor?" The voice was barely above a whisper. Brad crouched beside the dying man, whose body seemed little more than an assembly of bones.

"Yes."

"Will you tell my Mary I was thinkin' of her at the end?"

Brad nodded. "I'll tell her."

The man seemed to relax into death. Brad closed the sunken eyes. He had no idea who the soldier was, or where he could locate his Mary. What irony that a stranger could offer comfort in his ignorance. He prayed that death would find him a kind stranger.

35

Rebecca laughed out loud at her son's antics. It was good to be outside again. The winter had been a particularly severe one. Thankfully, April, 1865, had brought with it mild temperatures and sunny days—and, finally, hope that the war would be over soon.

"Mary, bring him back over here. He's only going to get himself in trouble there."

Mary grabbed the squealing three-year-old and carried him toward his mother. Rebecca studied the unlikely duo. Mary, Rachel's oldest daughter, was twelve now. She was a study in grace and girlish charm. Rebecca thanked God for Rachel and her children. They had filled a void in the tragic days following Jacob's death. And in the darkest days of the war, they had given comfort.

She turned her attention to the child. The boy squirmed in Mary's arms until he finally set himself free. He came flying toward her, his black hair ruffled by the wind, dark eyes alive with mischief. It was this child who had kept her sane, this child who had kept the memory alive, kept hope alive.

She had prayed for a son, and her prayers had been answered. Yet, every time she looked at him, she was reminded of his father. She could not help it. It was a sweet torture, but torture nonetheless.

She jumped at the sound of the gunshots. There was one, then two. Suddenly the air was alive with them. She held the boy tightly to her. For a moment, she thought the terror of the war had found them.

"Mary, run, get my father." She would not release the boy from her arms. She could not think. Suddenly, there was a rider on the road. He was screaming. What was he screaming? He was still too far away.

She waited, horrified, unable to move, pulling the child still closer to her. She heard the mad rider's words but could not believe them. He repeated himself, screaming to anyone who would hear, riding as if the devil himself was after him.

She released the boy then in a kind of stupor. He looked puzzled by her strange behavior.

Rebecca's eyes were bright with tears as she moved her hand repeatedly over the child's tangled hair. "It's all right, darling. It's all right. It's over. It's finally over."

The train moved along slowly. The joints of the tracks set up a steady rhythm, but still Brad could not relax. He looked out the window. The river had come into sight several minutes ago. Now it sparkled brilliantly in the morning sun. The first trees of the island of Bois Blanc were just barely visible ahead. He rested his head in his hands and tried to deal with the emotions that threatened to overwhelm him.

It was the fourth of July, 1865, and he was not the only soldier returning from the war on the train today. His anxiety was shared in part by the majority of the soldiers who crowded the cars. They were returning to friends and family. What was he returning to? A figment of his imagination? It had been so long, perhaps too long.

While most of the men still wore the remains of their uniforms, Brad had selected a pair of dark trousers, an open shirt, and a buff suede jacket. He had packed his uniform away the day he had left Washington. It was a symbol of the past, carrying with it too many painful memories. He did not want her . . .

Did not want her to what? Remember all the hurtful things he had done to her? God! He must be mad to think she would welcome him back with open arms! He should never have come.

"Detroit! Next stop, Detroit!"

He watched the familiar sights materialize out the window. The city had changed, but not so dramatically that he did not feel a tightening in his belly at the appearance of the docks and warehouses. He waited until most of the others had left the train before he rose and headed out. The platform was a sea of people, crying and laughing and hugging. He felt like an intruder into their happiness. He stood for a moment, disoriented. The sense of déjà vu left his hands cold and clammy. Finally, he approached a porter.

"George Cunningham's home? Is it still out Jefferson?"

"Yessir."

"Do you know if his daughter, Rebecca Cunningham, is still living with him?"

"You mean Mrs. Ward, yessir, she's still there." When Brad made no move to leave, the man felt compelled to explain. "After her husband died in the war, she and her son had nowhere else to go. Shame, the boy will never know his pa."

The porter moved away, but Brad still could not move. In his head, he had gone over every possible reception he might receive. But this was something that he had never anticipated, that she had married. He wrestled with the thoughts that bombarded him. He moved off toward Woodward. He needed a drink.

Seymour Finney's hotel had changed little in the four years he had been away. As he walked through the door, he fully expected to see Finney himself behind the desk, but Finney was not there. Instead, there was a young desk clerk. Brad moved up until he stood before the young man who was eagerly poring over some books. He stared down at the red hair and smiled for the first time that day.

"I'm looking for a room. Would you have one?"

Joey Whiton looked up. Brad had to laugh at the startled look on the boy's face. Joey's face brightened with a wide smile, and his eyes lit up excitedly.

"Captain! Captain Taylor! Damned if it's not you!"

Joey moved around the counter and hesitated only a moment before he moved forward to hug the surprised soldier. Brad's arms went around the boy's tall, thin figure. For a moment he felt as those people on the platform must have felt. It was a strange feeling, to feel welcome.

Brad set the boy back. "Well, Joey, it seems you've grown at least a foot since I last saw you."

"Yessir."

"Have things been well with you?"

"Yessir. Been workin' for Mr. Finney in the hotel since the start of the war."

"Good. Do you think I could get a drink?"

"Sure, Captain. Then I'll show you to your room."

Brad nursed his drink as the boy babbled on happily. When he was finished, Joey led the way up the stairs. Brad almost stopped him as he reached the door of the room.

"It's the same one you had before, Captain. Thought you might like that."

Brad did not have the heart to tell him.

The boy turned to go and then stopped near the stairs. "You're going to see her, aren't you? She won't believe it."

"Rachel, go check and see if Bertie has the picnic basket ready. The children are so excited, I fear if we delay any longer they will burst."

"Are we going, Mama?"

"Yes, my little imp. We are going now. Go find Ezra and Charity. Tell them we are ready to leave."

Rebecca stood in the parlor, looking out toward the low west sun. It had been almost three months since Appomattox. She had watched as the soldiers had come back, first in only a trickle and then a steady flow. At first she found herself timing her trips to town to coincide with the train arrivals, but the heartrending scenes of welcome had hurt too much.

She had tried to establish a new routine. Her efforts were no longer needed at the hospital. The summer days dragged. With every day that passed, she came closer to acknowledging that it was over. It had been over four years ago when he had said good-bye. She had just been too naive to understand.

The noise of the children overflowed once more into her thoughts, and she turned to face their excited faces.

"Has Samuel gotten the carriage ready?"

"Yes, ma'am." It was nine-year-old Ezra who answered. "He's bringing it around front now."

"Now listen to me, all of you. I want you all on best behavior, or we shall come home before the fireworks even begin. Is that clear?"

The four somber young faces nodded.

Rebecca smiled. "Come, then, it's time."

They made a cheerful group as they headed into the city to Grand Circus Park. There was joy in the air as Detroit prepared to celebrate the country's unity again after four long years. A day-long celebration had been planned. There had been fairs and parades earlier, and now the city buzzed expectantly. Elaborate fireworks had been planned for after dark.

Rebecca had promised everyone they would go early to ensure themselves a good place in the grassy park. Her father had preceded them. As a member of the committee in charge, he was finalizing the last of the arrangements.

They settled onto the quilt and watched the parade of people wandering here and there, spreading blankets and picnic dinners. As the sun slowly set, the excitement mounted. In the growing darkness, the children's giggles kept the air alive. Rebecca set her impatient son down beside her and lay back to stare at the starry night.

It was still warm, a balmy evening perfect for the fireworks. The stars were spread across the sky like wild daisies in a field. Rebecca lost herself in them for a moment. Their magnificence diminished the importance of her problems. She closed her eyes, until a sudden burst of light brought them open. The black canopy filled with a breathtaking scarlet sunburst. She could hear the "oohs" and "aahs" around her and the squeals of the little ones.

She didn't know why she turned away then, perhaps because the brilliant display only increased her sadness.

She heard the explosion as the next shell burst. In the light she saw him. Her heart stopped for a moment.

Then darkness came again. She blinked, frightened by the trick her mind was playing. She waited, heart pounding now, for the next shell. Surely it would prove her wrong. It was merely a resemblance. She had been fooled by the unnatural light. The night became a black abyss, and she was falling to its bottom.

She heard the whistling of the rocket. She held her breath. In the startling burst of light, he was still there, watching her. She struggled to sit up then, desperately fighting the urge to run into the darkness. She could still make out the dim figure as she rose to stand. She felt ill. She must be going mad. God was playing some terrible trick on her. It was cruel and unfair.

Again the whistling. Again the blinding light. He was there. He made no move, gave no sign of recognition, but his eyes burned into her. There was darkness again.

She needed to see his eyes. His eyes would tell her the truth. She set off on the journey, across the grass, across four years and hurts too numerous to mention. Through pain and loss, death and childbirth, passion and hope. A journey to the man she loved.

Brad had hesitated when he saw the child in the distance. He was not a part of this life of hers. Perhaps he should never have come, but now it was too late. She was coming to him. My God! She was beautiful, more beautiful than he'd conjured up in his most desperate moments. She was thinner, he thought. Her features and curves had changed from beautiful to exquisite.

He sensed no hesitation on her part. She appeared in and out of the flashes of light, her movement jumping forward until at the last she seemed to materialize suddenly in front of him.

How could he begin? He was afraid to even try.

She sensed his hesitation. It held her back from flinging herself into his arms. All this time, all this wait, and now they stood apart like two strangers, each waiting for the other.

"Mama! Mama!" The small boy had noticed his mother's absence and came running over to pull at her skirts. She couldn't leave his eyes to look down. She was afraid he would be gone if she did.

"Mama!" The small voice became more insistent. She saw Brad look down. There was a giant flash of white light. She saw Brad studying the boy.

"Here, Mama." The boy was eager to return to the others. He thrust the wooden object he clutched into her hand. "Keep Papa's soldier for me." Then the boy was off again.

She watched the recognition grow on Brad's face. Her heart was breaking for him. He looked down into her hand then. He took her hand in his and brought the small toy up for inspection. A new burst lit the bedraggled wooden soldier. He looked at her, and she saw amazement and confusion and pain.

"Why didn't you tell me?"

What could she say? Why hadn't she told him? She found the words then for why she hadn't. Her voice was barely above a whisper and choked with emotion.

"I loved you." Was it enough? Would he understand?

Another burst of light, and she saw his eyes were as glassy as her own.

"Oh my God, Rebecca! I'm so sorry! I've missed you so, my love."

She was in his arms. She could smell him, feel him. He held her tightly against his chest, as if unwilling to ever part from her again. She could hear her own sobs mixed with the wild beating of his heart. She pulled back slightly to touch his lips, to explore his thin face with her hands, to be certain he was really there with her and not a dream.

"I'm here, my love. I'm here," he reassured her

as multiple rockets exploded, sending vibrant cascades of color across the sky.

The tearful words that followed were lost amid the noise of the fireworks, but it did not matter, for the love that was once impossible, now was possible.

AVAILABLE NOW

MORNING COMES SOFTLY by Debbie Macomber

A sweet, heartwarming, contemporary mail-order bride story. Travis Thompson, a rough-and-tough rancher, and Mary Warner, a shy librarian, have nothing in common. But when Travis finds himself the guardian of his orphaned nephew and niece, only one solution comes to his mind—to place an ad for a wife. "I relished every word, lived every scene, and shared in the laughter and tears of the characters."—Linda Lael Miller, bestselling author of *Daniel's Bride*

ECHOES AND ILLUSIONS by Kathy Lynn Emerson

A time-travel romance to treasure. A young woman finds echoes of the past in her present life in this spellbinding story, of which *Romantic Times* says, "a heady blend of romance, suspense and drama . . . a real page turner."

PHANTOM LOVER by Millie Criswell

In the turbulent period of the Revolutionary War, beautiful Danielle Sheridan must choose between the love of two different yet brave men—her gentle husband or her elusive Phantom Lover. "A hilarious, sensual, fast-paced romp."—Elaine Barbieri, author of *More Precious Than Gold*

ANGEL OF PASSAGE by Joan Avery

A riveting and passionate romance set during the Civil War. Rebecca Cunningham, the belle of Detroit society, works for the Underground Railroad, ferrying escaped slaves across the river to Canada. Captain Bradford Taylor has been sent by the government to capture the "Angel of Passage," unaware that she is the very woman with whom he has fallen in love.

JACARANDA BEND by Charlotte Douglas

A spine-tingling historical set on a Florida plantation. A beautiful Scotswoman finds herself falling in love with a man who may be capable of murder.

HEART SOUNDS by Michele Johns

A poignant love story set in nineteenth-century America. Louisa Halloran, nearly deaf from a gunpowder explosion, marries the man of her dreams. But while he lavishes her with gifts, he withholds the one thing she treasures most—his love.

COMING NEXT MONTH

DREAM TIME by Parris Afton Bonds

A passionate tale of a determined young woman who, because of a scandal, wound up in the untamed Australia of the early 1800s.

ALWAYS . . . by Jeane Renick

Marielle McCleary wants a baby, but her prospects look slim—until she meets handsome actor Tom Saxon. Too late, however, she finds out that Thomas isn't as perfect as he seems. Will she ever have the life she's always wanted?

THE BRIDEGROOM by Carol Jerina

A compelling historical romance set in Texas. Payne Trefarrow's family abandoned him, and he held his identical twin brother Prescott responsible. To exact revenge, Payne planned to take the things his brother loved most—his money and his fiancée.

THE WOMEN OF LIBERTY CREEK
by Marilyn Cunningham

From the author of *Seasons of the Heart*. A sweeping tale of three women's lives and loves and how they are bound together, over the generations, by a small town in Idaho.

LOST TREASURE by Catriona Flynt

A zany romantic adventure set in Northern California at the turn of the century. When her dramatic production went up in smoke, actress Moll Kennedy was forced to take a job to pay her debts—as a schoolteacher doubling as a spy. Then she fell in love with the ruggedly handsome Winslow Fortune, the very man she was spying on.

SAPPHIRE by Venita Helton

An intriguing historical tale of love divided by loyalty. When her clipper ship sank, New Orleans beauty Arienne Lloyd was rescued by handsome Yankee Joshua Langdon. At the very sight of him she was filled with longing, despite her own allegiances to the South. Would Arienne fight to win the heart of her beloved enemy—even if it meant risking everything in which she believed?

Harper Monogram **The Mark of Distinctive Women's Fiction**